MURDER ON THE BEACH

THE CHLOE CANTON MYSTERIES BOOK 2

DAISY WHITE

Copyright © 2021 Daisy White

The right of Daisy White to be identified as the Author of the Work has been asserted by her in accordance to the Copyright, Designs and Patents Act 1988.

First published in 2021 by Bloodhound Books

Apart from any use permitted under UK copyright law, this publication may only be reproduced, stored, or transmitted, in any form, or by any means, with prior permission in writing of the publisher or, in the case of reprographic production, in accordance with the terms of licences issued by the Copyright Licensing Agency.

All characters in this publication are fictitious and any resemblance to real persons, living or dead, is purely coincidental.

www.bloodhoundbooks.com

Print ISBN 978-1-913942-84-7

ALSO BY DAISY WHITE

THE CHLOE CANTON MYSTERIES

Murder on the Island (Book 1)

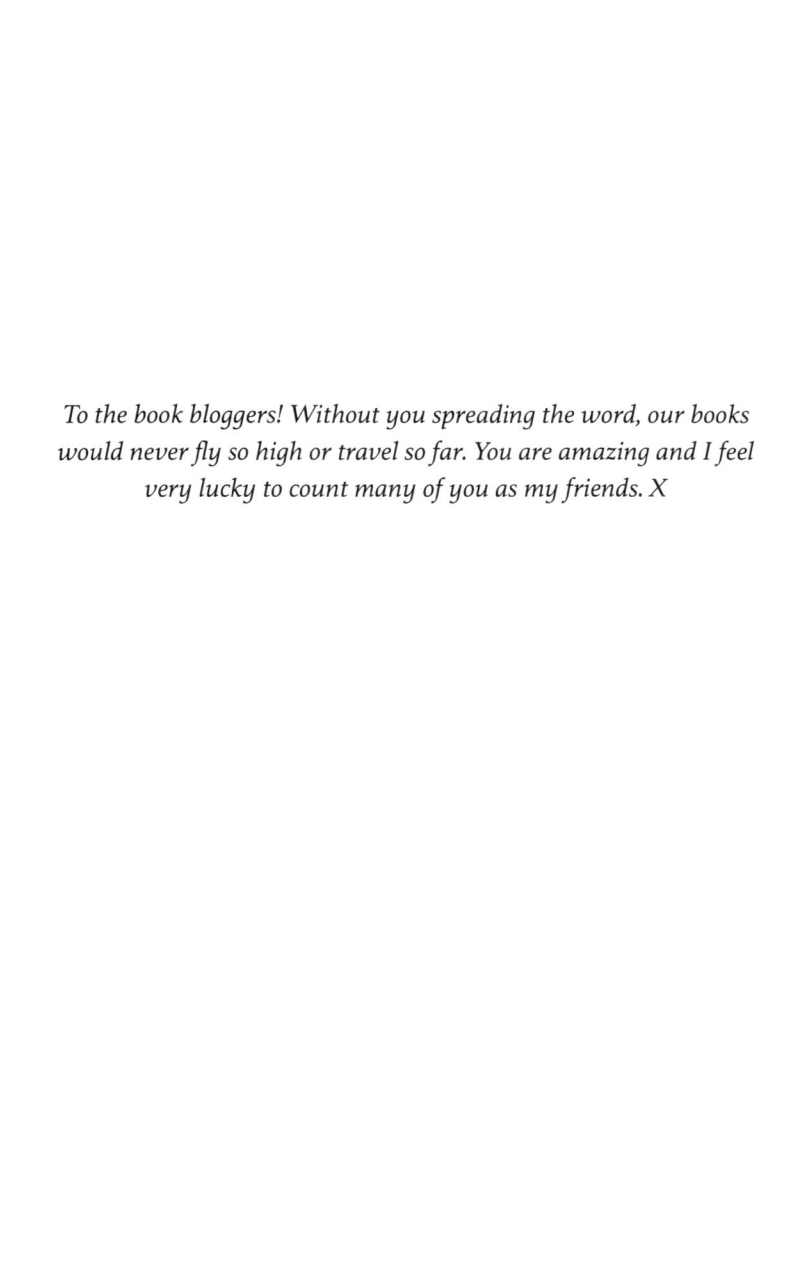

To the book bloggers! Without you spreading the word, our books would never fly so high or travel so far. You are amazing and I feel very lucky to count many of you as my friends. X

'We visited a wonderful cave... The most beautiful cave in the world, I suppose. We descended 150 steps and stood in a splendid place... with a brilliant lake of clear water under our feet and the roof overhead splendid with shining stalactites, thousands and thousands of them as white as sugar...'
— *Letter from Mark Twain (1908)*

1

The boy's body lay motionless on the dusty ground. His red shirt was torn from one shoulder and his torso was awkwardly twisted in the harsh midday sunlight.

'Get up, Jordan, and stop pretending you're hurt!' yelled Antoine.

Chloe, who had been standing at the gate, frozen in horror at the scene, let out a long breath of relief as the boy sprang to his feet, rubbing his arm. She was too far away to see the expression on his face but she guessed he would be scowling – probably with good reason.

Antoine had offered to teach the teenager to ride, but Chloe was slightly dubious of his methods. She was pretty sure her grandmother, the original owner of Beachside Riding Stables, hadn't just thrown her on a horse and expected her to get on with it. Or maybe she had...

Satisfied her interference was unnecessary, Chloe turned away, leaving the boys to argue over whose fault it was that Jordan had been thrown off again. Dre, her grandmother, or to be accurate her step-grandmother (there was no actual blood tie), had gifted Chloe her debt-riddled property on the beautiful island of Bermuda in her will. Just six months ago Chloe had sold her flat in London and returned to the island of her childhood. It was only four months ago, on her fiftieth birthday, that her husband had told her they needed to get divorced.

It was funny how you could jog along for years, not realising how much you were missing, and then suddenly, bang, your life could change completely, Chloe thought now as she walked back to the stables. Her old life with Mark in London already felt worlds away. Now she was living her best life on a paradise island, surrounded by friends and animals. It was like waking from an unpleasant dream, and discovering a whole new consciousness. A new happiness, even.

Her sandals scuffed the green fleshy foliage that lined the dusty path, releasing a sharp, minty scent into the hot summer air. A sudden noise and thundering paws on the hard earth made her turn quickly, heart pounding. Her dog, Hilda, was standing behind her, tail wagging, mouth open and panting hard, one ear flopped over, the other standing upright, having clearly emerged from the undergrowth at top speed.

'Silly dog, what have you been hunting down there?' Chloe scolded, bending down to pat the creature, who wriggled in delight and followed her owner towards the stables. Hilda was a Staffie cross, acquired from the local rescue kennels. She had settled easily into her new home and was adored by everyone who met her. Chloe, who had never had a dog, often found herself having conversations with her new pet, and felt soothed by her presence.

Dog and owner emerged in the brilliant sunlight, and Hilda darted off towards the white buildings, sending the ginger stable cat up onto the tack-room roof. Freshly painted in the spring by Chloe and Antoine, the little stable block looked beautiful and was currently smothered in purple bougainvillea. The fenced yard gave onto a stunning view of the beach, and underneath a weeping fig tree stood a little wrought-iron table and chairs. A new feed room made the yard into a sheltered L-shape, with the muck-heap tucked away under a lush green-leaved vine.

As ever, Chloe felt a rush of pleasure at the sight of five enquiring heads poking out of their half doors. It had been a shock when she first arrived, to discover she was now responsible for six horses, a few chickens, a stable cat and a couple of goats. Not to mention stable manager Antoine. But now, as she settled into life in her island home, it felt good; a ready-made family, especially as she had added Hilda and Jordan, the wayward teenage grandson of her neighbour, Ailsa.

A happy, busy family, who all ate far more than she did, she thought with a fond smile, but they were so much part of her new life in Bermuda. She was filling water buckets when her mobile rang, and she quickly turned off the tap, wiping her hands on her blue cotton sundress before answering.

'Chloe! Darling, it's been ages. How are you?' There was no mistaking that overloud, slightly shrill voice.

'Hallo, Maria. Fine thanks, still working on turning the stables back into a financially viable business. How's London? How's Mandy?'

'Oh the usual chaos and constant pouring rain in the city. I can't believe there was a heatwave predicted.' Maria tutted at the cheek of ineffective weather forecasters, before moving swiftly on with the conversation. 'Mandy's great and she's just been promoted. She's head of cardiology now.' An affectionate note of pride crept into Maria's voice as she talked about her wife.

'Congratulations. Do send her my love, won't you? Rain at this time of year sounds about right for London,' Chloe told her. 'You both need to come and holiday out here! I'm standing in glorious sunshine.'

'I know, and I did get your last email. Sorry, it's been utter chaos with work! Anyway, darling, I didn't just call for a chat, I might be able to help you out with your business. Do you still have that gorgeous palomino horse that was in the Palm Bay Hotel brochure?'

'Goldie? Yes, of course.' Chloe smiled affectionately across the yard as the mare in question peered out over her half door. 'Don't tell me you want her shipped to the UK for one of your celebrity weddings?'

'Don't be silly, darling, but excellent news you still have her.' Maria paused, and Chloe heard paper scuffling. 'Now, the next thing is... Have you heard of Lara Turner and Eddie Bristol?'

Chloe frantically searched her brain. 'Um... no, sorry. Unless Lara was in *Game of Thrones*?'

Maria was cackling down the phone. 'Not quite... They're reality TV stars. They won that Welsh dating show, *Tough Love*, six months ago and they've been raking in endorsements ever since,' Maria told her. 'Nice young couple and very ambitious.'

'It's not really my thing, I'm afraid,' Chloe said apologetically, thinking of the endless reruns of *House Restoration* or *Buying a Historic Ruin* she liked to secretly indulge in during the long summer evenings.

'I didn't really think it was, but it doesn't matter, darling. They got engaged last month and now they want to get married in Bermuda *next* month, on September the 12th.' Her friend sounded faintly harassed, and Chloe could totally understand why.

'But that's less than two weeks away! Why so soon? Doesn't it normally take years to plan these things?' she enquired, stroking Hilda's soft ears as the dog, bored with chasing the cat, came and sat at her feet.

'*Yes!* I mean I love a challenge but this is ridiculous,' Maria said, despairingly. 'But then again the budget is huge, and if I can pull it off...' She sounded as though she was trying to convince herself. 'Mandy reckons with her increased salary and my fee from this job we might even be able to afford that farmhouse in Wales, which would be a total dream come true.'

The pair had long been searching for their dream holiday home, and as Maria had spent much of her childhood in South Wales, they had narrowed their search to that area. Chloe's business brain clicked into gear. 'How far have you got with the planning? I mean, if they are set on getting married in Bermuda, the Palm Bay Hotel would be a perfect base, and I know they have a licence for a beach wedding. It sounds very romantic, if that was what they had in mind? Or are they more likely to go for a big hotel or a city wedding? Hamilton has some great options too,' Chloe suggested. She was also good friends with the new manager of the Palm Bay Hotel, Fiona, and felt she would love to push some business her way. 'I'm sure if they have a vacancy they'll be happy to fit you in. It would be good publicity for the hotel, wouldn't it?'

'I think the clients are both dreaming of sand and sunshine, so a beach wedding would be the preferred option. You are my first call so far, and I've literally come straight from a meeting with the happy couple,' Maria told her. She paused and Chloe detected more tension in the silence.

'Is the bride pregnant or something?' Chloe asked, still pondering on the speed of the wedding planning.

'No! At least I don't think so, and that would be terribly old-fashioned, wouldn't it?' Again, Chloe felt Maria seemed about to say something else, but instead rattled on with the details. 'Money is no object for these two at the moment because everything is being sponsored, from the bride's dress and knickers, to the groom's hair gel and pre-wedding waxing. Sorry, TMI. These are super savvy individuals considering they aren't even twenty-two yet.'

'Wow, I was still in a dodgy flat-share with my university mates at that age, wearing cut-off denim shorts and tie-dye crop tops. In fact, didn't we practically share a wardrobe?' Chloe said, laughing. 'Good for them though!'

'So I'll email the list of requests over and get in touch with the hotel, if you don't mind introducing me via email?' Maria said briskly, ignoring Chloe's reference to their shared questionable teenage dress sense. 'I have a whole selection of local suppliers to get through. At the moment Lara wants a five-tier marbled chocolate cake shipped from a boutique bakery place in Liverpool, but I might be putting the brakes on that one.'

'I can't imagine the cake would arrive looking very photogenic.' Chloe was giggling again. 'Or even edible! Besides, if they're getting married in Bermuda, why not use local artisans and suppliers? Actually, I've seen a florist's card on the board at the garden centre. Can't remember her name but I did look at the picture on the card and it was a stunning wedding bouquet.'

'Anything you can throw at me, please do.' Maria was sounding slightly more relaxed now. 'Neither of them have ever been near a horse, so God knows why she wants to ride into her wedding on one. You are sure Goldie is super quiet and not likely to throw her off or anything?'

'She's an angel in equine form,' Chloe assured her, 'and I'm sure I can borrow a trailer to get her to the hotel. We're down in Warwick Parish on South Shore Road, so it would be a bit awkward getting her over there if we were walking. There isn't a direct route unless I go along the beach, which is only possible at low tide.'

'Great stuff. Oh, Chloe, there is just one thing I should mention, and you can get up to speed online with the news stories if you want to. Lara in particular has some overenthusiastic trolls online and some trouble with a fairly persistent stalker recently. The police are aware but he, or she, of course, hasn't been caught yet.' Maria's voice was flat and cautious now, far from her usual brisk confidence.

'Right... I suppose that might be another reason for heading out of the UK for the wedding?' Chloe queried, thinking there was more to this story than her friend was letting on. Surely most famous people had stalkers?

'Possibly. Anyway, I wanted to let you know because security will have to be extra tight, mainly because of... because of the stalker thing. Thank you so much, darling, and I'll be in touch!'

2

Chloe had barely finished her call when a sulky-looking teen and a good-looking older boy appeared from the path to the field, and stopped in the middle of the yard. 'Hey, Antoine, how did he do today?' she asked, judging it better to pretend she hadn't seen the fall. Star, the grumpy black mare was following, docile and obedient, behind Chloe's stable manager, reins hanging loosely from his hands. But an evil glint in the horse's dark eyes showed she was still in a temper and she swished her tail crossly at the delay in returning to her stable.

'He says he wants to quit the job,' Antoine told her, slapping the boy affectionately across the shoulders. 'It's a shame because he could be really good. You gotta put the work in, though, to manage a mare like Star properly.'

Jordan glowered from under his thick fringe but still said nothing. Chloe hastily intervened. 'Well, you can't quit. We have a celebrity wedding to prepare for! My friend, Maria, is a wedding planner and she just called and asked to use Goldie for the big day. Some reality stars want to get married in Bermuda...' Chloe tried to remember. 'Um... Lara... something and Eddie Bristol. They were on...'

'*Tough Love!*' Antoine said, and then laughed at Chloe's surprise. 'Louisa is glued to the TV whenever that's on. She's like, obsessed with the whole thing. Trust me to end up with a fiancée who would rather watch reality TV than football.'

'She watches you at matches,' Chloe pointed out. Pretty, ambitious Louisa worked part time for Bermuda Tourism, as well as being halfway through a graphic design degree.

'So she should. We're fifth in the Premier Division now!' Antoine grinned, his face bright with his other passion. 'Somerset Trojans are going all the way. Anyway, tell us more about this celeb wedding. When is it?'

'Two weeks' time,' Chloe told them.

'Wow!'

Even Jordan looked more animated at the news, his eyes alight with interest. He bent down to stroke Hilda's ears, and when he eventually looked up, the grumpy expression gone from his face, he said, 'You know, from every angle this dog looks exactly like a frog...'

'You wouldn't be the first to say that,' Chloe admitted, and then jumped in pain. Star, neglected for long enough and hungry for her feed, had bitten her squarely on her shoulder.

Hilda lay panting in the shade as Chloe finished carrying water buckets and the boys mucked out and fed the animals. She popped inside and brought out a tray of lemon shortbread and iced orange juice, which she laid on the little table at the far side of the stable yard. Behind the fence, the land dropped sharply down to the beach, in a tumble of pine-scented shrubs and flowering weeds. In Bermuda's subtropical climate, with its predominantly alkaline soil, the flora and fauna at this time of year was quite beautiful, Chloe thought. She paused briefly to enjoy the view from her backyard. It was incredible to think this time last year her balcony in London had given out to seemingly endless blocks of flats, and an industrial estate full of green haulage lorries.

The vividness of the turquoise sea was so peaceful. The waves rolled gently up the beach in a froth of creamy lace, and the sun sparkled and danced across the water all the way from the rich blue sky to the rosy pink sand. Perfection. She sighed happily. She could easily see why Lara and Eddie wanted to get married here. But Maria was definitely hiding something, and whoever heard of two weeks to plan a wedding abroad?

Antoine was leaning against the fence now, munching shortbread and scrolling through messages on his phone. 'Louisa is so excited about Lara and Eddie's wedding.' A flicker of worry crossed his face. 'It wasn't meant to be a secret, was it?' His black hair fell in spiky waves over his forehead and he pushed it back impatiently.

'No. At least Maria didn't say so,' Chloe told him. 'I should think trying to organise a last-minute celebrity wedding in another country would be practically impossible to keep quiet.'

Jordan, who had downed his drink in a few thirsty gulps, was also looking at his phone. 'Eddie says on his Insta feed that he's getting married in Bermuda in September, so I guess they don't care who knows. He's tagged, like, almost *every* jeweller in Hamilton, *and* Palm Bay Hotel, and Grotto Bay, and pretty much every other hotel on the island. Wow!'

'That was quick. I only spoke to Maria half an hour ago. She must have got straight on to them and told them my suggestion was the Palm Bay Hotel. Can I see?' Chloe sipped her glass of juice and studied the proffered screen, interested to see what the bride-and-groom-to-be actually looked like.

Eddie Bristol was tall, broad-shouldered and blond. He was smiling lazily at the camera in most of the pictures, while his fiancée, Lara, was tiny and delicate, with long, wavy dark hair, a heart-shaped face and a dusting of freckles across her button nose. Her serious pouting contrasted with his generous smile. They made an extremely photogenic couple.

'She's gorgeous,' Antoine said. 'Not as gorgeous as Louisa, of course,' he added hastily, loyal as ever to his girl.

'They had fights all the time on the show,' Jordan said, his round face bright with interest. 'I didn't watch it but my mum loves it, so I sort of know what happened, and I follow Eddie on Instagram. He's a top bloke. He was a footballer, I think he even had a trial for Chelsea, but he runs a couple of gyms now.'

'And does a lot of endorsement work, I suppose,' Chloe suggested, remembering her conversation with Maria.

'Lara's known for being a right madam,' Antoine put in. 'Louisa said she saw a newspaper article saying she was lucky not to get kicked off *Tough Love*, because she scratched another girl's face and they got into a fight after one of the challenges.'

'Great,' Chloe said, her spirits dimming slightly. 'I hope she's going to behave herself with the horses.'

'She'll be fine,' Jordan said with a cheeky grin. 'Just put her on Star instead of Goldie. Look at this article... It says, "Troubled Lara, nicknamed 'Hellcat' on reality show *Tough Love* reports ex-boyfriend, Danny, for harassment".'

'Hellcat?' Chloe looked at the diminutive girl with the serious expression, intrigued. Was there something else behind her prettiness? The strain of perfection beginning to tell after her rise to fame perhaps? The couple were very young, but then Antoine and Louisa were also planning to get married, and were the same age. Funny, they seemed so much older, Chloe thought. Maria also hadn't mentioned an ex-boyfriend was possibly the stalker.

'Look, this is from last month,' Jordan said. 'This person kept leaving freaky stuff around for Lara when she did appearances at clubs, and even got into their apartment once and laid all her knickers out on the bed in a weird pattern with crossed knives... Look!'

Chloe studied the photo. It was a luxury bedroom, with lots of pale pink-and-silver silk and faux fur, but on the bedcover a spiral of skimpy underwear was laid and in the centre, as Jordan had said, four kitchen knives arranged point to point. She felt another niggle of worry. No wonder Maria had rung off so quickly after dropping her stalker comment into the conversation.

'Looks like some kind of satanic ritual,' Antoine commented, brows raised. 'Imagine knowing some stranger has been in your house messing with your underwear!'

Chloe skimmed the rest of the article. Apart from a vivid description of the 'terrifying' scene and quotes from both Lara and her fiancé, there was a line at the end stating the intruder had not been caught by police, but that this was the latest in a string of recent strange happenings. Apparently, Lara had found bloodstained flowers in her dressing room before a TV appearance, a dress had been delivered slashed beyond repair, and finally, when she had arrived early for a fashion shoot the floor had been littered with torn up, disfigured photographs of herself and Eddie.

Her ex-boyfriend, Danny Bolan, a rather famous soap actor, was mentioned, but a disclaimer stated there was no evidence to show he had anything to do with the incidents, and the harassment charges had now been dropped by Lara's legal team. It was a gossipy, bitchy article, pulling no punches in the descriptions of Lara and Eddie. She glanced down to the end of the piece.

It took a moment to sink in, but when it did, Chloe swore under her breath. The name underneath the article was Mark Canton. She might have recognised his overdramatic style.

'You okay?' Jordan asked, clearly noticing her shocked expression.

'Fine, yes I'm fine. Sorry.' Chloe hastily dragged her thoughts together. Mark! God, the last thing she wanted was to see her ex-husband's name associated with anyone she was supposed to be going to work with.

'Tough price to pay for being famous?' Antoine was saying now, clearly assuming she was just shaken by the article. 'I'd hate people writing loads of lies about me and Louisa, even if I was making a ton of cash out of it.'

Chloe blinked, looked away from Mark's byline, and studied the photograph of the crossed knives again, before shrugging the shivers away. It was business, and beyond ensuring Goldie was well treated during her role in the wedding ceremony, she wasn't part of any potential drama. 'Come on you two, get off home while I go and read Maria's email. She's always been the most efficient person I know, I'm quite sure it's waiting in my inbox.'

'It's a shame the last ride was cancelled,' Antoine said. 'Are you sure you don't mind doing evening stables on your own?'

'Perfectly happy, but thank you for asking.' Chloe smiled at him, heart still beating a little too fast at the thought of her ex-husband. 'It's okay, we're busy for the next three weeks, and now we have a celebrity wedding too. I'm keeping a close eye on the accounts.' Antoine, having run the stables single-handedly in the months before and after Dre's death, had known exactly how dire the finances had been, and how close the business had been to complete collapse.

'Sure. See you tomorrow then,' Antoine called, as he and Jordan headed off down the road. Both had scooters, and quickly departed in a roar of engine noise and dust; Antoine to the house he now rented with his fiancée in Somerset Parish, and Jordan to Hamilton, where he lived with his mum.

Chloe closed her eyes for a moment and breathed in the soft summer evening air. Odd how just seeing his name could affect her so much. But, she told herself sternly, she had come a long way since the divorce, and could certainly cope with Mark's bitchy articles popping up occasionally. He was a collector of dirt, and loved nothing better than writing about other people's misery. Although Mark was officially freelance, he specialised in sensational stories for the red-top tabloids and gossip magazines. Lara and Eddie would be considered perfect subjects.

Feeling slightly better, Chloe bent down and rubbed Hilda's furry head, thinking hard. The idea of someone invading your home, knowing your schedule better than you did, was terrifying, but not her problem. She felt sorry for Eddie and Lara as she would feel sorry for anyone who was in trouble, but it was none of her business.

Luckily, nobody was going to care what the owner of Beachside Stables did or where she went, even if she was loaning a horse for the wedding day. Mark, well Mark could do whatever the hell he wanted. She didn't care... But already she discovered she was feeling that pang of sympathy for Lara and Eddie.

Straightening, she collected the empty glasses and picked up the tray. Hilda trotted after her as she made her way through the scented garden, bright with summer flowers, to the long, low, tangerine-coloured house. One of the many things she loved about Bermuda was the colours; the pastel and vivid shades not only in the natural surroundings, but in the buildings, the food, the pink buses, the shop fronts... Soon after she arrived she had found herself pushing aside her black-and-grey outfits, dressing in bright yellow, pink and blue, just because it reflected her new mood, her new life.

Just as she reached the back door, balancing the tray

awkwardly, her mobile rang again, and she frowned at the unknown number. All bookings for the riding stables were made on a dedicated line, keeping her mobile phone free for personal use.

She wedged the phone between chin and shoulder. 'Hallo?'

'Chloe? Is that you?'

It was not a voice she had wanted to hear again, and despite the months that had passed since she was last in contact with him, her heart beat painfully hard, and she found she was clenching her hand on the door, nearly dropping the tray. The sunlight and the sea seemed miles away suddenly, and his voice dragged at her memories. For a second it almost seemed as though she had summoned him by reading his article, and now here he was, like an evil presence in her sunlit garden.

She pulled herself together with effort, and cleared her throat, focusing her gaze on her dog. As if sensing her confusion and fear, Hilda was now sitting at her feet again, large comforting brown eyes fixed on her owner's face. 'Hallo, Mark. How did you get this number?'

'Maria is organising Lara and Eddie's wedding, isn't she?' Chloe's ex-husband ignored her question and got straight down to business. His voice was as smooth and charming as ever.

Chloe didn't answer, but instead watched a line of chickens sneak under the hedge from her neighbour's garden, and stroll nonchalantly towards the small vegetable patch she had recently cultivated. Slowly, her frenzied panic cleared, her heart rate slowed down.

'*Chloe?*' He sounded slightly annoyed now at her lack of response, and she regained her composure.

'What do you want, Mark?' She was pleased to hear her voice now sounded cool and detached. She pushed the back door open with her foot and set the tray firmly but gently down on her kitchen table. *Her* table in *her* house, she thought with a sudden rush of confidence.

'I'm coming over for the wedding and I'll need some inside information. You live in Bermuda, right on site so to speak, so it makes sense Maria must have already spoken to you.'

Even knowing him as she did, Chloe was astounded at his breathtaking arrogance. How had she once been married to this idiot? She wandered back outside, and placed her hand gently against the wall of the house, *her* house. Her fingers touched the roughness of the paint, the reassuring solidity of the structure. Warmth from the sun spread a gentle cloak around her bare shoulders, and she inhaled the salt and sweetness of the coastal air for additional courage. 'Mark, we are divorced, and I think it's fair to say I actually never want to hear from you again. I don't care if you pitch up on the island by private jet with the happy couple, just don't come near me. I have no gossip, no information, nothing. Don't call me again. Ever.'

He started to speak, but she pressed the button to end the call and swiftly blocked his number. It wouldn't matter, because if she remembered correctly Mark had at least four phones and different numbers on the go, all the time.

Annoyed to find she was shaking and her heart racing again, she bent down to stroke Hilda's ears. Glancing across the garden she saw Ailsa's chickens merrily digging up her small vegetable plants and marched towards them.

The last thing she wanted was Mark coming to Bermuda, she told Hilda as the dog bounded towards the avian intruders, but if he did, she would be ready. He'd better not try any of his sly journalistic tricks on her again, or there would be murder.

3

Mark's call disturbed her usual evening routine, and even after she had settled all the animals, done a last walk around the garden and checked off some long overdue bookkeeping, Chloe still felt restless and emotional. More than anything now, she was angry that he had presumed so much, and also seemed to have totally disregarded their painful recent past.

Maria had indeed sent an email, copying in Fiona at the Palm Bay Hotel, confirming dates and adding a few details. The couple would be arriving in two days, assuming flights could be booked, and Lara would need Goldie for the wedding day, the wedding rehearsal, and possibly a photo shoot... maybe two. Maria herself, along with the couples' manager, publicity person and a couple of members of the TV production crew would be arriving on the Saturday evening flight from London.

Tomorrow is Saturday! Chloe thought, suddenly engaging her brain properly. She couldn't believe how fast things were moving. It was like being caught up on the edge of a whirlwind, and the niggling unease she had felt yesterday was rapidly overtaking any excitement at the plans. Why was it all happening so fast? What about the wedding guests, and the TV crew? Surely people needed time to make plans and to schedule things in...

She looked down at her diary and half smiled. No doubt about it, she was a planner. Although she supposed since she arrived in Bermuda she had discovered a slightly more impulsive side. But nothing on the scale of planning a wedding with two weeks' notice.

Her phone rang, and she snatched it up, checking the number, relaxing as she recognised the caller.

'Chloe! What's going on with this wedding? Is it a wind-up?' Fiona's voice was high and excited.

'No, it's for real. Sorry, the Palm Bay just popped into my head when Maria was asking about venues, and now I'm feeling guilty for landing you with a bit of a circus.'

'Don't be crazy, this is great for us. We had low bookings for September anyway because I'm having the older rooms refurbished after building work. I can easily shift my existing guests over to the pool side, which leaves the whole of the other wing, with the beach view, for the wedding party.'

Relieved, Chloe told her a little more about Maria's conversation. 'Are you going to be okay with the filming? She didn't mention that part earlier but looking at the email it seems to be a given...'

'Of course. We just need to make sure everyone keeps in touch, and honestly, Chloe, don't worry, I'm thrilled you thought of us first!'

Less than two weeks to get ready! Chloe said goodbye to Fiona and moved the paperwork around on her desk, shuffling bills into a folder while her mind dealt with the logistics of this last-minute event.

It was possible, but Chloe could see an entire seven days disappearing with this new booking, so she went through her lists and blocked out most of the days ahead of the wedding, leaving a few regulars that Antoine could probably deal with. Her previous limited experience of working with her friend was that Maria was an all-or-nothing kind of person, and organising a wedding of this size at short notice was going to take all her skills. Still, the sum mentioned to procure Goldie for the proceedings was far above what Chloe would have charged.

She sent an email back as requested, attaching copies of her business insurance, and got a reply straight away:

> Chloe, this is going to be so much fun! You are a shining star to help with the organising, and to offer to pick me up from the airport. Will confirm flights tomorrow. Lara and Eddie can't wait to meet you. xx

Hmmm... thought Chloe, hoping the young couple wouldn't be the precocious, spoilt brats her ex-husband had portrayed them as in his article.

Finally closing her laptop, she picked a few books at random and sat in bed, reading, hoping she could distract herself and calm her whirling thoughts. But only when Hilda hopped up onto the bed and curled at her feet, did she feel herself relax a little.

She woke early, eyes tired and gritty from her lack of sleep, annoyed with herself for letting Mark upset her so much. She told herself firmly it was simply because it had been unexpected, not because she still felt anything at all for him.

This morning she had a few hours off and an outing planned

after she had helped the boys with morning stables. The calming routine of coffee and toast soothed her, and she began to recover enough to consider nipping down to the beach for a quick swim. It was still only half past five. Without giving herself any time to think, she pulled on a swimsuit, grabbed a towel and called to Hilda.

The sea was silky smooth and icy cold early in the morning and she plunged in, gasping and laughing. Hilda disliked the water, and stayed at the tideline, investigating seaweed and the pale bleached bones of driftwood. The Longtails swooped overhead and gulls called raucously across the beach. Chloe floated idly on her back for a few moments before putting all her effort into a fast front crawl back to the sand. As she strode through the shallows dozens of tiny silver fish swirled around her legs, their scales gleaming and glittering in the early sunlight.

Panting from her exertions, but feeling a whole lot better after the exercise, she rubbed her hair with her towel and started to walk briskly back to the house. Hilda, much to the dog's annoyance, was persuaded to part with a four-foot long piece of driftwood she had brought home.

'Leave it in the garden,' Chloe told the dog, aware Hilda would still manage to sneak her treasure into the house at some point during the day. At least it was better than clumps of seaweed, which gave off the most peculiar smell of burnt rubber if she didn't discover them until a few days later.

Hilda dropped down onto the grass, wood between her front paws, sharp white teeth attacking the end. Chloe laughed at her antics, shutting the door firmly as she headed for the shower. She heard her phone ring briefly as she was washing her hair, and checked her voicemail as she dashed out into the kitchen. She hoped it wasn't Finn cancelling their morning plans. Instead, it was Maria:

'Hallo, darling! It's all moving very fast, so I think the best thing to do is get over to Bermuda and crack on while I'm on site. I'm booked on the BA2233.'

'Great! I'll come and collect you if you still want me too?'

'Of course, I'm dying to see your house. Kellie, that's Eddie and Lara's manager, and the others will get a couple of taxis straight to the hotel, or Fiona said she might be able to organise minibuses,' Maria said briskly. 'The time change from the UK is what? Three hours?'

'Yes, I think so.' Chloe glanced at her watch. Late morning in London.

Morning stables completed and a quick meeting with Antoine about the day's rides, and Chloe was back inside for a change of clothes. She left Hilda down in the yard with Antoine, knowing the dog would be happy pottering around with the horses, and he would tie her up in the shade if he took a ride out.

Ready for an excursion, standing in her front garden, Chloe breathed in the sweetness of the sunshine and the sea, glad to have a distraction after Mark's call. She suspected her involvement in the wedding might now be slightly less straightforward than she hoped. It would be lovely to see Maria again though. With Alexa, she was one of her closest friends. The three women had met at university and been pretty much inseparable ever since.

Maria was a hugely successful wedding planner, and Chloe was very proud of her achievements. She had checked her emails earlier to discover an additional four from her friend, asking questions, listing potential suppliers, sponsors for caterers, airport transfers... Naively, it hadn't occurred to her Maria would expect any more than her to chauffeur Goldie around and make sure the horse was well behaved and beautiful for the camera. Now it appeared she had been appointed as Bermuda liaison officer. Still, at least she had lots of friends to call on for help.

'So Goldie is going to be a TV celebrity?' Finn greeted her, as she slid into his car, leaning in for a quick kiss on the cheek. He was tall, broad-shouldered, with a shaven head and quick brown eyes. Chloe had once told him he looked more like a rugby player than an inspector in the Bermuda police. Finn was part of the Serious Crimes unit, who covered the island investigating murder and serious assault. She had called him last night to confirm today's outing, and also to tell him about the celebrity wedding.

'Yes. I didn't realise they were going to be filming the wedding, but there is also a magazine covering the whole event and a photo shoot the day before, I think...' Chloe said. 'Actually, I'm beginning to think the whole thing might be a bit of a nightmare.'

'How so?'

She felt slightly uncomfortable telling him about Mark, especially at the start of their morning out, so she brushed off his queries with some quick comment about demanding famous people, and changed the subject abruptly. 'Thanks for this. I can't believe I haven't been to the Crystal Caves before.'

'Well, it is very much a tourist destination, but still interesting. Strictly speaking it's the Fantasy Cave *and* the Crystal Caves, but everyone just calls them the Crystal Caves. No old buildings, I'm afraid,' he teased, knowing her love for historic houses, and derelict destinations. 'But the caves on the island do date back to the ice age.'

'I remember a bit from history lessons at school,' Chloe said. She and Finn had briefly shared a classroom as children. Although she could barely remember things that happened last year, she had experienced vivid flashes from her Bermuda childhood ever since she returned to the island. It was another reason she felt so comfortable with Finn – he seemed to be part of her past, but unlike her ex-husband, a good, strong, happy part.

'Actually, I love the tale they tell about how the Crystal Caves were discovered by a couple of boys playing cricket,' he said.

'Because it's related to cricket or because it's a good story?' Chloe teased him back, knowing his absolute dedication to the sport. With Finn it was a toss-up between his boat restoration and building or cricket as to which got highest billing.

'You don't remember that part?'

'No. You might as well tell me,' Chloe said, watching the view from her window as they drove past John Smith's Bay. Every moment, it seemed she marvelled at some new view to treasure on the island that was now her home and she couldn't imagine that ever changing.

'Okay, so in 1907 two kids were playing cricket, one of them missed a catch and they found the ball had gone down near a hole. The hole was pushing out warm air so they scrabbled around and discovered what lay underneath. The family who owned the land got to hear what had happened, went to investigate, dug down a little further and found the caves themselves,' Finn recited in a schoolmasterly tone, but with a glint of mischief in his face.

'Wow, they must have got such a shock, seeing what was underneath their backyard!' Chloe exclaimed. She might not have visited yet, but she had seen pictures of one of Bermuda's most incredible tourist destinations. 'All that darkness and huge stalactites hanging down.'

'I should think they were terrified to start with, but what a great adventure. And imagine telling your grandchildren about it,' Finn said, swinging the car down a gravel track, which was lined with majestic royal palms and gave out onto a lush green garden area.

Huge signs announced the entrance to the caves, and Chloe couldn't help but feel a rush of childlike excitement. Luckily, only a small queue had formed and Chloe and Finn were able to purchase tickets for the next tour.

Chloe took hers and smiled at Finn. Their little excursions and days out had become a regular event, and she enjoyed exploring with him, whether it was little-known paths around Cooper's Island Nature Reserve on the south-eastern tip of the island, or the intriguing bustle of the Royal Naval Dockyard and The West End.

The small, bubbly tour guide led them down the steps into the semi-darkness. After the bright sunshine of the day, it was a shock to be descending into the shadows. The air was warm, but surprisingly clear. Chloe had expected a musty, damp smell, in keeping with other caves she had explored.

They went further and further down into the limestone caves, following wooden walkways, listening to the tour guide, but distracted by the sight of thousands of ancient stalactites stretching towards a still lake of turquoise and silver.

The other people on the tour murmured in awe, snapping photographs, and spreading out to explore. Reflections of the stalactites above threw beautiful shapes across the water, and Chloe leant on the walkway railings, lost in the magic of the place.

'Beautiful, isn't it?' Finn said softly.

Everyone was still speaking in hushed voices, as though out of respect for the wonders of nature. The cave was like a huge underground cathedral, peaceful and glowing softly, as though hundreds of candles had been placed in the crevices of the rocky walls.

They inspected the other paths along the tourist trail, careful not to touch any of the incredible formations, which were, as Chloe remarked to Finn, as much like works of art as sculptures in any gallery anywhere in the world.

'How am I going to top this excursion?' Finn laughed as they reached the light at the top of a long flight of steps, and emerged into the warmth and the brightness of the sunshine.

'I'm not sure you can,' Chloe said, blinking in the sudden harsh daylight, her eyes adjusting slowly. 'That was incredible.'

'Have you got time for a coffee?'

She glanced at her watch. 'Yes, but a quick one. Sorry, I've got to take a ride out at three.'

'Don't be sorry, it's your job, and it's great to see the stables doing so well. Dre would be so happy,' Finn told her as he joined the queue for drinks.

Chloe sat down at one of the little wooden tables and gratefully accepted a steaming cup when he returned. She hadn't been totally sure she would tell him, but now, the words were coming out before she even thought twice. 'My ex-husband is coming to Bermuda. He called yesterday.'

4
―――

Finn watched her, concern evident in his expression. He spoke a moment later, having made an instant connection. 'You said he was a journalist? Is he covering the wedding?'

'Yes. He asked me if I could give him any gossip, even offered me money.' Chloe found herself getting annoyed all over again. 'I don't want him here, Finn. I know he isn't coming to see me, but I feel like Bermuda is such a part of my life, my new life and him coming here is wrong.'

She had been going to say having Mark here would be like tainting her new-found happiness, but checked herself at the last moment. It was true, but sounded a bit silly, especially admitting that Mark's visit would affect her so much. Finn might start to wonder just how much she had actually moved on since her divorce. She glanced at him, and brushed a strand of hair from her face, waiting.

Finn sipped his coffee, a half-smile on his face, sunglasses pushed back, brown eyes sparkling with intelligence and interest. He was leaning back in his chair, dressed for off duty in a faded pink T-shirt and stone-coloured shorts, long legs stretched out in the sunshine. The fingers of his left hand traced a pattern on the wooden tabletop, and the lines in his face when he smiled made her heart give a little leap. 'I don't think you need to worry. You have enough friends here now, so if he does make a nuisance of himself we can always have a little word. Any of us.'

'I'm not sure it would be a police matter.' Chloe smiled in spite of her worries. 'At least I hope not.'

'I was thinking more of your neighbour,' Finn told her gravely. 'Nobody would want to mess with Ailsa, and she treats you almost like family now. Mark has zero chance of hassling you. The chances are, he just thought he'd try his luck. How does he know you are involved with the wedding?'

She sighed, twisting a length of hair between her fingers. 'We have enough mutual friends who probably told him Maria was organising the event, and he must have guessed she would get straight in touch with me.'

'Okay, but you said no, and turned down his offer of money, so he'll have to find another source. For an event that size there will be plenty of other people who are prepared to make a quick dollar or two,' Finn said comfortingly.

'That's true.' But Chloe knew how persistent Mark could be when he was on the trail of a story. He would do almost anything to get what he called 'front page dirt' and the niggling worry distracted her for the rest of the day.

That evening, leaving a grumpy Hilda with a chew bone to entertain her, she went with Peter, the taxi driver to collect Maria from the airport.

It was a lovely drive, and she couldn't help but relive her own arrival, remembering the smells, the warmth and the feeling of homecoming.

Maria had travelled business class, and was one of the first passengers to clear the immigration channel and pass through customs, even beating the airline crew, who stood with their passports in a cordoned-off channel.

'Darling!' Maria dumped her handbag on the trolley and hugged Chloe with such violence she nearly toppled them both into her luggage.

'Oh, Maria, it's so good to see you!' Chloe realised she had tears in her eyes. 'Look at me, I'm such a softy. Where are the others? You said Eddie and Lara's manager was coming today?'

'Still arguing about bags, I think,' Maria told her airily. 'They're getting taxis anyway, so we don't need to wait for them.'

'Shouldn't I say hallo or anything?' Chloe queried. 'Maria?'

Maria was marching onwards past several potted plants, and as Chloe caught up, she lowered her voice. 'Believe me, you don't want to meet Kellie until you have to. And Ben is a pain in the arse.'

Chloe frowned, glanced back at the throng of noisy passengers pouring through from baggage reclaim, and then shrugged.

'Mandy is wild she couldn't come too,' Maria told her as Chloe began to lead the way across the airport and out of the double doors. 'She can't get any time off until December, though, so perhaps we might be able to pop out and see you before Christmas?'

'That would be wonderful. Have you seen Alexa recently?'

'Last week. She's coming to stay soon, isn't she?'

'End of October,' Chloe said, waving to Peter as they approached with the trolley full of luggage. 'I wanted to get everything sorted out before I had friends over, and the winter will be my low season, so less work and more time to play tourist with my visitors.'

'Sounds perfect,' Maria agreed. 'Hallo, you must be Peter! Chloe's told me all about you, and it's lovely to actually meet you at last.'

'And you.' Peter beamed at her, pushed his old hat to the back of his shiny bald head and began to load the cases into the boot.

As the taxi pulled smoothly away and began the drive across the narrow causeway, Chloe enjoyed Maria's sigh of pleasure as she took in the view. The turquoise-blues of sea and sky mixed with the lush greens of coastal vegetation made for a stunning visual welcome.

'Chloe tells me you're here to organise a wedding?' Peter said, his dark eyes shrewd in the mirror, almost hidden by the wrinkles which lined his face. 'One of these reality TV stars, isn't it?'

News had spread fast and as Chloe and Peter had already discussed, there were plenty of rumours going around already, including one that the couple were going to be married in the Crystal Caves, and another that they would exchange vows underwater whilst scuba-diving in one of the coastal wreck sites.

'Yes, Eddie and Lara are apparently thrilled at all the positive press in the last day or so,' Maria said, still staring at the view. 'God, I can hardly believe these colours are real. If only I could paint! The blues and golds on the skyline are just intense.'

'One of my boys works in security,' Peter said to Maria. 'I'll give you his card when we get to Chloe's place. I imagine you might need something extra in that department. I've seen plenty of famous people on the island and it can get out of hand with all their fans following them around.'

'Oh, thank you,' Maria said gratefully. 'I think the hotel have arranged their own security team, but we are going to need a lot of people for the actual wedding day. You wouldn't believe how popular these two are!'

'Oh, I know, my granddaughter works at the paper and she's written a piece about it already. Lovely girl, and very professional. I'll give you her card too, just in case you want to arrange an interview or anything.'

Chloe grinned to herself. Peter and his wife had been so kind to her, and their large, bustling, extended family held down every possible job imaginable. If you needed a plumber, a lawyer, a photographer or a gardener, Peter would recommend a family member. He had stacks of business cards and neatly arranged folders that he kept in the glove compartment in his taxi.

Once they arrived at Beachside Stables, and Maria was furnished with a wad of the business cards, Peter left, waving out the window, narrowly avoiding Ailsa's chickens, who had popped out of the hedge, changed their minds and scrambled back to escape the car.

Maria, who had watched Peter's exit with a slightly bemused expression, was now laughing. 'Gosh, are those your birds?'

'No, next door's. I have some too, but mine stay down in the yard. Now I thought we'd have a quick drink and I'll show you round the place before Fiona picks you up at ten. Are you exhausted?'

'Me? No. Dying for the loo, but I can't wait to look around. I mean, wow, Chloe, this place is just heaven, and I've only had a ride from the airport. And your house is *tangerine-coloured*. Oh, and the white roof! Perfection! What do you have to drink?' Her words were spilling out, enthusiasm and emotion overflowing. She hugged Chloe again.

'First night on the island so it has to be a Rum Swizzle,' Chloe told her, returning the hug. 'Bathroom is that way.'

Maria enthused over the interior of Chloe's new home. 'It's

just so you in a way London never was, and look at you! The space, and beach vibe, and the homeliness...' Her quick green eyes flashed over Chloe's face, taking in her new clothes, new shape and general air of happiness. 'I should have said it before but you look amazing, and you have muscles!' She squeezed Chloe's forearms and made her laugh. 'I thought when I saw you at the airport how happy you looked.'

'It must be all that mucking out. Seriously, though, I am happy. It's wonderful here, and the business is slowly getting back up to speed. Come and see the yard.' Chloe mixed them both their drinks and they clinked glasses, before she led the way down the garden to the stables.

Maria enthused about everything, taking pictures of the horses, the view down to the sea in the soft evening light, even the goats in their pen.

'It's such a shame you can't stay here,' Chloe told her as they leant against the fence that separated the yard from the cliffside, sipping their drinks, enjoying the balmy scented air.

'I know, darling, but it really is a work trip, even though it doesn't feel like one at the moment, and I need to be on-site ready for any emergencies. At any wedding there are always disasters, but with celebrity clients even a chipped toenail is a nightmare of extreme proportions.' She sipped her dark drink carefully. 'This cocktail is delicious. I must recommend it for the wedding reception.'

'I made it a bit weaker than it should be, just in case Fiona wants to talk business when you get to the hotel,' Chloe said, as they admired the horses one last time, Maria cooing over Goldie and the stable cat, but slightly wary of the chickens.

Chloe watched her friend closely before she said, 'Maria, why *is* the wedding going ahead in such a hurry?'

Maria straightened and leant back against the stable wall, the picture of elegance. But tiny frown lines had appeared between her eyes, and she looked strained, Chloe thought. 'Darling, I honestly don't know. When Kellie originally approached me she gave me a two-month window, but she was back on the phone the next day in a bit of a state, pushing for the quickest date we could do.'

'She never said why though?'

Maria shook her head, dark glossy hair catching the evening sun. 'No. I have to admit I was a bit worried, myself. I mean, I wondered if it was some kind of PR stunt and they would cancel the wedding before the big day. It's been done before.'

'It just feels a bit odd,' Chloe told her.

'I know. But don't forget I've met with the happy couple a few times now and they seem genuine. They are just so excited for a beach wedding,' Maria told her.

'No more stalker incidents then? I read about the house invasion,' Chloe told her. 'It must have been terrifying.'

'Well, Kellie did say nobody has been arrested, and I suppose although it was fairly threatening, nobody was hurt. They seem inclined to believe it *was* Lara's ex-boyfriend, Danny. He's been making a bit of a nuisance of himself ever since she hooked up with Eddie,' Maria said with a sigh. 'I do hope it's all sorted out by the wedding. Lara apparently reported him for harassment but then decided not to pursue it.' She broke off and fiddled with a line of horseshoes Chloe had nailed onto the wall for luck, tracing the metal curves with a careful finger.

'I read about that, and I'd be surprised if they weren't still taking it seriously. Perhaps they're just putting on a brave face?' Chloe suggested, moving closer so her friend looked up sharply. 'Oh, I should probably mention that Mark called me. He was hoping for gossip on the wedding,' she added in what she hoped was a casual manner.

'*Seriously*?' Maria's eyes flashed and her mouth tightened in anger. 'I suppose someone told him I was involved.'

'And that it was being held in Bermuda,' Chloe added. 'Honestly, don't worry. I was pretty thrown when he called, but I'm okay now.'

'Sure?' Maria looked hard at her friend, obviously concerned. 'I'm sorry, it never occurred to me he would get in touch, and now you have to put up with him coming here. God, Chloe, are you sure you're all right with it?'

Chloe nodded. 'I wasn't at first, but I am now. After all, he's coming to work, not to hassle me, and at least I've had a warning and he isn't just going to turn up at the house.' She squeezed Maria's hand gently. 'Now come on, girl, you've got a wedding to plan!' She ushered her friend back up the garden, and into the kitchen.

'I'm hoping I can just settle in and get straight down to work tomorrow morning. Fiona seems very organised and efficient and she's agreed to do so much in exchange for the publicity, I'm desperate to deliver for her,' Maria admitted, pushing her long dark hair back. As usual it was fashionably cut, with a jagged fringe showing off her green cat's eyes, hanging to her shoulder blades at the back. Her nails were short and varnished a brilliant red and she picked up one of Chloe's handmade candles, holding it to her nose, 'This is gorgeous. It smells like the beach.'

Chloe bent down to the cupboard under the sink and pulled out a cardboard box. 'Take one for your hotel room. Remember that course I did ages ago? I found the notes and ordered some new scents.' She smiled. '"Bermuda, and island life in general, are great for creativity.'

'Thanks, I will.' Maria chose two candles, before heading to Chloe's bathroom again. She returned ten minutes later, make-up immaculate, scent applied and a determined look on her face. 'There,' she finished off with a slick of scarlet lipstick. 'How do I look? Able to pull off the wedding of the year?'

'Gorgeous as ever, and yes, you are more than capable of

pulling this off,' Chloe told her friend. 'Look, I can see Fiona's car out the window.' She waved and picked up the handle of one of Maria's bags to help her friend.

Fiona, who was small, pretty, and vivacious, called out a greeting as the two women stepped out of Chloe's house. 'Hi, Chloe, and nice to meet you, Maria! We're all set our end, and I just can't wait to show off Palm Bay. I sent one of the hotel minibuses for your other guests. They are just having a quick drink and nibbles on the terrace before we chat business. Let's go and get you settled in, before the hard work begins.'

Once Maria was dispatched to the Palm Bay Hotel with Fiona, Chloe tidied up, enjoying the peace but also revelling in the pleasure of introducing her friend to her little home. She had put a lot of effort into making the house somewhere between calming and cosy, and was pleased with the results. The framed photographs of Dre, of her childhood, the prints she had bought from the Stone Gallery at Dockyard, and the stack of antique tobacco boxes, all meant something to her. It was home in a way her London flat had never been and it was fun to show it off.

She was just going to bed when she received a text from Maria. She opened it, smiling, expecting a chat, but froze, her eyes fixed on the picture attachment:

OMG, just got to my room and found this outside. Freaked. Hotel security are checking it out Xx

The picture showed a huge flower arrangement, full of beautiful white roses and lilies. But the arrangement was a funeral wreath, and the whole thing appeared to be splashed in blood. The pure white petals were stained with scarlet drops and streaks, and some of the lilies drooped, bruised, as though their crisp beauty had been crushed by a vicious hand.

There was a little printed card attached to the flowers, and Chloe zoomed in to read it:

Lara and Eddie,
Welcome to your dream wedding.
xox

5

An early start was ensured as Maria texted at 6am with more about the funeral wreath drama from last night. Chloe, who had tried to call her friend several times after she received the text, groaned and rolled out of bed for her morning coffee.

Sorry I bothered you last night. Security are great and they are sure it's a prank. Ha! So not funny. Take care and speak later x

Chloe, who had spent a long time worrying about Maria's safety last night, felt glad her friend was feeling confident, but not entirely sure if the confidence was misplaced. It seemed a little odd to brush off what was a fairly horrifying gesture. She sipped her coffee and thought she would speak to Maria later, and find out exactly what was happening and if the police had been notified.

Hilda bounced out into the garden to bark at the stable cat, who was climbing the fig tree, and Chloe got on with her domestic chores, enjoying the breeze and sunlight streaming in at the windows. Late summer on the island really was heaven, whatever else was going on. When she first arrived in early spring the weather had been changeable, with heavy rainstorms and high wind as likely as the golden sunshine. But since June the sun had settled on Bermuda for a long and beautiful few months, and Chloe loved every moment of it.

She was showered and dressed by the time Antoine started work in the yard. He waved and she was just about to go out and join him when her phone rang. 'Chloe, I've just started doing the revised schedule with Fiona. Can you confirm the times I sent over, please?'

'Sorry, Maria, I haven't had a chance to even look at my emails, but thanks for waking me up with your text this morning,' Chloe told her friend, yawning. 'And I tried to call you after last night. Are you really okay?'

Maria laughed, but it sounded slightly forced. 'Of course, darling. Sorry, I was just tired and the whole thing freaked me out, but I'm sure it was just one of those things. I feel super safe at the hotel, there are security guards everywhere, and Fiona was very reassuring.'

'That's all right then. Did you tell Lara and Eddie?'

'I suppose Kellie will, but I won't mention it. I mean, it was clearly aimed at me, as it was left at my door. Probably a journalist trying to rattle my cage. Probably Mark! Kellie and the team don't want any negative publicity so if you don't mind keeping it quiet?'

Something about her tone didn't quite ring true. It was as though she was trying to convince herself a blood-splashed funeral wreath was a pretty everyday occurrence. 'I won't tell anyone. As long as you are okay, I suppose,' Chloe said doubtfully.

'Yes, darling, and thank you, but as soon as you get a chance please let me know about those times.' Her voice changed again, low and brisk. 'Actually, I am having a bit of a stressful day even without the little flower delivery last night. Lara had some guy on her social media messaging her, telling her she would never make it to Bermuda and the plane would crash. They somehow got hold of the flight number and everything. Now she's been googling the Bermuda Triangle and she's panicking.'

'That's an awful thing to say!' Chloe was horrified. 'Who would do that? The stalker? Her ex-boyfriend?'

'Oh, Lara and Eddie both get death threats all the time, really awful messages as well as the usual attacks on their looks and lifestyle,' Maria said. 'I think Kellie will be able to calm her down, but I've had to brief the security team, and we had to tell the airport and the airline, which caused a huge amount of fuss.'

'God, I'm so glad I'm not famous,' Chloe said. 'I can't imagine putting up with that kind of thing on a daily basis. Speaking of stress, have you heard anything from Mark?'

'Bastard!' Maria said furiously. 'How dare he even contact you, or me, after what he did. I'll make sure it gets back to that stupid girlfriend of his that he's been pestering his ex-wife. He'll regret he tried anything with you.'

'Maria, calm down! Thank you, but I think just ignoring him is the way to go. He is only after a story on Eddie and Lara, which obviously I won't give.' Chloe ran a hand through her hair, combing out the tangles, pulling a face in the mirror. She really needed a haircut. Which had nothing to do with Mark making her insecurities bubble to the surface once more. Obviously.

'Still, I don't need any excuse to kick him in the balls, because I've been dying to do it for years, so let me know if he gives you any more hassle,' Maria said protectively.

'I'll do it myself, but honestly don't worry. It was a shock when he called, that's all.'

Chloe ended the phone call and went down to the yard with Hilda, tying her long blonde-grey hair up into a high ponytail as she went. Insects chirruped lazily from the lush flower beds, full of Bermudiana and phlox. She inhaled the scent as she walked. A bird was having a dust bath under the hedge, watched beadily from across the lawn by the stable cat.

'Did your friend arrive okay?' Antoine asked. He was cleaning tack, and she inhaled the luscious smells of saddle soap and leather as she, too, picked up a stirrup leather and attacked it with a wet sponge.

'Yes, she started work early this morning and texted me at 6am!' Chloe told him. She decided not to mention the funeral wreath. The less people who knew the better if it *had* been done to rile Maria herself. Maria hadn't mentioned the fact that the card had been a message to Lara and Eddie, but Chloe supposed she must be used to handling things like this. She truly hadn't seemed unduly bothered during their call earlier.

Antoine looked impressed. 'Bet she's stressed out planning the wedding though. What if something goes wrong? It's all down to the wedding planner, isn't it?'

'I suppose so and she's always been super organised. She hardly slept when we were at university together, just lived on coffee, and I don't think much has changed,' Chloe told him, dunking bits into buckets of warm water, and beginning on Candy's saddle. The tack was soon gleaming and ready for clients, so she grabbed the body brush and started on Star.

Antoine and Chloe each took an early ride out, and Chloe dashed back to the house to check her emails and respond to Maria's request for timings. She also needed to do her accounts properly, she thought, looking at the neat stack of receipts on her desk. Although she was careful to update the bookkeeping every Friday, she made an effort to go through everything once a month and do a quick forecast for the next few months. They were slowly getting out of debt and with business picking up in June and July she had been able to save for things like buying hay in bulk and getting the horses shod on a six-week basis. She was also putting a bit away to give Antoine a Christmas bonus for all his hard work, and a few hundred dollars as an extra wedding gift.

She was just going back outside, her mind already on the afternoon bookings and more tack cleaning, when there was a sound at the door and a figure appeared, throwing a large shadow across her path.

'Mark!' Chloe, having almost walked into him in her haste, now shoved him away, and steadied herself against the door, heart pounding. Hilda barked, rushing up to him so ferociously he backed even further from the house.

'Hallo, Chloe. I just thought I would pop in and say hallo.' He was brushing down his shirt as though her headlong rush might have dirtied his clothing, but he was smiling. His brown hair was spiked with gel, black-rimmed glasses and stubble giving him a kind of aging rock star look, and he wore a black leather jacket slung over his shoulders.

'What the hell are you doing here?' Chloe said, recovering, furious at her fast-beating heart and instinctive retreat back into her kitchen, which allowed him to take a step over the threshold. What part of 'I never want to see you again', did he not understand? But he had always been ruthless when he was on the track of a juicy story. 'When did you arrive?'

She remembered making him angry when she had expressed distaste at his subject choices; the famous singer who had a secret child, the actors who had their life choices questioned on the front cover of some magazine. It seemed very sad to Chloe, making a living digging up people's secrets and generating misery. But she supposed the other side of the coin was people couldn't get enough of celebrity gossip, and with online content to fill as well as actual physical copies of newspapers and magazines, Mark made a good living out of his chosen subjects.

He followed her into the kitchen, got halfway and stopped as Hilda began growling again. 'I came in on the same flight as Maria and the others. Cute dog. Is it yours?' He put out a hand but Hilda, picking up vibes from her mistress, continued to growl.

'Yes she is.' Chloe stood in the doorway, making no effort to discourage Hilda's guard dog instincts. Mark looked the same as ever, with his good-looking square face and big smile that didn't quite reach his grey eyes. They were nearly the same height and it had always been easy to be able to look him in the eye without tilting her head back. 'Mark, I really don't think we have anything to say to each other. I told you not to come here, not to contact me and yet you pitch up on my doorstep. Where are you staying anyway?'

'Fourways Inn. Nice place and very convenient. Come on, Chlo.' He had always shortened her name when he wanted something. She supposed he thought it sounded affectionate. 'Let's have a coffee and a chat. For old times' sake? I actually saw Maria at the airport back in London, but she really doesn't like me so I didn't try and speak to her. It took me ages to get through the airport in Bermuda but I saw you head off in the taxi together, so I figured it might be best to talk to you on your own.'

'How's your girlfriend? I'm sure she would be delighted to hear you'd been visiting your ex-wife,' Chloe countered and then almost groaned as she realised she sounded jealous. Actually, the best thing about seeing the man who had been her husband was discovering she had no feelings left for him. Not the slightest twinge. Annoyance, trepidation, and definite anger that he was trespassing in her new life, yes, but nothing else. All at once she felt better.

'She'd be fine about it,' he said. 'Look, do we have to do this on the doorstep?' He glanced to his left and Chloe heard the squawk of an approaching chicken.

'We don't have anything to talk about. Anything I have to do with Eddie and Lara's wedding is private, a business arrangement, and we have nothing to say to each other on a personal level.' She was pleased to hear her voice sounded cold and firm.

'Don't you think it's odd this is so last minute? How does Maria feel about organising something this big in a few days?' Mark pushed on.

'Are you all right, Chloe?'

Bless her neighbour, Chloe thought, as Ailsa sailed to the rescue, pink lace tunic top floating in the breeze, trousers muddied from working in her garden, and a chicken clasped to her breast. She snuck a glance at Mark and was delighted to see he looked totally wrong-footed, thrown off his smooth chat line.

The chickens, always keen to investigate strangers, beat Ailsa to the kitchen door.

'I'm fine thanks, Ailsa,' Chloe told her. 'This is Mark, my ex-husband, and he was just leaving.'

She made no attempt to introduce her neighbour properly and Ailsa merely nodded at the newcomer, beady black eyes bright with interest, lips pursed as she considered him. 'Chloe's told me all about *you*.'

He had recovered a little and smiled at her, trying to shuffle away from the chickens, who were now enthusiastically pecking at his shoelaces with their sharp yellow beaks, emitting little coos of satisfaction. 'All good I hope.'

Ailsa grinned wickedly, wrinkles collecting around her eyes and mouth. 'I wouldn't say it was good, no. You'll be just leaving then, Chloe said?'

'I'm over here to cover Eddie and Lara's wedding,' Mark told her, clearly, as many had done before him, underestimating the tiny, feisty woman.

'Well off you go and cover it then,' Ailsa told him bluntly. 'Wedding's at the Palm Bay Hotel not down here.'

Chloe bit her lip to stop herself laughing, and Mark stared, apparently at a loss. When Antoine called from the yard, also asking if she was okay, he gave up. 'Well, I'll see you around then, Chloe. We'll catch up another time.' He started to walk away, but stumbled over his shoelaces, which one of the chickens had completely undone. He swore and regained his balance without another word.

Chloe heard a scooter start up at the front of the house, and turned with relief to Ailsa. 'Thank you for that.' She bent down and smoothed Hilda's fur and added to the chickens, 'And thank you, Betsy and Onion, you might have made my day.'

Ailsa laughed, and Chloe waved to Antoine, who was still hovering by the gate to the garden. 'I'm fine thanks, tell you about it later,' she called.

He gave her a grin and the thumbs up and turned back to lugging straw bales into the feed room.

'Well, he's a bit persistent isn't he, your ex? I thought you told him not to come to the house?' Ailsa said. 'Want a cup of tea?'

Chloe went back into the kitchen and put the kettle on, dumping a packet of biscuits and two plates on a tray, and leading the way back out into the garden. 'I did tell him not to come here! He probably thinks he can charm his way back into my good books and get something to write about.'

'He's a reporter though, you said?' Ailsa munched a biscuit and scattered a few crumbs for the chickens. 'You must have to be nosy to be in that job. He probably still thinks you might give him some gossip on the wedding. I would say they're all the same these journalists, but Peter's granddaughter, Daphne, works for the paper and she's a lovely girl, very smart. *She certainly wouldn't be door-stopping people.*'

'Oh yes, Peter told me about Daphne. But this is a different form of journalism. Mark gets nasty stories, the things people want to keep hidden, the things certain publications pay a fortune to get hold of.' Chloe sighed. 'But I really don't want him here. I mean, there's no way I'd tell him a single thing about Lara and Eddie anyway, even if I hadn't signed all those non-disclosure forms my friend just emailed over. But it's more than that. I feel like he's part of my past and I don't want him here, intruding on my future. Does that sound silly?'

'No. Everyone makes mistakes,' Ailsa said comfortingly. 'Take my neighbour with her cockerel. She swears he can't get through the hedge but yesterday morning, I found him in my veg patch! Cocks or ex-husbands, they're all the same.' She waved her hand dismissively.

Chloe caught Ailsa's eye and laughed. 'I suppose they are.' She grinned at her friend. 'At least Antoine and Louisa's wedding is going to be lovely, just all their friends and family on the beach.'

Ailsa nodded approvingly. 'He's a good boy. I hope some of his work ethic is going to rub off on my grandson.'

'I think it already has,' Chloe told her. 'And Jordan's riding lessons are going well.'

'Business is good then? I haven't seen you much this past week, but I've noticed a good stream of traffic pitching up on the driveway.'

'Yes, it's pretty busy but it's certainly tailing off a bit in the last couple of days. I'm trying to do as many rides as possible before we hit the winter season, because everyone says the tourists dry up for a bit before Christmas, and again March and February time. Jordan will hopefully be able to take rides out by next summer, if he keeps working here.'

'The tourists will start to ease off soon, you're right. Less cruise ships and we're not the Caribbean, no matter how many people think we are, so we don't have the weather to tempt them in,' Ailsa told her.

'I think the stables will be okay. The fee for Eddie and Lara's wedding will see us through until at least February, and pay off a few more debts, so I'm keeping my fingers crossed,' Chloe said.

Ailsa was watching her garden. 'It's that blinking cockerel again. Right, I'm off but let me know if that idiot ex-husband bothers you again, and I'll be round.' She winked and rushed off across the grass, her avian entourage pursuing her enthusiastically.

Chloe carried the tray inside, checked the time and called Hilda, who had been lying panting in the shade. Jonas and his sister had booked a private trail ride, and she was looking forward to catching up with them. They had become friends after the happenings earlier in the year and every month or so the three of them would enjoy an hour's ride together.

As usual, they were punctual and professionally turned out, with smart shiny boots and hats. Melissa's brown hair was tied neatly into a ponytail and Jonas carried a gift from the gallery they owned in the Naval Dockyard.

'How lovely to see you!' Chloe smiled, accepting the little pack of greetings cards with thanks. 'You're so kind but really you don't have to keep bringing me presents.'

Melissa, who seemed to be finally recovering from the traumatic events of the spring, kissed her on both cheeks. 'It seems ages since you came to visit the gallery. We're having a little party next week, maybe you would like to come?'

The thought didn't terrify her as much as it would have done once, and really, as business was good, she might be able to treat herself to some more artwork for her house. 'I'd love to see you both, next week is a bit busy. Have you been painting again, Melissa?'

'Yes! I've done a few studies of the coastline at Cooper's Island Nature Reserve, and some lizards, and...'

Jonas interrupted her, laughing. 'She doesn't stop painting now, I'm left to run the gallery by myself. She even took a tent up to Cooper's Island and got permission to spend a weekend up there, camping out.'

Melissa hit his arm, also laughing. 'You have no idea how much I'm enjoying rediscovering my creative side.'

The ride was lovely, passing the romantic novelist's ruined house, which sat in the jungle area to the west of Chloe's house. A swift trot along the Railway Trail, and they ended with a gallop along the beach, hooves splashing up salty spray, drenching the riders.

'So are you all set for the celebrity wedding of the year?' Melissa asked as she helped untack Star. The little mare liked Melissa and she was one of the few people who was spared her teeth.

'God, I don't know.' Chloe smiled at Melissa. 'Eddie and Lara are arriving on the island tomorrow morning and coming over to see Goldie. My friend Maria, who's organising the whole thing is beyond stressed and you should see the schedule! It's packed. I suppose that's what happens when you want to get married at such short notice.'

'Seems a bit odd to suddenly decide to get married on Bermuda without time to plan,' Melissa said, heaving the saddle across one arm and giving Star a hug, smoothing her wild black mane back onto the correct side.

'Maybe she's pregnant?' suggested Jonas with a hint of mischief touching his voice. He had moved away to smoke a cigarette. He was leaning elegantly against the wrought-iron table that looked so pretty positioned under the bougainvillea.

'Don't be so silly, Jonas. We aren't living in Victorian times!' Melissa told him severely.

'No, I don't think it's that. From what Maria says they are just pretty impulsive and enjoying their fame. When you suddenly have so much money, I guess it might be fun to decide on a beach wedding seven hours from your hometown, with two weeks' notice,' Chloe said.

'Well, I think it's a bit sad,' Melissa said decisively as she picked up a beer from the cooler she and her brother had brought, and popped the top. 'You should get married in a place that means something to you, not just because it looks good on Instagram.'

'Ouch!' Jonas was laughing now.

'It's true,' Melissa said passionately. 'There is so much more to Bermuda than location and beautiful beaches. The island has a heart and soul, not to mention an incredible history and culture. It's disrespectful to think it's only worth coming here because it's a "destination".'

'I do agree,' Chloe said, 'but I haven't spoken to Eddie and Lara yet. They might well have other reasons for wanting to get married in Bermuda. And my friend is trying to persuade them to use all local suppliers so I guess it will be good for economic reasons, if nothing else.'

Antoine was coming back with the other ride, and he waved at them. Melissa had widened her friendship group since the events of earlier in the year, and often joined Antoine and his friends for a night out. Jonas, older and smoother, stayed within his society circle, but he seemed far more relaxed and at ease, confident at last in his abilities to manage the family business.

Antoine called a greeting as he came nearer, but Melissa was staring out to sea, her whole body suddenly tense. 'Can you see that? Over on the rocks?'

Jonas and Chloe hurried to her side, shielding their eyes against the sun, blinking at the place she was pointing.

The beach curved away to the left, divided from the next cove by a line of limestone, which stretched out into the waves. The object was lying half on the rocks, half in one of the natural rock pools created by the geography of the island.

'It could be a fishing net and seaweed?' Jonas ventured, as they stood staring out to sea.

'It's a body!' Melissa said shrilly. 'I'm sure it could be the wreckage of a small boat... Look! A bit further along the rocks. And there's something else... A body. I think there's a body down there!'

6

Chloe pushed her hair back from her hot face. She didn't have the best eyesight, especially in bright sunlight, but she had to agree it could be a body. 'Let's go down and check before we call the police or coastguard.'

Antoine, half attentive to his clients, half watching Melissa, called out as the three were starting down the trail to the beach. In a few short sentences Chloe told him what had happened.

'I couldn't hear what you were saying, but it was obvious something was wrong. It does look like a body and Melissa's right, an upturned boat maybe,' Antoine said, after directing his gaze towards the rocks.

'Can you make sure the clients go as fast as possible? If it is a body, one of us will phone for help, but I need you to direct any emergency vehicles,' Chloe told him quickly.

'Of course!'

Chloe started running, catching up with Jonas, who had stopped to wait for her, feet sinking in the deep powdery sand under the cliffside. 'You don't have to come if you don't want to,' he told her breathlessly as they continued onto the blessedly easier going wet compacted sand.

'Of course I do. That poor person could still be alive. If they took a boat out and got into trouble...' It was a common occurrence during high season. People forgot the tides, were caught in treacherous undercurrents and quickly became exhausted in their panicked efforts to get back to land.

Melissa was already scrambling across the rocks, and she reached the body first. 'He's dead!' she called out to Jonas and Chloe. 'And it's a paddleboard, not a boat.'

'Poor man!' Chloe inched along the rocks and halted above the tragic little scene. The torso was lying half out of the water, spreadeagled across the rough rocks, arms outstretched, but the man's legs were still in the water, the material of his bright red shorts moving gently in the tidal rock pool.

Jonas was already on the phone to the authorities, explaining their position, giving details.

Melissa was right down next to the body, pressing tentative fingers into his neck. 'I definitely can't feel any pulse!'

Chloe leant over, balancing precariously, and touched the man's back. He was stiff and cold.

'Should we turn him over? I mean if he's drowned but not quite dead, he might need to cough water up or something?' Melissa said hopefully. Her face was pale and her hands shook a little.

'I don't think we can,' Chloe told her, shivering slightly, biting her lip. 'One of us might easily fall and slip, the angle he's at.'

Jonas waved an arm at her, finished his call and relayed the information. 'It's too dangerous to try and move him. They said wait for the medics and police, and don't touch anything.'

The Bermuda Fire and Rescue Service, an ambulance and two police cars could soon be seen by the three on the rocks. The BFRS had a large four-by-four which made light work of the sandy terrain, and Chloe was extremely glad when she,

Melissa and Jonas were able to head back to the safety of the beach, allowing the experts access to the scene.

After answering a few standard questions as statements were collected, Chloe led the others back up to the yard, where Antoine was waiting.

'I sent them all straight down. Is he really dead?' Antoine asked quickly.

'Yes. His paddleboard was on the rocks a little further along. It's terrible,' Jonas said soberly, as he and Melissa accepted the drinks Antoine offered.

Chloe took hers and gulped the cold water gratefully. She felt slightly sick and still quite shaky. 'I suppose when you drift out to sea and get into trouble it must be hard to attract any help. People would think you were just waving or something.' She bent down to hug Hilda as the dog skittered out of the undergrowth, nose sandy and paws stained green.

'I let her out when I came back with the ride,' Antoine told Chloe and she nodded gratefully.

Jonas gave her hand a quick squeeze. 'It's awful, but sadly when you live surrounded by the sea, there will always be tragedies associated with it.'

'We should go, we have a private viewing at the gallery in an hour,' Melissa said, glancing at her watch and changing the subject abruptly. 'Thanks for the drink, Antoine, and Chloe, ring us if you need us, won't you?' She was still very pale, her cheekbones standing out sharply under her tanned skin, her grey eyes strained.

Chloe hugged her, and sat watching them go. 'My legs feel like jelly,' she told Antoine. 'I keep thinking how terrible, whether that man had any family, any children, a girlfriend...' Ailsa's chickens were pecking around in the dust, and they clucked companionably as she waited for the emergency services to return.

Finally, a sombre group, led by the four-by-four, bumped slowly back up the sandy trail. The responders were on foot, and they paused to get their breath and finish up paperwork. A young police officer called to Antoine and Chloe.

'Hi Josanne.' Antoine waved back at his cousin, who came towards them.

'Are you feeling all right?' Josanne had the same brilliant smile and brown-eyed good looks as Antoine. He had recently made the transition from Bermuda Fire and Rescue Service to the police.

'Do you know who he is?' Chloe asked the young man.

He shook his head. 'Not yet. The paddleboard comes from the Elbow Beach Resort, so he may be a guest there. We'll chase it up. I take it none of you recognised him?'

'No, he was face down. Young, physically very fit. We gave statements to one of your colleagues on the beach,' Chloe told him, standing up, feeling strength return, the shock finally receding. 'Thanks for coming so quickly. I really must get on with these horses, and I just remembered I'm supposed to be out for dinner tonight.'

Antoine immediately offered to do evening stables, and Chloe gratefully accepted, staying only to help distribute feeds, which was far easier when two people were doing the job. The horses kicked at their half doors and whickered hopefully as Chloe added vitamins to the bowl and inhaled the sweet smell of barley, chaff and molasses.

～

Finn called as Chloe was changing for dinner, and sipping a hastily mixed Dark 'n' Stormy. It was still one of her favourite island drinks, and tonight she felt the need for a strong alcoholic boost to her rapidly dropping energy reserves.

Murder on the Beach

'Are you sure you're okay?' Finn asked, as she reassured him that she was fine, and that Jonas and Melissa had only left so quickly because they had a business meeting.

'Melissa was very shaken but trying not to show it, and Jonas was his usual cool, calm self. Do you know who he was yet, Finn?' Chloe took another sip of the drink, letting the dark, sweet liquid roll around her tongue.

'His name was Danny Bolan. He was a guest at Elbow Beach Resort. We were able to identify the paddleboard as one from their water-sports centre.'

'Poor man...' Chloe's sluggish brain caught up. 'Oh hang on, I know that name...'

'Do you? I suppose you might. Danny Bolan was a British actor. He flew into Bermuda last night. He was also Lara Turner's ex-boyfriend.'

Drops of Dark 'n' Stormy spilled onto the table as Chloe sank down into a chair. 'Oh God, yes! I read about him in that article Mark... my ex-husband wrote. The implication was that he might have been Lara's stalker, I think?'

'Really? I can't comment on that. Call me if you need anything, Chloe.'

'Thank you.' She put her phone down thoughtfully, before downing the rest of her rum cocktail in one go.

∼

'This was a lovely idea,' Fiona said, smiling at Chloe as she manoeuvred the car into a parking space on the hill. Like Maria, she was high energy and full of enthusiasm for the wedding. Not surprising, the wedding was a definite coup for a small hotel.

'Such a beautiful place!' Maria said. 'Although I seem to keep saying that about everywhere I go on this island.' She was in a lacy white maxi dress tonight, and her black hair was pinned up, showing off perfect cheekbones. 'Chloe, are you all right?'

Chloe took a deep breath of soft summer air, and told them both about Danny Bolan.

'Bloody hell! I'm so glad Lara isn't on the island yet,' Maria said. 'That poor man. And you, you poor love, finding a dead body on the beach. That's not a good way to end the day.'

'Or start it really,' Chloe told her dryly. 'I'm fine, honestly. Melissa and Jonas were with me, and the police and medics turned up so quickly and dealt with everything.'

'That's horrible. And you found him? Are you sure you're all right?' Fiona added, her eyes wide with shock. 'Do you want to eat? We can always cancel.'

'No, I'd like to get out. If I stay at home I'll spend the evening googling Danny Bolan and that won't help anyone.' Chloe paused for a second before leading the way up the road.

Gibb's Hill Lighthouse stood high above Southampton Parish, its ironclad form standing out against the gentle evening sunlight. The three women began walking slowly up the hill, enjoying the views.

'So, are you all ready for tomorrow?' Chloe asked her friends, trying to force normality back into the conversation after her bombshell. She had already decided it would be better not to share with Maria that Danny had been on her flight. Her friend wasn't stupid and Chloe could already see her sharp brain working out the implications of Danny's death.

'Maria is definitely the most organised wedding planner I've ever met.' Fiona laughed. It sounded a bit sharp, and her face still registered the shock Chloe herself was feeling. 'So I am pretty confident, and super excited to meet Lara and Eddie, of course.'

'Look at that weird insect! It's like a massive woodlouse climbing up the wall,' Maria said suddenly, effectively distracting them all from the steep climb by peering down at a stretch of white-painted rendering.

Chloe looked down. 'Don't touch it! I think it's a St David's centipede and if it bites you, it's just as painful as a bee sting. My neighbour had some in her garden and she told me all about them.'

Maria moved hastily away. 'I'm not that great with creepy-crawlies anyway and that one is massive.'

Fiona was rummaging in her bag and extracted her phone to answer a call. The others walked slowly to let her catch up, and when she did so her face was grim again.

'What's wrong?' Chloe asked quickly, her mind back on dead bodies.

Fiona showed them both a photo on her phone, and they squinted at the screen. The symbols were painted in scarlet, and in several places the wet paint had dripped downwards, giving them an eerie, bloody appearance. There were two symbols, one comprised of two half circles with a line down the centre, and the other two crossed lines with wiggly lines above, like flames from a bonfire.

'What the hell is that?' Maria asked, clearly shocked.

7

'I don't know but someone painted it during the shift changeover between the security guards. It's down on the garden terrace,' Fiona said angrily. 'I won't have this intimidation at the hotel. Some little idiot who thinks it's fun to play games and get everyone all riled up... Sorry, excuse me a moment...' She moved away to make a call.

Maria and Chloe stood awkwardly, waiting for her to finish.

'I assume the police have been notified?' Maria said eventually as Fiona slipped her phone back into her bag and returned. Maria was fiddling with her lucky charm bracelet, in the way Chloe knew so well. Despite her initial dismissive comments regarding the funeral wreath, her friend was extremely worried. Why wouldn't she confide in her?

Fiona was speaking again, her words brisk and clipped, and her tone sharp with annoyance. 'Yes, that was James, you know, my head of security. It's possible the painter was disturbed before they could finish their pictures, because he said the paint was still wet, and the guard who discovered it thought she heard a scooter drive off at speed as she approached the terrace on her first routine walk around.'

'The garden terrace is next to the road, isn't it?' Chloe queried, remembering from her visits to the hotel.

'Yes, so an easy getaway for our graffiti artist.'

'It looks like a fire.' Maria was still peering at the symbols. 'I hope this person isn't planning more mischief. I mean, Lara and Eddie haven't even arrived yet!' Her face was tight with frustration. 'I hoped they could escape everything just for a few days, just leave the chaos behind for their wedding day.'

Fiona dropped her phone back into her patchwork bag and threw the strap over her shoulder. 'You mean the stalker and unfriendly house invader? I know we moved on fairly quickly from the elephant in the room. This Danny Bolan could easily have been Lara's stalker, couldn't he? I've done a lot of research since you asked me to take on the booking.'

'Of course... I mean, yes he could have been.' Maria sighed and ran her hands through her hair, taking it down and shaking it out, allowing the soft evening breeze to coax out the shining strands.

'He came out on your flight,' Chloe said reluctantly. Probably better Maria heard it now they were all discussing the issue.

'Oh my God. He was coming over here to find Lara, wasn't he? Perhaps to try and interfere with the wedding?'

'Perhaps. But he was sure as hell not the person who just painted my terrace area,' Fiona said. 'Someone else must be responsible. Does this couple have many obsessed, crazy stalkers, and if so, how many are likely to have trailed them to Bermuda?'

'I don't know!' Maria's voice was strained. 'Of course, they have a massive fan base, and with that comes stalkers, trolls, people who are just curious about their lifestyle. Hell, Lara's Instagram account has two million followers. Anyone could be set on ruining the wedding, not just Danny.'

'Maybe, but we won't let them win,' Fiona said, her small

chin set in a way Chloe had come to recognise as being when her friend meant business. 'Come on, security is amazing, the police are aware and they are on the case. I'm not having some petty, small-minded loser spoil these kids' wedding. It's tragic that this Danny drowned the day after he came to the island, but the tides and currents do need a bit of respect and accidents happen. It's awful, but I think we should move on and let the police do the investigating as to who left the wreath and who painted my terrace.'

'She's right,' Chloe said, putting an arm around Maria and giving her a gentle hug. 'I've never dealt with any stalkers, online or offline, but earlier this year someone was spreading rumours about my stables, trying to put us out of business, so I know how damaging gossip can be.'

'You're both right. Kellie is just obsessive about negative publicity. When she found out about the wreath last night she even accused me of sending it myself.' Maria smiled, and Chloe was pleased to see the fire was back in her green eyes. 'What happened to the person who tried to put you out of business?'

Chloe shrugged, already starting to walk towards the lighthouse. 'Oh, he's dead now.'

'Really?' Maria's eyes were wide with shock when Chloe turned back to the path.

'Long story, and not one for just now. Come on, let's eat, go through the schedule for tomorrow one last time, and enjoy the view,' Chloe said firmly.

∽

'Do you want to climb to the top before we eat?' Chloe asked Maria as they stood in the shade, waiting for their table. The lighthouse was always popular but luckily Chloe had booked ahead and secured the last table of the evening.

'Of course,' her friend said promptly, visibly pushing her worries away. 'It's stunning and I can't wait to see the view.'

'Wait until you've been up and down all one hundred and eighty-five steps,' Fiona warned, laughing. 'I'm going to stay down here and wander round in the sunshine. I could do with a rest after all that drama.'

Chloe coaxed Maria to the top as her friend groaned about her aching legs. 'And I thought I was fit. How are you not out of breath? No, don't tell me, it's all that mucking out!'

'Now look,' Chloe told her as they reached the very top, 'you can see South Shore and Little Sound right here and over that way.' She pointed, narrowing her eyes in the low evening sunlight. 'Over there you can see Hamilton and the Royal Naval Dockyard. If you have time you must go there.'

'It is incredible,' Maria admitted. 'But I'm not looking forward to the climb down again!'

Downstairs in the restaurant, they ordered pizzas, salads and a bottle of wine. The restaurant was full of chattering families and couples, and the heavenly smells of oregano, tomatoes and pizza dough filled the small area. A stray sunbeam, dancing through the window, caught Chloe's wine glass, turning her wine blood red, rich and deep.

'Early start again tomorrow, but I feel like we are ready to get going,' Maria said, tearing off a piece of bread from the tempting display in the basket between them. 'Once we get the whole team together, I'll start sending out daily schedules to everyone.' She caught Chloe's startled look and grinned. 'Don't worry, it's just routine to send them out to the main team, and most of it won't affect you, but we also have security, the florist, the happy couple's manager and PR chap, the caterers... the list goes on.'

'We are all set,' Fiona told her, 'and looking forward to meeting Lara and Eddie tomorrow. You said they're arriving at 9am on the private jet?'

Maria sipped her wine and tapped the sheets of paper she had distributed. 'Yes, we thought we may as well charter a jet after the chaos with the prank caller, so instead of arriving on the British Airways flight from Heathrow tomorrow evening, they'll fly through the night and arrive ready for a full day's commitments. Much better!'

∼

After Fiona dropped her back home, Chloe sat down at her kitchen table, Hilda at her feet, and studied the schedule properly. If she was reading correctly every hour was packed with photo shoots and meetings, but Goldie would only be needed for a bit of riding practice, a pre-wedding photo shoot, and the wedding itself.

Yawning, Chloe checked the times against her client bookings. She would be busy, but she could just about do it. In a week, things would be back to normal and she would have been paid enough to pay off some more debt, and even save a little for the quiet months.

'The thing is, Hilda, is this mystery stalker going to cause any more trouble?'

Hilda wagged her tail, eyes bright with intelligence.

'I can't believe I'm talking to my dog. I always laughed at people who had a chat with their pets,' Chloe told her, stroking her soft head.

Restless, Chloe opened her laptop again and began to read the news stories about Danny Bolan. Some of the comments were vicious, and clearly Lara had many supporters who were just as obsessive as her haters. Many said if Danny went to Bermuda to cause trouble for the couple, he deserved everything he got. Others speculated he had been the stalker all

Murder on the Beach

along, and now he was dead Lara could get on with her dream wedding.

Danny's poor family, Chloe thought, slightly shaken by the vitriol online. She was trying to ignore the idea that had just popped into her head. She tapped out a quick text to Maria:

Just checking you are ok? Has Lara said anything about Danny? x

The reply came back half an hour later:

Kellie said Lara was devastated for him but underneath I think they are a bit freaked he was over here at all. Honestly, all fine, darling, and I can't wait for tomorrow! xx

She clearly didn't want to talk about it, and hadn't mentioned any other disturbances, so she could stop worrying, Chloe told herself firmly. As for the thought still worming its way through her consciousness…

An hour later she was sitting cross-legged on her bed, and back on the phone to Maria. 'Were you still awake?'

'I am now, but I was actually thinking about Danny… There is so much online now, seems like almost all the news sites have picked it up. So sad if he did come here with the intention of wrecking the wedding. There are some horrible things written by Lara's fans: "He deserved to die" and "I would have killed him myself rather than put Lara's wedding at risk". What are these people on?' Maria's voice was slightly hushed, but the underlying sadness came through clear enough. 'I'm not sure who I would find the scariest if I were Lara, the trolls or the adorers!'

'I suppose they feel like they really know Lara and Eddie, even though they don't and won't ever meet them. Thinking about Danny, I mean.' Chloe took a deep breath. 'Maria, what if Danny's death wasn't an accident? What if he was murdered?'

8

'What do you mean? By who?' Maria's normally sharp voice was shrill.

'Don't you think it's a bit of a coincidence he arrives on the island, probably with the intent to cause trouble for Lara and Eddie...'

'But before he can, he dies in an accident,' Maria finished her sentence. 'I... I suppose if he was on my flight, anyone else could have come over here too. I mean, the happy couple haven't exactly been keeping things a secret. That's one of the reasons we had all the trouble with their flight.'

'They put everything on social media,' Chloe said. 'I'm guessing that's how someone, not necessarily Danny, managed to locate their home and break in. Imagine how many millions see their posts!'

Maria was quiet for a moment, but Chloe could hear her quick breathing. 'Can you talk to Finn? You've already told me how great he is on a personal level, so I'm sure he wouldn't mind you just suggesting Danny might have been... murdered.' Her voice caught on the word. 'Kellie would go mad if I even suggested talking to the police. She's phobic about what she calls bad publicity, and a dead ex isn't great, but if they find out it wasn't an accident...'

'I get it,' Chloe said. 'Look, I will talk to Finn. The police in Bermuda are very professional, and the crime levels are extraordinarily low. I'll ring him in the morning.'

They said goodnight, and Chloe settled down with Hilda, her mind whirling with possibilities. When she eventually slept, she dreamt of hordes of Lara fans sailing to Bermuda on a pink ship.

～

Another early start for Chloe and her stable staff meant the yard and occupants were polished and immaculate by the time the VIP guests arrived. According to Fiona, who called to alert Chloe they were on their way, Lara and Eddie had successfully travelled to Bermuda by private jet, and thanks to Maria's immaculate arrangements, had been met at the airport by the hotel's driver and people carrier with blacked-out windows. There had, she added, been no sign of any journalists.

'I hope Lara doesn't fall off.' Jordan, ever the optimist, was sweeping the yard again, making final preparations for the arrival of the reality star couple. His thick fringe fell heavily across his eyes, and his mouth was quirked with mischief.

'She couldn't fall off Goldie, so shut up, and put the tools away in the feed room,' Antoine told him sharply. He flicked an expert glance around the yard and horses. 'Looks as good as it ever will.'

Chloe yawned. Last night, talking to her friend it had all made sense – if Danny came over on Maria's flight, it was entirely possible more of Lara's fans had come too, possibly to thwart Danny's plans.

But Chloe hadn't yet called Finn. This was mainly because

she felt silly, now, in broad daylight, talking about murder, but also because, as she told Maria, Finn and his team were extremely professional and she felt sure if there was any sign Danny's death might be anything but a tragic accident, he would find out.

She was always a bit sensitive about appearing to be a nosy busybody, even though she laughed off the term when any of her friends suggested it. She wasn't nosy... just... interested, she thought, dragging her mind back to the scene in front of her. She would call Finn later.

The horses had all been bathed, manes and tails brushed out into silky waves, and Chloe felt extremely proud of them as she studied each gleaming head in turn. The concrete yard had been power-washed by Antoine, who had borrowed the equipment from a friend. The washer had turned out to be more violent than they had expected, and soaked all three of them, but the yard looked great, and now they were changed into dry clothes. Chloe darted over and removed a fallen flower from Star's forelock and the mare flashed her ears back in annoyance.

'It will be fine. Oh, just don't mention anything about Danny Bolan, okay?' Chloe reminded Jordan and Antoine hastily. Kellie had rung an hour ago to say she had already talked through Danny's death with the couple and they would prefer if it wasn't mentioned during their visit.

'Especially not that you found him over here?' Jordan suggested, waving a hand towards the rocks below.

'Exactly,' Chloe told him firmly.

'Not funny,' Antoine told the younger boy, who just shrugged, and turned away.

The people carrier, complete with uniformed driver, bumped up the track to Beachside Stables at 10am, exactly on schedule, and Chloe went to greet them, smiling but stomach fluttering with nerves. Goodness, it was like entertaining royalty. She had kept a sharp lookout for Mark since his first visit but luckily he seemed to have got the message. Nobody pursued the vehicle and Chloe hoped maybe Lara and Eddie might cause less fuss than had been anticipated. Either that or the last-minute change from scheduled airline flight to private jet had foxed all the journalists.

Lara was the first out of the vehicle, banging the door open, and leaping from the people carrier in a whirl of energy. She looked just like her photos, Chloe thought, smiling. She was small and slender, with a mass of dark-brown hair, and hazel eyes. Her make-up was heavy but slick, emphasising her pouting lips and sharp cheekbones. Dressed in gym gear, which was carefully cut to emphasise her figure, she was glowing with energy and excitement.

Chloe was very surprised when the girl rushed up and kissed her. 'You must be Chloe. Thank you so much for making my dreams come true with the horses! It's like a fairy-tale photo shoot, isn't it?' She seemed slightly breathless and her eyes sparkled with genuine enthusiasm. She pulled back and stared hard at Chloe, her lips slightly parted as though she was surprised.

Chloe, naturally more reserved, but always ready to respond to a friendly gesture, and give anyone the benefit of the doubt – smiled back. 'Pleasure, and Goldie is super easy to ride. Even with the dresses your stylist has lined up, there won't be any problems with the long skirts.'

Lara was still staring at her, big dark eyes full of emotion, the shock still evident in the line of her mouth and set cheeks.

'Lara? It's okay, you needn't worry about the riding part,' Chloe said gently. 'Are you okay? Goldie really is bombproof!'

Lara still stared and Chloe began to feel uncomfortable. It was a childlike stare, frozen and wide-eyed.

'Glad to hear the horse is up to the job.' Maria also emerged from the people carrier. 'This is Kellie, she's Lara and Eddie's manager, and Ben is from their PR agency, and Lizzy, the producer on their TV show. The rest of the team are arriving tonight on the BA flight.'

Kellie was stick-thin with a long thin nose, and caramel-brown hair pulled into a severe plait. She nodded at Chloe, before continuing a conversation on her mobile phone. Ben was short, spiky-haired with large glasses and a very white fake-looking grin.

Lizzy was the only one who looked properly friendly and fairly normal, Chloe thought. She was tall, with freckles and messy blonde hair piled up on top of her head. She wore jeans and a T-shirt.

Chloe hoped she could remember all the names. Apart from Lizzy, they all seemed incredibly jumpy, and stressed. Even Maria, who was used to handling royal weddings and Hollywood stars, was biting her lip and studying her wedding jotter. She had caught her friend's enquiring eye when they first stepped out of the vehicle, and discreetly shook her head. No, she hadn't made the call to Finn yet. But she would as soon as this was over.

'Nice to meet you all,' Chloe said at last, turning away from Lara. 'This is Antoine, my manager, and Jordan, who works with us.'

The two boys nodded and although Jordan mumbled something unintelligible, his face flushed, Antoine smiled charmingly. 'My fiancé is such a huge fan, Lara. It's lovely to meet you. Welcome to Bermuda.'

Lara snapped back from whatever trance she had vanished into and batted her lashes at him, returning the charm. 'Thank you so much, I can't believe how beautiful it is here and everyone has been so nice. We're super excited to be here.' She spoke fast, words tumbling over one another, with an endearing kind of childish haste.

'Let's get moving then,' Maria said, glancing at her phone. 'We have a tight schedule today and I know Kellie is hoping to squeeze in a quick meeting with the jewellers after this.'

Kellie, still talking firmly into her phone, glanced round and nodded briskly, before walking away from the group and leaning against the people carrier.

'Eddie!' Lara yelled suddenly, startling the horses, who threw up their heads and fixed beady eyes on the newcomers. 'Get over here and see this place. It's sooooo pretty and cute!'

'Hurry up for God's sake, Eddie!' Ben, the PR man added, getting ready to snap a photograph on his phone. He sounded extremely irritated, but flashed another insincere smile at Chloe when she met his eyes.

Realising now that the groom had so far been absent from the introductions, Chloe watched as the last occupant squeezed his way out of the people carrier. He was holding a sandwich box, and folded it carefully, turning back to leave it on the seat.

The photographs she had seen hadn't truly done justice to Eddie's size, or the way he and Lara complemented each other's physical appearance so perfectly. If she was a little Disney princess, he was the prince on the magic carpet. Grinning amiably, he ambled over and shook Chloe's hand, covering it with his own for a second.

He was tall and broad-shouldered, with messy white-blonde surf-boy hair, bright blue eyes she had seen on online, and the slightly clumsy movements reminiscent of a bear.

'Sorry,' he chewed and swallowed, 'I was starving. Travelling always does that to me, and Kellie never gives us enough time to eat, so I have to take whatever I can get. Nice to meet you all.'

As soon as he walked into the yard, Lara hurled herself into his arms and covered his face with kisses. 'Isn't this just the best?'

She seemed to have completely recovered from whatever had shocked her. Chloe wondered if she had taken something drug-related.

Antoine and Jordan, who had been openly staring at the glamorous group, now turned away and started gathering Goldie's tack. Chloe went straight over to the mare's stable and popped her head collar on, making a brisk remark about cracking on with the rehearsal.

Luckily, the happy couple took the hint and prised themselves apart. They were soon cooing over the horse as though she was their treasured firstborn. Goldie did look gorgeous – her coat shone the exact shade of a gold coin, brilliant in the sunshine, and her white mane and tail drifted in the breeze like froth from the waves.

'The hotel have been so helpful,' Lara said, as Chloe began to lead the horse down to the sand. 'They've arranged to have gazebos on the beach for our hair and make-up teams, and they said they can keep the other guests away from the bit we want to do the photo shoot on. Of course, for the actual wedding day we'll have the place to ourselves.' She beamed happily, and reached out a manicured hand to pat Goldie's neck. 'It's just so perfect, and I'm so lucky.'

Chloe hoped the hotel thought they were pretty lucky too. To have landed a celebrity wedding was the equivalent, as Fiona had told her last night, of a year's paid advertising, but a lot more work. But recent events seemed to suggest it might be harder work than anyone could have imagined.

Still, Lara and Eddie seemed perfectly nice, and the fee being paid to Beachside Stables would put them back where they needed to be for this financial year. The niggling fear of financial ruin had considerably lessened in the last couple of months, but it was still there. It would be at least three years before the debts were all paid off and the business could move from survival to profit.

The one thing which had not been mentioned was the stalker. Had Maria and Fiona decided not to tell the couple about the wreath and the red-painted symbols? Lara seemed perfectly happy now, singing to herself, taking deep breaths of the salty air and bubbling with non-stop chat. Eddie was walking behind, talking to Antoine, but when she looked round Chloe could see him watching Lara indulgently.

Definitely no sign of stress from the famous pair, but plenty for their team, Chloe thought. Kellie and Ben were also making their way down to the beach, slipping and struggling on the soft pale sand, in rather inappropriate shoes. They were talking intently, faces serious. Occasionally, Ben would gesticulate wildly and Kellie would make shushing movements with her hand.

Down on the beach, Chloe legged Lara up onto Goldie's smooth back. She wriggled and squirmed her way to a sitting position, giving excited squeaks, like a small child.

'Doesn't she get a saddle?' Eddie asked, frowning at his fiancée, who was finally perched precariously on Goldie's withers. 'Like, she hasn't ridden before… I don't want her to fall off or anything.'

'No, because of the dresses, she needs to ride bareback for the shoot and for the wedding, so she needs to practise,' Chloe told him, positioning Lara's hands on the reins and leading her a few steps down towards the sea. She thought that despite all her squealing and waving of hands, the girl was athletic enough to be able to sit up there without any problems, she just needed to calm down a bit.

It was slightly off-putting that despite everything, Chloe kept turning round and catching Lara's eye as the girl stared at her.

Chloe had even snuck over to Lizzy and asked if she had a make-up mirror. But no, she had nothing smeared across her face, nothing that should make the reality star stare like she had seen a ghost. It really was rather uncomfortable, Chloe thought, but maybe it was a nervous thing.

Prompted by Antoine, Goldie carried her rider gently and carefully twice around the beach. It was going so well, they even let Eddie lead his fiancée along by the water's edge. Poised to grab the horse if anything should go wrong, seeing Antoine out the corner of her eye in exactly the same attitude, Chloe let out a tiny breath of relief.

Antoine called out, 'Eddie, don't let the reins dangle so much. You don't need them tight, you just need to keep a feel on them. At the moment Goldie could get them tangled in her front legs. And Lara, can you try and sit down on your bum and not hold on.'

'She can't hold on to the mane in the photos,' Kellie said, her forehead creasing. 'It would look unprofessional.'

Ben, who was taking quick photographs of the session with his phone, nodded in agreement. 'It's going to be very relatable for their followers to show some bits of her struggling to ride on social media, but the magazine will want something very different. She needs to look polished and professional.'

'She's doing well for a beginner,' Chloe pointed out. She was starting to feel slightly sorry for Lara, who, in between staring at Chloe, was obviously trying extremely hard. 'It's tough getting your balance up there if you've never ridden before.'

Kellie turned her cold, pale-blue gaze to Chloe again. 'She can't hold on. I've already spoken to the magazine and the photographer. We know exactly what we need and Lara and Eddie need to look relaxed and happy. Like she could go off for a gallop along the beach if she wanted to.'

Chloe felt that was a pretty tall order, but she just shrugged and went to meet Goldie as they turned up the beach again. 'Lara, try just putting your hands on your hips as Goldie walks, grip with your thighs not your heels. Just get the feel of her movement as she walks.'

The girl *was* concentrating, she could tell. The stream of exclamations had stopped and she was biting her lip, forcing her shoulders back, long hair blowing out behind her. Chloe noticed she seemed quite out of breath after the exercise, holding her chest and taking big breaths as though she had just run a race. Maybe she wasn't quite so athletic after all, or perhaps it was nerves.

'She'll get it,' Eddie told Chloe with a smile. 'She's a tough little bird really and for this deal she would have ridden a giraffe if she had to. It's massive for us, which is why Kellie and Ben are freaking out.' He snapped his fingers lazily, white-blonde hair blowing in the breeze. 'Mega bucks.'

'Right. Well, let's just make sure she's happy,' Chloe said, squeezing Lara's hand reassuringly, which made the girl beam. 'Go up towards the cliff path one more time.'

By the end of two hours even Kellie was looking pleased. Ben had gone back up to the car, but as soon as they were released from riding practice, the couple were busy with their phones.

Goldie took the whole thing in her stride, even allowing Lara to get a selfie with the girl's lips pressed against the horse's nose. Chloe hoped the pink lipstick mark left on Goldie's immaculate coat would wipe off.

Back up in the yard, Ben was proffering paperwork and pens.

'Right, before we go I need everyone here who hasn't yet signed the non-disclosures to get on with it,' Kellie said, scowling round. 'You, of course, Chloe, have done yours but your stable staff need to sign here.'

Antoine let out a snort of laughter, and turned it into a

cough, and Chloe bit her lip to stop herself from giggling. Honestly, it was really hard to take this seriously with Lara pouting and posing next to a chair and Eddie snapping pictures of every horse, plant and seashell he could find. She told herself sternly to be businesslike as the two boys signed the documents. These were quickly snatched away.

The whole lot was zipped into an expensive-looking leather folder and Kellie stalked over to the people carrier. She let out a yell and ran back.

Chloe felt her heart hammering against her ribs and her stomach clench in fear. What could have happened now? She fumbled for her phone just in case they needed to call the police...

9

'What's wrong?' Eddie had stopped snapping photos and was looking thoroughly alarmed.

Chloe felt her heart jerk again, and the hand not holding her phone clenched tightly on to Goldie's head-collar rope.

'There is a... a *chicken* on my seat!' Kellie yelled furiously. 'Get rid of it!'

Luckily, everyone apart from the unfortunate Kellie thought this was hilarious. Another chicken was discovered in the driver's footwell, and both birds appeared to pose for the inevitable photographs before being ejected and shooed back into Chloe's garden. Ailsa was nowhere to be seen, but Chloe couldn't wait to see which chicken, Betsy or Onion, would make it onto Eddie and Lara's social media.

Finally, the whole entourage departed in their people carrier, bound for the studio of Bermudian artist Alexandra Mosher to discuss a possible collaboration with her beautiful island-inspired jewellery pieces.

Before she left, Lara gave Chloe another heartfelt hug, again pausing just a moment too long for manners. She seemed about to say something, but Eddie grabbed her hand and, laughing, hustled her away.

'Honestly, my girl would chat for England! Thanks for the riding lesson.' Eddie beamed from out the open door. Lara waved too, but her expression was serious, and contemplative.

Chloe let out a long breath and sat down on one of the chairs, legs stretched out. 'Wow, that was hard work. I feel like I've just done a twenty-mile trail ride or something.'

Antoine laughed at her and collapsed on a straw bale. 'The chickens were brilliant. Must be tough being a superstar and having to put up with all kinds of shit, then you hire a luxury vehicle and the chickens hijack it. Goldie says she's knackered too,' he added jokingly. 'Wasn't she well behaved?'

'An absolute dream,' Chloe agreed. 'God, I sound like Lara. They're very sweet, aren't they, our wedding pair? I'm so glad she didn't fall off or anything. It's lucky our best-behaved mare is also our prettiest.'

'She's looking forward to being a TV star,' Jordan told them, as he leant against Goldie's stable door and stroked her velvet nose.

'And nobody mentioned Danny at all. I find that totally weird.' Antoine shrugged. 'Still, Lara is totally gorgeous, but I'm not sure about Eddie.'

Chloe was surprised. 'But he seemed very relaxed, and very protective of Lara.'

'When Lara was riding by herself at first he was taking a phone call and having a right go at someone. Total personality change. He looks like a chilled-out surfer type, but firstly, I bet he's never been near a board in his life, despite dropping those hints about catching waves, and secondly, on that call he was bitchier than any girl I've ever heard.'

'Maybe he was just nervous about everything. Must be hell having your wedding turned into a business transaction. He did say the magazine deal was worth a lot, and Kellie seems to be pressurising them both to a massive extent. I guess that's her job though... Come on, let's get the stables done and you can head off. I'm far more excited about your wedding anyway,' Chloe told him, hauling herself up and heading for the water tap with a bucket on her arm.

He laughed. 'Me too, and yeah, I better not be late tonight, because Louisa will want all the gossip.'

Half relieved nobody else seemed to have noticed, but also now half wondering if she'd imagined the invisible link between Lara and herself, Chloe popped into the house to make a sandwich. She found Ailsa and her chicken entourage at the back door.

'They all gone then?' Ailsa asked, peering down towards the yard.

'Yes. Back to normal for a bit. Do you want a drink? I'm just making a quick lunch because we've got two rides booked this afternoon. You're welcome to join me.'

'No thanks, I've got something in the fridge. I just wanted to let you know while you were all down on the beach, your ex-husband came round.'

Chloe paused at the cupboard, and straightened slowly, plate in hand. 'Was he looking for me? Did you talk to him?' How awful if Mark had managed to sneak in and take photos or something. Kellie would probably kill her.

'He was coming up the driveway, and then he sort of ducked in behind the fig tree, and went round the corner of your house to the garden. I saw you all go down to the beach so I went to have a chat with him,' Ailsa said, straight-faced.

Chloe sliced cucumber. 'What happened then?'

'Oh, he got a shock when I went over to say hallo, but he's a smooth talker, isn't he?'

'Invariably,' Chloe admitted with a sigh.

'Anyway, he asked all kinds of questions. He obviously knew Lara and Eddie were here, but I told him he was trespassing, and if he wanted to wait, he could do so out the front, and you would be along soon.'

'Did he actually go?'

Ailsa laughed. 'No chance. He went and sat on the porch, making calls on his phone. Eventually, someone came up from the beach, a man with glasses and Mark went to talk to him.'

'That would be Ben, the PR guy. Did he actually speak to Mark?' Chloe asked.

'Not for long, but they shook hands and seemed very friendly,' Ailsa told her. 'Don't worry, your ex went off on a scooter after that, and the other man just sat in the car.'

'I can't think why Ben should have been friendly towards Mark, but maybe he has to be nice to any journalists,' Chloe said, slapping some fish pate into her sandwich and slicing the bread neatly. She suddenly darted a glance at Ailsa. 'I don't suppose you heard any of their conversation?'

Ailsa smiled innocently, wrinkles and dimples showing in the harsh sunlight, grey-streaked hair blowing in the rising breeze. 'I wasn't trying to listen or anything but I may have heard a few words... Something about a curse on the wedding?'

∼

By evening stables, Chloe and the boys were working increasingly slowly. Not only was there a lot to do, but their progress was impeded by constantly checking their phones, mainly to see which of their animals was featuring on Eddie and Lara's social media feeds and stories.

As well as this harmless pastime another, less innocent story had broken at four that afternoon. Chloe had come back from a ride, to find Jordan excitedly poring over the online article:

Is Lara and Eddie's wedding cursed?

Since the couple decided on a last-minute wedding on Bermuda, speculation has been rife as to why Lara and Eddie chose to get married so quickly. We can exclusively reveal, Lara visited a tarot card reader last month, who predicted the star would need to marry quickly or never achieve her dream of having a family.

A string of terrifying events have dogged the couple's relationship and wedding plans, including a home intruder. Now we can exclusively reveal the trouble has followed them to Bermuda, as a bloodstained wreath was delivered as an early wedding gift, and graffiti daubed on the wall of their room.

Most significantly of all, Lara's ex-boyfriend Danny Bolan appears to have followed Lara to Bermuda and was found dead yesterday evening, in an apparent water-sports accident. Police are currently investigating...

The article ran for three pages, dredging up Danny's previous drug habit, Lara's harassment charges, and Eddie's four-year-old son with an ex-girlfriend.

'What a load of rubbish. The graffiti was on the terrace not the wall of their room!' Chloe exclaimed, turning away from the phone.

Mark's name was at the bottom of the online article and the article had already been shared thousands of times.

'Do you think this stalker is in Bermuda and maybe it wasn't Danny after all?' Jordan asked. 'Because someone's got it in for them.' His expression was thoughtful. 'What kind of weirdo would do that?'

∽

Much later, having waved goodbye to her last clients of the day, Chloe started to untack Candy and Mars, the little chestnut, and realised she still hadn't called Finn.

Jordan took Mars' saddle and returned with a fresh water bucket for him. 'There's more stuff about Lara. It says the wedding curse is coming true and someone painted witch symbols on the wall of her bathroom before they arrived!'

'They weren't in her...' Chloe began, trailing off as she realised there could well have been another freaky incident as Lara and Eddie arrived at Palm Bay Hotel. Oh God, she hoped not. Maria had said Kellie hated bad publicity and this was truly awful.

Antoine brought his last ride in half an hour later and once his lovely clients had kissed all the horses, reminisced about their Texan childhoods and presented Chloe with a beautiful box of chocolates, almost every gossip columnist seemed to have the story of the cursed wedding and Lara's fear she wouldn't be able to have a family unless she married as soon as possible.

Chloe dashed through tending to her animals, fed Hilda and rang Finn.

'Hi, Chloe, is everything all right?' His calm, measured tone as usual made her relax a little. She had never seen Finn stressed out.

'I was talking to Maria, my friend, you know...'

'The wedding planner, of course,' Finn said. 'I'm sure everyone involved is struggling to take in Danny's death.'

'It's about that actually...' Chloe paused, and then brought the words out in a rush, telling Finn everything that had happened since the wedding venue and dates were announced on social media. 'But I'm sure you already know about everything. I don't want to seem, you know, like I'm being nosy...' Chloe trailed off uncertainly. To her relief Finn laughed.

'You do like the amateur detective stuff, don't you? I prefer inquisitive to nosy. Does that sound better?'

'It does,' Chloe agreed.

'Okay, to set your mind at rest, I do know what has been going on at the hotel. The security team are excellent, and James, who runs the show at Palm Bay, is a personal friend.' He paused, as though considering his words. 'Regarding our investigation into Danny Bolan's death, let's just say we are still asking questions. Don't ever be afraid to tell me things, especially if something is worrying you.'

'Thank you, Finn.' Chloe felt herself relax for what felt like the first time since Maria had mentioned the wedding. 'As soon as this is all over, I'm looking forward to our next day out.'

'Me too,' Finn said warmly, 'and my sisters are having a party at the end of September. You know their usual Cup Match "do" was cancelled? Well, I understand this is to make up for it. I'd love you to come along.'

Chloe felt herself smiling. 'I'd love to accept.'

'Call me if you need anything in the meantime, okay?'

She promised she would and rang off. Hilda was sitting at her feet, studying her face. 'He means nosy really, doesn't he?' she asked the dog, smiling a little to herself.

Outside, the wind was picking up, and Chloe took the precaution of closing her shutters. Rain started just before she went to bed, rattling on the window panes, and drumming on her roof. Glancing at the pictures of Goldie on the beach that had made their way onto Lara and Eddie's Instagram feeds, Chloe shivered a little. Bad weather was the last thing they needed for a beach wedding, and she was sure the forecast had been fine. These sudden storms blew up quickly around Bermuda and usually passed through fairly swiftly, but she could imagine Lara and Eddie might be feeling rather as though the curse was scoring another direct hit.

10

The next morning was filled with darkening skies and rain. Chloe, thinking of the rides planned for the day, sighed. Consistent bad weather was rare, but she had had a couple of days this season when she had no choice but to cancel.

Her phone rang as the rain started again, battering the windows.

'Hi, Maria, how are you?' Chloe sat at the table and sipped her coffee, smiling at Hilda, who was stretched out upside-down on the rug, grinning toothily.

'Lara and Eddie were devastated after that story broke. Bloody Mark, how did he get hold of those details? And he got the last bit wrong. The graffiti symbols were on the garden terrace!'

'I know... Maria, my neighbour saw Mark yesterday at my house. He was sneaking around while we were down on the beach. She told him to get off my property, but said he went up to where the car was parked and talked to Ben. I forgot to tell you with all the chaos going on.'

'The PR guy?' Maria sounded perplexed. 'He can't have told Mark anything. He must have been telling him to get lost.'

'I don't know, but worth mentioning to Kellie maybe?'

'Of course. Did you speak to Finn?'

'I did, and he was reassuring in his usual lovely way. He just said thanks for the info and to let him know if anything else came up.' Chloe kept her voice light.

'I absolutely need to meet this guy!' Maria said.

'You will. He understands we have a lot going on here, and he's in the middle of investigating Danny's death,' Chloe explained.

'I guess it was too much to hope that he might have let slip a few details...'

'Maria! Of course he wouldn't. He's far too professional...' Chloe stopped short in her indignant defence of Finn as Maria laughed.

'Okay, I get it. Back to business, darling. Number one, I was calling to ask if you could come into Hamilton this morning to look at flowers. It's raining so you surely can't be riding.'

'Come on, Maria, why do I need to come into Hamilton to look at flowers? It's not on the schedule and even if I have to cancel the clients, I still need to look after the horses, and...' Chloe, already stressed, felt the last thing she wanted was to drag over to Hamilton in the rain.

'...And muck out! I know, darling, and I'm so sorry but could you possibly make it just for an hour?' Maria sounded harassed. 'Lara wants to ask if Goldie can wear a necklace of flowers both for the shoot and the actual wedding, and says you need to talk to the florist and approve the choices. She's really taken a shine to you.'

'I've only met her once! Can't I just look at some pictures online? Seriously, I would love to help but I'm hoping the rain will clear so I can juggle the rides with the weather, and I was hoping to catch up on the accounts,' Chloe told her, aware she was weakening. Poor Maria sounded so stressed out and she did really want her friend to make a success of this.

'Please come, Chloe! In just a few days this will be over and you can get back to normal. I think Lara wants to make sure the flowers aren't poisonous to horses or something.'

Chloe made a huffing sound, listened to the downpour outside, and checked the weather radar on her open laptop. It looked like this rain was here to stay, but it was predicted to clear at two. She pulled a face, hating herself for being so weak. Hilda, crouched at her feet, wagged her tail. 'Okay, I'll come.' She supposed she might be able to pick up another wedding gift for Antoine and Louisa while she was there. Her heart was set on one of the pictures in the Stone Gallery, but maybe some pretty photo frames or something might be a nice extra.

'Okay, great. Second thing, the wedding date has been brought forward. You can understand it with everything that's happening I suppose, but I feel sick every time I think of it. The big day is now Thursday.'

'*This Thursday?*'

'All the paperwork was approved apparently and yes, they are all ready to rock and roll.'

'Bloody hell. Is that even possible?' Chloe poured herself another coffee.

'Well, you said you'd cleared the diary, so I assume we have Goldie, and I'm just working through a tick-list of suppliers and producers. Luckily, the TV crew have been filming all ready, and they have this great Bermudian location manager who has brought in some extra help,' Maria explained.

'I still don't understand why the great hurry to get hitched. Do you think Lara really believes the tarot card reader?' Chloe was sceptical.

'Not sure. If I had to guess, I'd say the whole thing is being driven by a desire to amass as much money as possible in the shortest amount of time. Probably Kellie's desire, but Lara and Eddie seem happy with it. Got another call coming in, see you later, darling!'

～

Chloe and the boys got extremely wet doing the stables, and sorting out the animals, but bang on time, she zipped up her spare raincoat, and caught the bus into Hamilton. Walking down from the bus station, her spirits lifted. The rain was salty and the stiff breeze had blown her hair out into a wild mane. There was something uplifting about this mid-Atlantic weather. Peering into a few shop windows, she checked her watch and directions as she searched for the florist.

She finally spied the ornate metalwork sign with relief. It was opposite a hairdressers' and underneath a health-food café. The sugar-pink door was garlanded with tropical greenery and flowers, and inside was like a vast white cave, with an overpowering earthy smell. Chloe jumped as a frond from a hanging fern in a red pot stroked her ear.

Maria spotted her, came forward and hugged her, whispering, 'Thank you so much, darling. I owe you for this one!'

Lara was talking to a small slim woman with serious hazel eyes and long mousey-brown hair set into two plaits. 'Chloe! I'm so glad you made it. Isn't the weather vile? I hope the sun is going to come back for the photo shoot and my wedding day, or I'll have to order wellies and a raincoat! Come and meet Isabelle.' She gave Chloe a quick hug, gazed intently into her eyes and then dragged her across the shop.

Unable to get a word in, Chloe instead made her way over to the far corner, carefully avoiding a stack of glass jars, and a table heaped with delicate rosebuds and candles. The florist shop was small but beautiful, with colourful blooms and foliage displayed in metal buckets around the sides, and shelving stacked with homeware and vases. As well as the earthy smell of plants, incense was burning on the pay desk and Chloe coughed, trying to clear her throat.

'Isabelle is going to find out if she can get these lilies – aren't they gorgeous?' Lara said. 'I want to garland them around Goldie's neck, and maybe wind some of these daisies in her bridle.' She peered at Chloe like a small child asking a favour. 'Do you think that would be okay?'

The delicate pink lilies were stunning but Isabelle issued a note of caution after smiling at Chloe. 'These are imported, of course, so the price is a little higher. We grow some of these roses here actually on Bermuda. I try to make as much use of island flower producers as possible. After all,' she added to Lara, 'if you wanted to get married on Bermuda it must be because you fell in love with the romance of the island, so why not use Bermuda flowers at your wedding?'

Kellie was scowling round, apparently tapping out an email on her phone while she kept an eye on the proceedings. 'It needs to be extravagant, over the top. We want pink and mauve, and lots of it.'

Lara caught Kellie's eye and said hastily, 'Of course. I totally agree... Perhaps if you could get the lilies, too, it would be just perfect. They wouldn't be poisonous to Goldie would they, Chloe?'

'Probably not unless she ate them and I hope we can prevent her from doing that,' Chloe said cautiously.

'Don't you think they will look amazing against her golden coat?' Lara persisted.

Chloe agreed they would and assured her all the flowers were a perfect choice. She saw a couple of wooden picture frames on the shelves and picked one up to examine it. The wood was intricately carved with symbols or runes, and smooth to the touch as she ran a thumb over it.

'Do you like those?' Isabelle asked her, as Lara moved away to talk to Kellie.

'Beautiful,' Chloe agreed. 'What is the wood?'

'Just driftwood originally! The carvings are ancient symbols of love and hope. Look, this star is creation, and this one is a bind rune to encourage eternal love, this is for a happy family and marriage...' Isabelle said enthusiastically.

'What about this one?' Chloe asked, intrigued.

'A protective symbol, a pentacle,' Isabelle told her. 'Everything we make and sell combines a mixture of runes and symbols to bless our happy couples. The flowers all have a little token hidden in the bouquets or garlands. I only do flowers for weddings, not any other event, so I have done a lot of research into the subject of love and eternity.'

'That's a lovely idea,' Chloe said. She noticed other symbols carved on the inside of the doorway, and couldn't help but feel a slight chill. Isabelle was sweet but rather intense, and the odd mismatch of witchcraft and wedding flowers made her uneasy.

Lara whirled back across the shop, nearly knocking the picture frame from Chloe's hand. 'That's pretty. Oh, Isabelle, do you think you could add a few more bags of rose petals for the tables? Kellie says the supplier in the UK is under-stocked and can't make the order.'

Isabelle nodded briskly and made a note on her clipboard. 'Now the rest of this order was all prearranged but I do like to double-check... You wanted flowers on the horse for the shoot and the wedding? Buttonholes, of course... Table arrangements... And, of course, the date has been brought forward...' She raised an eyebrow at Kellie, who ignored her.

'Don't forget the flower wall, and the flower arch we get married under.' Eddie wandered over, and was also introduced to Isabelle. 'Lara loves her flowers,' he teased his fiancée and she slapped his arm gently and rolled her eyes.

'Shut up, Eddie, I'm sorting out the flowers. You go and ring Karim and Eli to make sure they've picked up the suits. Oh, and tell Eli if he misses the plane I'm going to personally hunt him down and kill him.' Lara accepted another smacking kiss from her fiancé and then slapped his butt. 'Tell him those exact words, Eddie!'

'Yup, I will deliver your message,' Eddie promised, grinning. He nodded at Isabelle and Chloe before ambling out of the shop, holding his phone in his hand.

Chloe gently replaced the picture frame. It was lovely but not quite what she wanted for Antoine and Louisa. At the back of her mind was the fear Isabelle might have somehow misunderstood the symbols and be giving a gift with a curse attached to it. Not the best way to start a married life!

Isabelle was making further notes, and Chloe glanced at her watch. Apart from trying to research the flowers on her phone to make sure the blooms on Goldie's bridle weren't ones that would poison her if she ate them, her contribution was limited and she was fretting to be back at the stables. The weather had definitely brightened up, so she needed to get the ride out and Antoine could have a break.

'That's my list almost complete,' Maria said, relief in her brisk tones, as she consulted a sheet from the wedding file. 'You need to pick up your rings at three, and Kellie says she has a whole load of emails for you to deal with, mainly PR opportunities.'

'All in hand,' Eddie said. 'We can have a chilled afternoon and send someone to get the rings.'

'We can't because we promised the jeweller some pictures in his store,' Lara reminded him.

'Oh yeah. Let's see if we can pick them up earlier, get some lunch here, and then go back and deal with the email mountain.'

Chloe, listening with half an ear, couldn't help but feel massively grateful that her life wasn't as stressful as theirs seemed to be. She pulled a bus timetable out of her raincoat pocket and studied it carefully. If she left now she could get the next bus...

Finally, it appeared everything was done, and Lara was back to hanging on to Eddie's arm and babbling with excitement while he smiled indulgently. They headed back out to the people carrier, and were approached by two teenage girls, who wanted selfies with the happy couple. The sun was starting to appear from behind the thick rain clouds and the drizzle had stopped. More shoppers and tourists had braved the weather, filling the pavements in search of bargains or lunch.

Chloe watched impatiently as Eddie and Lara posed and pouted. She barely noticed a crowd of teenagers walking along the pavement, mingling with the shoppers, until they suddenly brought out cans of spray paint and leapt directly at Eddie and Lara.

Lara was screaming, and Chloe ducked away in horror, half blinded by the rainbow colour of paint spray that filled the air.

11

She was dimly aware of Isabelle, the florist pulling her and Maria back into the safety of the shop.

But Chloe wiped a shaking hand across her face and went straight to the window, checking the young couple were okay. Eddie was holding a crying Lara, his face striped with a million blood-red droplets, and the pair were now flanked by their two security guards. The other appeared to have set off in pursuit of the gang.

The pavement was covered with a multitude of colours including red, blue, orange, green and pink, and the puddles mixed the paint into rainbow whirlpools as the excess water hastened towards the gurgling roadside drains.

'Are you okay?' Isabelle was offering damp cloths and paper towels to clean their faces and Chloe's bare arms. Her hands were shaking and her face looked thin and pinched. 'Such a horrible thing. I would ask Lara and Eddie back in but I don't want to interfere with their security team...'

'What happened? I mean, why would anyone do that?' Maria demanded, her cheeks red with fear, as she scrubbed furiously at green paint spatters in the mirror.

Chloe opened the door, and called to Kellie, asking if Lara and Eddie wanted to come and clean up before they left.

Kellie's face was tight and her lips set in a thin line, but one of the security guards shook his head. 'They just want us to take them back to the hotel and I think it would be best to get them out of here.' He jerked his head at the crowd forming on the perimeter of the paint spillage, almost all snapping pictures with their phones. 'Maria, if you want to come and jump in we can get going.'

'Chloe, will you be okay? I mean, they should have thought and sent a car for you,' Maria said, clearly worried for her friend.

'I'm quite happy on the bus,' Chloe told her firmly. 'Honestly, go for it before they leave without you.'

Chloe wondered if Mark was lurking amongst the chattering, excited, shocked onlookers, already writing his story in his head as he watched the devastated couple. She went with Maria to the car, and waved at Lara, who was hiding her face behind dark glasses, as the doors were shut and locked. Eddie was sitting with his face in shadow behind the tinted windows, but his shoulders were set and tense.

Isabelle offered tea, but Chloe could see she was busy and still shaken. She made her goodbyes and left, glad to be away from the whirlwind circus that appeared to be Eddie and Lara's life.

She walked quickly towards the bus station, blessing the efficiency of Bermuda's public transport system as she sank gratefully into her seat on the pink bus, and enjoying the scenery on the way home as the bus rumbled through the picturesque, bustling city and finally down into the parish of Warwick.

Thanking all her lucky stars that the weather had cleared to a pale wash of pristine blue, Chloe was back in time to take her ride out. During evening stables, she and the boys discussed this latest attack on the celebrity couple.

'I don't understand. They must have known Lara and Eddie would be there. Fair enough they've been putting loads of their itinerary up on social media even though Maria told them not to.' Chloe dumped a wheelbarrow full of dirty straw onto the muck-heap and trundled back for a bale of fresh bedding. 'But why attack them in the first place? They're just kids making a go of things.'

Jordan was sweeping muddy water towards the drain, his hair dried wavy and more than ever like a horse's mane. 'What if someone paid them to do it?'

Antoine dumped water buckets in the stables and agreed. 'Teenagers don't just suddenly walk along a street with spray cans and let fly on people, whoever they are. It's not like Lara and Eddie have said or done anything controversial, have they? They're just reality stars having a glitzy wedding. They're using local businesses, they're promoting the island and saying good things about it. I reckon Jordan's right. This was a job. Someone who doesn't have the guts to do their own dirty work.'

Chloe considered this comment long after the boys had gone home. She spent some more time on her vegetable bed, and on her garden, whilst accepting with a dog and wandering chickens it was never going to be a pristine plot.

'Evening, Chloe!' Ailsa slipped neatly through the gap in the hedge, pursued by Betsy and Onion. When the birds immediately began scratching in Chloe's newly dug soil, she nudged them gently with a foot. They squawked indignantly, fixing bright beady eyes on the humans.

'Looks like all that fame has gone to their heads,' Chloe said, laughing.

'Jordan showed me the pictures on Lara's Instagram

account.' Ailsa grinned. 'Trust them to get in the car. They are so nosy! How are things going with the wedding plans anyway?'

'Fine, I think. They've brought the date forward again, so the big day is on Thursday now.' Chloe stopped work and leant on her fork.

'That's crazy!' Alisa commented. 'I wondered if you'd seen the papers today?'

'No, just the online versions. Why?'

'Danny Bolan's death is now a murder investigation,' Ailsa said, brandishing a copy of the *The Royal Gazette*.

Chloe studied the front page, heart pounding. There was a photo of Danny, smiling at the camera, giving a thumbs up to whoever was taking the photo, and separate pictures of Lara, Eddie and Danny's parents. But the article was far from Mark's gossipy style, and Chloe noted the journalist who had covered the story was Peter's granddaughter, Daphne.

The evening sun enveloped the garden in a soft glow, and the sky, rinsed clear again by the recent rain, stretched high and baby blue. Only a few wisps of cloud danced on the horizon. The peace and tranquillity seemed at odds with the shocking news.

'See, it says they have established he had a high concentration of heroin in his system,' Ailsa pointed out.

'One of the online articles I read did say he was known to use drugs. I think he even admitted going to rehab before he met Lara,' Chloe said doubtfully. But her heart was pounding. She finished reading and handed the paper back to Ailsa.

'But the police have now said they have evidence of a struggle, and that he was dead before he went into the water.'

'So someone killed him and tried to make it look like he had taken drugs, gone out on a paddleboard and drowned?' Chloe suggested.

Ailsa shrugged. 'From what I can see this wedding has been

nothing but trouble, and as soon as the whole circus moves off the island the better it will be for all of us. That poor boy. Whatever he had or hadn't done, he surely didn't deserve what happened to him.'

They were both silent for a while, watching the chickens pecking at Chloe's vegetable plants. Chloe sighed, put her fork down and admitted defeat. 'I think I need a drink. Do you fancy a Dark 'n' Stormy, Ailsa?'

12

It was gone six by the time Antoine finished combing out Goldie's mane and tail, and Chloe was starting to worry they were going to be late.

'At least the weather has cleared. They would have had to try and fit the shoot in tomorrow if it was still raining,' Chloe said to Jordan, feeding the mare some carrot slices.

'Maybe they should have checked the weather before they booked the wedding dates,' the boy suggested. He was wearing a navy hoodie and board shorts, his face half hidden in the dark fabric folds.

'I'm going to just pop one of those lightweight travel sheets over her to keep her coat clean,' Antoine said, wiping sweat from his face.

At last the hired four-by-four bumped slowly up the track past the house, towing the rickety old trailer. It smelled strongly of pigs and Goldie snorted crossly, but eventually allowed herself to be led inside.

The driver, Harry, grinned cheerfully as they settled themselves on the dusty seats, boxes of equipment and tack perched precariously on their knees. 'Never thought I'd be taking a horse to a photo shoot, let alone a celebrity one!'

'Thank you so much for fitting us in,' Chloe said, smiling at him in the rear-view mirror.

'No problem. My granddad sends a lot of work my way, and I used to do a bit of work for Dre when she was alive, before the feed store did deliveries and that,' he said, his dark eyes and bony face giving a strong look of his grandfather.

'Peter is my go-to for any advice on finding pretty much anyone,' Chloe admitted, casting an anxious glance behind at Goldie in her trailer, bumping along the road behind them. But the mare seemed unphased, and was busy pulling at her hay net.

The Palm Bay Hotel was busy, with guests scattered across the manicured golf course on either side of the driveway, strolling down from the main building towards the lush gardens and pool, or enjoying late lunches under pink-and-white-striped awnings on the patio. The hotel security guards, with their distinctive yellow badges, were much in evidence.

'You need to go the back way, yeah?' Harry queried, pausing at the end of a sweep of gravel.

'Yes, follow it round past the deliveries sign,' Chloe answered, feeling another twinge of nerves as they rumbled round a corner and saw more security guards and a cordoned-off area.

However, the hotel and Maria had worked hard to ensure everything ran smoothly, and after Chloe showed their passes they were directed straight over to a gazebo, with plenty of shade and a bucket of water for Goldie.

The trailer was parked neatly and Harry helped lower the ramp, while Antoine led the mare out onto the gravel.

Chloe and Jordan unpacked grooming brushes and the gleaming tack, which included both an English snaffle bridle and a Western bridle, plus the saddle just in case the bride lost her nerve and decided she really couldn't face the shoot bareback.

The photographer and his team came over briefly to introduce themselves, and Maria hustled past and waved, clipboard and jotter stacked in her hands and a cardboard box wedged under her left arm. 'Hi, Chloe, everything okay? Goldie looks gorgeous!'

Eddie, dressed in a grey suit and pink-striped tie wandered into the gazebo and smiled at them. 'All ready for the shoot? Can I pat her?'

'Of course, but don't let her rub her head on your arm like that, she'll spoil your lovely suit,' Chloe told him warmly, thinking privately he seemed a bit distracted, his ready smile flashing white, but not quite reaching his eyes. 'Are you both okay? After earlier I mean...' She had lowered her voice, but she saw Harry, sitting on a deckchair on his phone, glance up with interest.

Eddie smiled ruefully. 'Nothing a shower couldn't fix but I'm still fuming about all the negative press. Not so much for me, but why can't they leave Lara alone? Seriously, I know she can be a bit wild and OTT but that girl is just the sweetest most genuine person I've ever met. Like, she is also a pain in the arse, but that's my Lara.' He was laughing now, but his blue eyes were serious.

He still hadn't mentioned Danny, Chloe thought, as she gave Goldie's neck a final polish with the soft cloth. She was tempted to broach the subject. He must know that she knew the police were now conducting a murder investigation. She opened her mouth to speak but Antoine got there first.

'Are you nervous about the shoot?'

'Nah... not really.' Eddie shrugged his massive shoulders. 'We had to get used to this kind of thing early on... Kellie's had our schedule sorted ever since we got engaged.'

Antoine and Chloe exchanged a glance. Neither of them had taken to cool, patronising Kellie but she did seem to be making the couple lots of money.

'Where is Lara anyway?' Chloe asked.

'Oh, still having her make-up done, I think.' Another genuine flash of amusement. 'Getting it trowelled on, I expect. I'll see you in a bit.' He patted Goldie again and ambled out, exchanging a joke with the security guard outside the gazebo.

'Cool guy,' Harry offered, from his seat near the door. He was busy on his phone, but kept darting interested glances at the activity around them.

'Yes, he is,' Chloe replied. 'I do agree about Lara too. She's lovely, but I suppose for some people that must be what gets them riled up.'

'My granddad always says if you can't say something nice, then you should keep your mouth shut until you can,' Harry told them. 'I reckon some of these people online should think of that before they hit the keyboard with their comments.'

Jordan, hood still up, phone in hand, nodded his agreement. 'Glad I'm not famous. All the money in the world isn't worth having everyone chipping away at you all the time.' He patted Goldie's neck, and she turned and nosed at his pocket, hopeful for treats.

Chloe smiled at him. He was at that awkward age where sometimes things he said came out wrong and his behaviour immature, but more and more he would come out with comments that suggested not only a growing maturity, but also a high degree of intelligence.

Half an hour later a harassed-looking Maria came over to say they were ready for the horse. Chloe slipped the bridle on, while Antoine gave the shimmering golden coat an unnecessary final polish. The box of flowers from Isabelle, the florist, contained a magnificent wreath for the mare's neck, and Chloe asked Jordan to carry it down to the beach.

As they walked down the path, various people were snapping pictures on their mobiles, and Chloe felt most uncomfortable. It was very crowded, not at all like the professional shoot she had taken part in earlier in the year.

Passing the hair and make-up tent they were joined by Lara, who was almost unrecognisable in thick, flawless make-up, her loose dark hair curling down her back. She was dressed in her first outfit, a long pale-pink silk dress, and was holding it up around her ankles as she walked.

'I hope Goldie won't mind all this fuss,' she said to Chloe, anxiously, slipping an arm in hers and squeezing her hand gently. 'But it will be quieter once we start shooting.' She seemed to be lacking a little of her exuberance and sparkle today, but Chloe supposed it had been a stressful couple of days for the poor girl.

Chloe returned the pressure on her hand, and was about to say something comforting when a man leapt out of the shrubs and crouched in front of them, pointing his camera in Goldie's face and taking a series of quick-fire shots. Lara screamed, clinging to Chloe. There was a flurry of activity and shouts and the horse swung round on her haunches, one hoof landing squarely on Lara's sandaled foot.

Chloe and Antoine were comforting the horse, who was snorting and swishing her tail, making the crowds move nervously away. Kellie could be heard berating someone for the intrusion, Ben was talking urgently to one of the security team, waving his arms around, and Lara was leaning against a palm tree, teeth gritted in obvious pain, one foot lifted.

Her hair stylist ran over, grabbed her hand and began asking her questions. Chloe could see to her relief the girl was soon moving her foot, and even putting it back to the ground to walk a little.

'Lara, I'm so sorry. Are you all right?' Chloe called to her, whilst soothing the jumpy horse with soft words and gentle pats.

Lara called back something Chloe couldn't catch, but she smiled bravely and gave her a thumbs up to reiterate.

'We need to take the horse down to the beach without all this fuss,' she said firmly to the photographer.

'Agreed. Take her down to the rocks on the right-hand side and we'll start as soon as Lara's ready. The first-aid team will check her out. Even if her foot needs bandaging, the dress will hide it.' He was a quiet-mannered man, with a deep, soothing voice, and his team were waiting with various shades and lighting equipment.

His comment seemed a little callous, but Chloe desperately hoped Lara's foot wasn't broken. A trip over to the hospital would ruin Kellie's schedule and they would lose the light. Not to mention the implications of hopping down the aisle at her own wedding. Again, she felt a rush of sympathy for the girl.

Luckily, after the press intrusion, the shoot went smoothly, and the whole team seemed delighted with the results. Goldie managed not to eat any of Isabelle's beautiful flowers and the light, all soft, rosy, romantic pink and gold, had the photographer raving. Lara's ankle had been tightly bandaged, as a bruise had spread across her entire foot, but she had carried on posing for the camera, draping her long dresses across her injury. Chloe felt new respect for her. Having been trodden on by the horses frequently herself she knew exactly how painful it was to have 900lbs of equine land on your bare foot.

Before they departed, Chloe went in search of Lara, finding her, phone in hand, standing at the top of the beach, watching the sun sink low over the ocean. 'I just wanted to make sure you were okay,' Chloe said gently. 'I'm really sorry, but when horses are frightened they don't think about anything except running away, and I know how much it hurts to get trodden on.'

Lara, face scrubbed clean of make-up, hair in a simple ponytail, smiled. 'It's fine, honestly. We got the shoot done, that's all that matters.'

She must have picked up on Chloe's expression, because she continued, 'You must think we're crazy to put up with this chaos around our lives.'

'It's your choice, and not up to me to judge anyone,' Chloe told her.

'It's my job.' Lara paused and snapped another picture of the beach. 'It's just so beautiful here, I don't even need a filter. Look, I wanted to tell you some stuff, if you don't mind.'

'Of course not,' Chloe said gently.

'My dad died in a car accident when I was three. My mum worked so hard, but she was on minimum wage, our benefits cheque never came in at the right time and she got into debt buying things for me. She never bought stuff for herself, only for me. Food, school uniform, not exactly designer purchases but God we struggled. I remember going to the local food bank with her, how ashamed she was to be taking handouts.'

Chloe started to say something but Lara raised a hand, her huge diamond engagement ring glittering in the last rays of gold, reflected up from the sea. 'I know she shouldn't have been ashamed, but she was a proud woman. She died when I was thirteen and I went to live with an aunt. She was nice enough but I did the whole teenage rebellion thing. I was still grieving for my mum, still am if I'm honest, and I made a promise to her and myself I would make enough money to buy whatever I wanted in life, and when I had that security, I'd set up my own food banks, make sure people knew asking for help is nothing to be ashamed of.'

'I'm sorry about your mum,' Chloe said. 'She would have been proud of you, but you didn't have to tell me all this. As I said, I don't judge.'

Her gaze was as vulnerable as a child's. 'That's why I wanted to tell you. I don't want you to think I'm this greedy spoilt brat who enjoys being famous. I never lied about where I came from. And... Chloe, this is a picture of my mum...' Lara showed her the screensaver on her phone.

The photo looked like a snapshot taken at a birthday party. Lara and her mum were cuddled together, smiling, arms wrapped around each other. But Chloe was looking less at the poignant attitude of the pair, more at Lara's mum. The woman was blonde with pale-blue eyes, and a round face. Her long hair was blowing in the breeze, mingling with her daughter's dark curls.

'It's a lovely photo,' Chloe managed at last. Still shocked. The woman could have been her double at that age. Same face shape, same colouring, same determined chin tilt...

'Do you see why I couldn't believe it when we met you for the first time?' Lara asked anxiously. 'You're practically her double. A bit older, of course, but she would have looked like you do now if she had lived. You must have thought I was a right weirdo just staring at you...'

'Oh, Lara, I do see the likeness, and I understand why you were thrown. I would have been too. It's funny, isn't it? They say everyone has a twin somewhere in the world.' Chloe smiled. When she looked back at the photograph there were differences, it was just the shock from the first impression.

The girl sighed. 'It was like seeing a ghost. But then I felt like maybe it was my mum saying I was doing the right thing after all. That's why I wanted you to help choose the flowers. I do believe in signs and the supernatural.'

Chloe scuffed a bit of sand with her toes. 'And tarot cards?' she said gently.

'Kind of. That was a bit blown out of proportion... But Danny's death, his murder, I'm grieving, Chloe.' Her dark eyes held Chloe's, sincere and fragile. 'Who could have killed him? Sometimes I feel like I'm stuck on this rollercoaster and I can't get off...'

Before Chloe could respond, a shout from behind them indicated Kellie requesting Lara's presence.

'I'm sure everything will be fine,' Lara said brightly, her tone and demeanour changing as she turned and waved at her manager. 'One of my best friends, Maisie-Lynn, is one of my bridesmaids and she'll be here soon. We were kids together and she knew Danny.'

Chloe thought she sounded as though she was trying to convince herself what she was doing was right.

'I do enjoy the fame and the money, most of the time, but at least I'm honest about why, and where I came from. Social media is a huge part of my life. I was scouted from my Instagram pictures for *Tough Love*. That was how it all began with Eddie.'

'*Tough Love* was the reality show where you met?' Chloe asked as they turned and began to walk back up towards the hotel.

'Yeah. Eddie actually applied, but the show's producers scouted a lot of people from social media. They want certain types, I guess,' Lara said quietly.

'Well, you only have two more days in Bermuda, so I'm sure you can relax a little bit and enjoy the island. Your wedding party is arriving on tomorrow's flight so you can catch up with your bridesmaids. Kellie must give you a bit of time off sometimes!' Chloe said cheerfully.

Lara smiled, but it didn't quite reach her eyes. 'The odd half hour, yes. Thanks for listening to me ramble on.'

'No problem, I wish you and Eddie all the very best and Goldie is looking forward to the wedding day. Lara, I got you a gift...' On impulse, Chloe pulled the little box she had purchased in Isabelle's shop and gave it to Lara. 'A little early wedding present.'

Intrigued, the girl carefully opened the box. 'Oh it's so cute! What does it mean?'

Chloe helped her fasten the silver bracelet around her slender wrist. 'The charms are for wealth, health and happiness, and this little symbol is for protection.'

'Protection against what?' She was wide-eyed, enchanted by the gift.

'Anything you like. Just protection,' Chloe told her firmly. 'I was going to give it to you tomorrow at the party, but it seems like you could do with it right now.'

Antoine was shouting that they were going to be late back, and Kellie was advancing, lips compressed with annoyance. Chloe hastily gave Lara a hug. 'I really must go, Lara, but I'll see you tomorrow.'

Lara hugged her back. 'Thank you so much for the bracelet.' Her huge dark eyes were almost black in the evening light. 'I feel like meeting you was kind of meant to be. Does that sound crazy? Maybe it's something in the Bermuda air. It's like... special.'

Chloe remembered something Dre used to say to her as a child. 'My grandmother used to tell me every meeting, every experience and every person that comes into your life is for a reason.'

'She must have been very wise.'

'Oh she was. See you at your party!' Chloe smiled at the girl before she turned and walked quickly back up the path.

'We thought you'd been kidnapped or something!' Jordan told her with some relish when she arrived back at the trailer. 'You know, with all the weird things happening. Me and Antoine were just going to come and rescue you.'

'Thank you for the thought, but nobody is likely to kidnap me. I was just talking to Lara, sorry it took so long.'

Harry had packed up their equipment and loaded Goldie up into her trailer so Chloe jumped into the back seat and they rumbled peacefully home. The boys settled Goldie, and shot off on their scooters, no doubt desperate to pass on as much gossip as they were allowed to various friends and family members.

Chloe released the delighted Hilda, brought a glass of rum down to the yard and settled the remaining animals for the night. The darkness was broken by the moon and dozens of sparkling stars, which seemed to hang over the sea. The wind had dropped and the sleepy murmur of the waves, and chirrup of night-time insects were the only sounds.

She yawned, empty glass in hand, walked slowly back to her door, pausing as she thought she heard a rustle near the side of the house. The little dog growled, and Chloe stopped abruptly, with her hand on the back door.

Hilda shot off, barking and Chloe followed, hearing what she thought was the sound of running feet. But when she arrived on the driveway she could see no sign of either vehicle or person.

13

Shrugging, her heart still beating too fast, hand clenched around her glass, she went back inside. Mark? Very likely, but surely he would have come and pestered her for some information. There were no celebrities lurking in the yard today for him to snoop around. She would bet the photographer who had leapt out the bushes earlier at the magazine photo shoot had something to do with him... The lights in Ailsa's house were out. Her neighbour liked to go to bed early, or she might have popped round to check if her ex-husband had been spotted on the prowl again.

Her heart sped up again as several notifications popped up on her phone. But luckily, Fiona and Maria were the only people who had left messages, thanking her for the evening, assuring her everyone was delighted with the pictures.

There were no other disturbances as she made preparations for bed, but she was extra careful to lock up that night. Leaving her mobile phone next to the bed as she always did, she found herself stretching sleepy fingers more than once to check it was still there. Hilda gave a great sigh and started snoring, but Chloe lay awake a little longer.

She was thinking about Eddie's words, about the reason Lara was hated so much. It made her uncomfortable to think of the vitriol directed at both of them, especially after Lara had been so sweet and honest about her mum when they talked on the beach.

Her phone buzzed, waking her from a deep, exhausted sleep, and she fumbled clumsily, knocking her glass of water and her reading glasses onto the floor, instantly worried about broken glass and Hilda's paws. But the dog was still on her bed, head on one side, eyes bright and alert at the sudden noise and movement.

'Hallo?'

'Chloe!' Lara wailed down the phone, and Chloe hastily took her mobile further away from her ear.

'Lara? What's wrong?' Chloe pushed her hair out of her eyes, breathing fast, anticipating all sorts of disasters.

'You'll never guess what happened! Maisie-Lynn was taking pictures in our final dress fitting and she tried to sell them to a rival magazine.'

'I... Your bridesmaid? I thought she was one of your best friends from when you were kids?' Chloe was incredulous, but still half asleep. Why was Lara calling her?

'She is... was,' Lara said. 'I can't believe it, but the magazine called just now to tell us what happened.'

'They called you at midnight?'

'Is it midnight?' Lara sounded shocked. 'Chloe, I'm sorry, I'm just so mad about it. Maria said I needed to calm down and Kellie thinks I'm stupid for choosing Maisie-Lynn as a bridesmaid anyway, and Ben wants her invitation cancelled, but she's flying out tomorrow lunchtime...'

It sounded as though the girl had pretty much called everyone on the wedding team to recount her tale of woe, Chloe thought, hazily. 'So will they publish the pictures?' Chloe could quite see how this would be a disaster for the lucrative deals lined up with rival magazines and suppliers, but also, what an awful personal betrayal.

'No, we managed to swap them for another bit of news about my ex. I've rung her and told her she can't be a bridesmaid after this, which means uneven numbers because Eddie's having eight groomsmen.'

'I'm not surprised,' Chloe told her. 'But you still have seven bridesmaids, don't you? That's quite a lot for any wedding. What did she say when you confronted her?'

'She said she needed the money and it was good PR for us,' Lara said, hurt clear in her voice. 'I'm so careful who I tell things to, and I just can't believe she's done this. Eddie's fuming, but I can't ban her from the wedding even after what she's done. Why didn't she come to me if she needed money?'

'I don't know,' Chloe said lamely. She had witnessed Lara's generosity for the week, and had absolutely no doubt she would have lent or even given her friend some cash if she had needed it. But clearly Maisie-Lynn had been trying to cash in not only for money but also for her own slice of fame. It was truly sickening, and Chloe's heart went out to the bride-to-be.

'Anyway, I just wanted you to know. Sorry, I guess I just wanted another person to sound off to, and you've been so sweet to me,' Lara said honestly.

'Why don't you let Kellie handle the PR, and you and Eddie go and have a nightcap or book in a massage at the spa for tomorrow morning?' Chloe suggested. 'You are the bride, so it would be nice if you have a little time just to enjoy the fact you will be getting married soon.'

'You're right... You're so right!' Lara said. 'Thanks, Chloe, and give Goldie a kiss for me!'

'I will.' Chloe rang off thoughtfully. No wonder Maria needed a two-week holiday at her yoga retreat every time she finished planning a wedding. It took her a long time to get back to sleep and she woke heavy-eyed in the morning.

She thought back to her own wedding as she made a cup of coffee and let Hilda out into the garden. It had been hastily arranged, because Mark treated the whole thing as an adventure, and she had been so in love she had agreed to a quick wedding. She remembered emerging in the rain from the town hall, at that stage thinking she was two months pregnant, laughing with Mark.

But she had lost the baby at twelve weeks, and there had never been another. It was over, and she shook off the cloak of dark memories, replacing them with the gentle touch of morning sunshine on her bare shoulders and Hilda's bright, happy face as she called her dog inside for breakfast.

Antoine was giving Jordan another riding lesson when she reached the yard. The boy was certainly improving, and was now able to point Star in roughly the right direction and stop when he wanted to, not when the mare decided she was bored.

Chloe leant on the gate and waited for them to finish. She ran her fingers over the rough wood, picking at the peeling white paint on the top bar. The gate and field fencing would be a winter job, she thought, mentally adding it to her growing list.

Funny to think that shortly the whirlwind carnival of the Eddie/Lara wedding would be over, the couple enjoying a long honeymoon, which took in New York and Barbados, and the stables would be back to normal.

As the boys came in from the field, Chloe swung the gate shut behind them. 'That was much better, Jordan,' she said encouragingly.

His face was glowing with pride and achievement. 'She tried to get me off under that tree branch but I stuck on and then she was fine!'

'She was testing you,' Antoine told him, laughing. 'She's only good with clients who can ride well, that's why we have to be careful who rides her.'

'Really, the only person Star likes is Melissa,' Chloe added as they walked back to the yard.

Her phone buzzed with a message as she began to dismantle some bridles for cleaning. There was only one ride today, and Chloe had already thanked God for her forward planning in shifting bookings to after the wedding.

Hi Chloe, fancy breakfast at the Ocean?

Chloe smiled, glanced outside the tack room at the glorious day, and decided she did fancy a coffee and bagel at the Ocean Café.

Love to. You say what time.

Half an hour later, having asked Jordan to take Hilda for a walk, and promised Antoine if he didn't want to take the ride out she would be back by two latest and would do tour-guide duty, Chloe was running for the bus in sandals and a yellow sundress, her long plait flopping over one shoulder, and shopping basket on her arm.

~

Chloe had fallen into the habit of wandering down to the Ocean Café for breakfast a couple of times week, and catching up with Finn for a quick coffee was always a treat. She tried to arrange work at the stables around her visits and time her food shopping to coincide with these days. The bus ride was only fifteen minutes either way.

It was Peter, the taxi driver, who had originally suggested a couple of diners she might like to check out for breakfast. At first, she had stayed close to home, feeling as well with her initial money problems that eating out would be a foolish extravagance.

Finn had mentioned the Ocean Café several times, but Chloe had gradually found the confidence to explore on her own. Walking past on her way to the garden centre, or the supermarket, she had been intrigued by the bright turquoise exterior with a wave design painted on the walls. It looked more like a surf shop than a diner.

The owner, 'Spider' Morris was a retired police officer. He was a massive man, well over six foot five, but limped from an old injury which had caused his early retirement. His real name was Michael, but his nickname had come from his time in the Bermuda Police Force and he told Chloe even he had forgotten its origins.

'Morning, Chloe!' Josanne and another officer were in the queue for tea and snacks.

It was a busy place, much frequented by the police and the Bermuda Fire and Rescue Service officers.

Finn was late, and Chloe was sipping her coffee, before Spider dumped a plate of bacon and eggs in front of her. He had a plentiful supply of staff but liked to do as much as he could himself.

'You on your own today, Chloe?'

'No, Finn's dropping by on his way to work.' Chloe thanked him for the breakfast and inhaled the luscious smells of cooking and the sea. 'How's business going?'

'Pretty good.' He paused, dishcloth tucked in his belt, sweat on his brow. The very picture of a busy diner owner. 'Actually, we've been seeing a lot of reporters with this celebrity wedding coming up. You know me, I'm happy to serve anyone, but there's been a bit of tension between the reporters. All different papers, you see, and all trying to get the scoop on the happy couple. Not to mention the murder investigation.'

Chloe had hoped to avoid wedding talk for the morning, but she expressed sympathy. 'I guess they'll be gone soon though. The wedding is on Thursday but I guess the investigation into Danny's death may take some time.'

'Yeah, that's a weird one. Someone did a pretty bad job of making it seem like an accident.'

'You're right, there's been so much coverage, I suppose the reporters are desperate to find out what really happened,' Chloe said, pushing a strand of hair back behind her ears. The sun was hot on her shoulders, and she reached inside her basket for the sun cream.

'Desperate is right. They can take it outside if they want to argue.' Spider grinned down from his great height. 'I told a couple of them yesterday and they ran off pretty quick.'

'Well, you do have a calming effect on most people,' Finn said, arriving at the table, brown eyes sparkling with amusement. He apologised for being late and turned back to Spider. 'Just the usual, please.'

'No worries, chief. You want takeaway?'

'Please.'

'I had a call-out early this morning, and as I was heading back this way, I thought how nice if we could grab a drink,' Finn told Chloe as he settled opposite her, yawning. 'Because we missed a brunch last week, didn't we?'

'That's okay. I've told you before, it's always lovely to see you, but if you can't make it that's also fine.' She smiled at him through a mouthful of mushrooms, relaxing in the sunshine. 'I'm enjoying the view and my breakfast. And we did the Crystal Caves last week so I don't feel too hard done by.'

He leant back in his chair, stretching his legs out from

underneath the table. 'I hear Spider's had a bit of trouble with reporters recently.'

'He just told me. I suppose Bermuda isn't such a big place really, though, and with the actual wedding at Palm Bay Hotel, this area is an obvious choice to hang out,' Chloe said. She really didn't want to drop Mark into their conversation, so she quickly changed the subject. 'So how are things going with you? Not just the Danny investigation, I mean other things too.'

She liked hearing about his work, the progress he was making on his boat, which was one he had renovated from dereliction. In fact, she had been to admire the results twice now, and shared his triumph at the beautiful polished wood, the fine lines of a vessel which would skim through the water under the Bermuda skies once again.

'The investigation is ongoing,' Finn said carefully. 'Bermuda is never heavy on serious crime, as you know, so this has shocked people. My sisters are busy with party preparations, and the boat will be ready for spring, I think. How's Goldie? All ready to be a TV star?'

'I guess she is.' Chloe laughed, pushed her plate away and sipped her coffee. 'That was delicious. I really shouldn't eat so much here, though, now I just want to fall asleep in the sunshine. Yes, Goldie behaved well at the shoot and she's ready for tomorrow.'

'I hear the security is going to be tight,' Finn nodded at a few acquaintances who walked past their table, 'especially after all these unpleasant happenings since they arrived.'

'A photographer scared us all on the photo shoot by leaping out of the bushes, but as far as I know nothing else has happened since the paint-spray attack in Hamilton. Maria is rushed off her feet now. I've hardly seen or heard from her or Fiona,' Chloe told him. 'Eddie and Lara are so young and really very sweet. I would hate anything to happen to them before their wedding.'

'I'll make a few extra enquiries. Just general chit-chat, and see what comes up.' Finn glanced at his watch. 'Sorry, I must get on to that meeting now. Do you want a lift home?'

'Thank you, but I'll stay here in the sun for a bit longer, and then I've got some shopping to do, so I'll get the bus. You would be going right out of your way giving me a lift.' She smiled at him, shading her eyes with her hand as he stood up, his tall figure silhouetted against the brilliant blue sky.

'No worries, see you soon. Maybe we could do another trip or dinner after the wedding?'

'That would be lovely!' Chloe said.

He hesitated a moment and then walked out, yelling goodbye to Spider, who was in the kitchen area.

Chloe lazed in the sun, people-watching for another ten minutes, then said her own goodbye to Spider and walked briskly down the dusty pavement. She remembered the tedium of shopping back in London, and almost shivered. She was so lucky to have this place as her home. People now seemed to know who she was after a summer on the island, and she was greeted by name in many shops. Slowly her confidence had developed, especially after shopping with Ailsa a couple of times. Her neighbour knew everyone and wasn't afraid to spend a bit of time chatting, which quite often turned into a couple of hours chatting and no shopping done.

Chloe had filled her bags and was on her way back past the Ocean Café, heading for the bus stop when she stepped aside to avoid a group of four men. The pavement was narrow just here and the men had turned out of an alleyway, talking intently.

'Chloe!'

She raised her head, made eye contact and her heart seemed to miss a beat. Bloody Mark.

'Sorry, Mark, can't stop, I need to catch my bus,' she told him firmly.

'Any quick quotes from the happy couple?' he said, laughing, his voice teasing.

She wondered if 'Get lost' would count as a quote, but smiled instead. 'Goodbye, Mark.'

His companions laughed and she heard one of them tease him about losing his touch with women.

'She's my ex-wife,' he told them.

They looked uncomfortable with this, but Mark, basking in his usual arrogance, continued to block her way. 'I wonder if you could pass a message to Lara direct, Chloe.'

'No, I already told you I couldn't.' Really, he was being obtuse in the extreme. She was going to have to walk into the road to get around his group soon.

'That's a shame. I'm glad the stables are doing well now. I understand they were almost bankrupt when you took them on.'

She said nothing.

'Which horse is the lucky mount for Lara?'

Really annoyed now, Chloe raised her voice. 'Mark, get out of my way. I have things to do, and as you just pointed out, a business to run. I don't have any gossip for you because I don't know any. All I'm doing is providing a horse for the wedding. There must be plenty of other people you can hassle for quotes. I feel very sorry for anyone who features in your stories. Just go away!'

He scowled, and opened his mouth to speak, when another voice came over the low turquoise wall.

'Is everything all right, Chloe?'

Spider, with his keen radar for trouble, had appeared nonchalantly next to her, apparently clearing tables, his expression serene, but his big body casting a shadow across the group on the pavement.

'Oh fine, thanks, Spider. I'm just going to catch my bus,' Chloe told him with relief. She had been wondering if she would need to physically attack Mark to get him to move out the way, and how satisfying it would be to hear her fist crunch against his nose. Goodness, she thought, half amused, she was getting as bad as Jordan.

'Good. See you next week for breakfast.' He smiled at her, before turning to the four men. 'You gents will be moving along then, I'm sure. Pavement's a bit narrow here, you're blocking the way.'

Mark's companions muttered something that might have been an acknowledgement to Chloe or an apology to Spider and began to edge past in single file.

Mark, however, scowled up at Spider and didn't move. 'This is a public highway, and I can do whatever I want.'

Spider beamed at him, arms folded. 'Not technically true. Would you like me to educate you on our highway code here in Bermuda?'

Chloe smiled her thanks at Spider, slipped past Mark and walked quickly up the hill, just catching her bus. As it rumbled back down the hill past the diner she could see Spider still talking and Mark, unable to get a word in edgeways, looking furious. His companions seemed to have deserted him.

She laughed to herself, settled her shopping basket and bags, enjoying the bumpy journey home.

Antoine was just finishing off tidying the muck-heap as she walked up her driveway and Ailsa was standing in her garden talking to her daughter, Jordan's mum. They both waved, and a chicken shot back under the hedge, a flower in its beak. Chloe inspected the damage as she pulled out her door key. Yes, clearly she wasn't going to be able to grow much in her garden. Almost all flowers and vegetables seemed to be a chicken favourite.

She greeted Hilda, who bounced up the garden from the

yard, and unpacked her shopping. A quick salad for lunch, and she changed into her riding clothes before going out to the yard. The dog trotted happily beside her, and as usual, after the shady, cool interior of her house, the sunlight warmed her soul.

Mark's moods didn't affect her anymore. He was, as Ailsa had pronounced, a part of history. Soon he would leave Bermuda, and life would get back to normal. Meanwhile, she had to cherish a tiny part of herself that had thoroughly enjoyed seeing him cut down to size by her friends, and the shock in his eyes at her appearance, her home, was well worth the worry she had endured over his visit.

Dre would have been proud of her. She had never said she didn't like Mark, in fact, she hadn't known him, but when they sent the wedding photo, a brief card had merely congratulated the couple, adding a note to Chloe, '*Very happy for you.*'

Given the chance, Chloe would have invited Dre to the wedding, or even had her own wedding on Bermuda. But that had never been an option.

The three clients were on a cruise and all novice riders. Chloe and Antoine had allotted their three gentlest horses: Candy, Mars and Goldie, while Chloe would ride Star.

After the usual chit-chat, Chloe and the boys helped them to mount. The eldest client, a tall, bony-looking woman with a sharp face slid her feet into the stirrups and leant down to Chloe. 'It was here, wasn't it?'

'I'm sorry?' Chloe moved slightly back.

'The murder. Can you take us down to where they found the body?' The woman's face was intense with curiosity, and her companions were nodding.

'We read about it in the paper. Can you show us where it happened?'

Chloe, speechless, opened her mouth, but was saved a reply as Star, impatient and bad-tempered as ever, lunged forward with her teeth bared. Poor old Mars was another of the black mare's sworn enemies. Mars carted his rider across the yard and Antoine leapt to the rescue as all three women twittered in alarm.

Chloe mounted, face grim with distaste as Star shook her head and licked her lips. This was clearly not going to be the easy ride she had anticipated.

14

The last dress rehearsal was at 3pm and Harry appeared promptly at 2pm with his four-by-four and trailer to transport Goldie and the Beachside Stables crew to Palm Bay Hotel.

Luckily for everyone's nerves (Chloe thought), the whole thing went extremely smoothly. Even after just a couple of rides, Lara was getting the hang of it. She was naturally athletic, like a little gymnast, and adored Goldie. The gentle mare accepted the hugs, the kisses, the garlands of flowers, the cameras, without batting a white-lashed eyelid.

Some of the TV crew fed the mare carrots, and were yelled at by Kellie for getting in the way, and Ben the PR officer was shouting into his phone. Apart from that, preparations were going just like clockwork, according to a sweaty, red-faced Fiona.

'I haven't heard from Maria for twenty-four hours, even though I've rung her twice,' Chloe said to Fiona as she offered her a bottle of water.

Fiona gulped the drink and pushed her hair back. 'She's fine. Run absolutely ragged, but we have two ace events teams working with us, plus another security detail. I keep telling myself it's just one more day.'

'Well, everything I've seen looks incredible,' Chloe assured her. 'Antoine and Jordan are glued to Lara and Eddie's social media and every time Goldie features they screenshot the evidence.' She laughed. 'Goldie thinks she's the superstar.'

∼

Afterwards, the photo shoot paraphernalia was removed, the beach was cleared, the sand raked by a tractor and hotel staff began to set up the massive gazebo for tonight's party. Twinkling silver lights were threaded amongst the palm trees on the terrace, and caterers were in deep discussion over three long trestle tables which had been carried out from the glass doors next to the turquoise swimming pool.

'At least the weather is good now,' the photographer said to Chloe, who was gulping her own bottle of water and wiping sweat off her forehead.

'I know, it would have been awful if it was raining,' she said, keeping an eye on how many extra treats Goldie was getting.

The photographer moved off into a huddle round a laptop with Kellie and the rest of Lara and Eddie's team as Jordan wandered over to show Chloe the latest gossip updates on his phone.

She scanned them quickly, wincing at the cruel things written in various columns and online blogs, especially about Lara. But would these be the kind of people who would get on a plane and chase her to Bermuda? Or even chase Danny to Bermuda... Surely these kind of bullies stayed behind a screen to hurl their insults, Chloe pondered.

Mark, no doubt basking in the glory of his exclusive the other day, had written a bitchy little piece about Lara and Eddie being fake and annoying all their wedding team with outrageous demands:

'... Lara will be riding into her wedding on a palomino stallion. Not content with a normal horse, the star threw a hissy fit during a meeting with the wedding planner, and shouted at us to find her a palomino,' a source tells us. 'Luckily there was a horse like that at a local stables or she wanted one flown in from America!'

'What a load of rubbish!' Chloe said indignantly. 'Bloody Mark and his stupid stories.'

'Goldie is pissed off he thinks she's a stallion,' Antoine informed them, chucking a light pink travel sheet over the mare's back. 'Can we head home now? There's plenty of time if we are still needed for something, but I need to check in with Louisa with an ETA... There's some party she wants us to look in at, and we need to do a bit more wedding planning of our own.'

'Of course. Let me just check with Maria and Fiona. Give me twenty minutes?' Chloe said to Antoine, Harry and Jordan. Team Beachside Stables, as she was beginning to think of them. She smiled. "I'll be as quick as I can."

'No worries.' Antoine leant casually against the side of the vehicle, and all three young men took their phones out, eyes narrowed in the late evening rays.

Chloe jogged back down to the various gazebos set up between the terrace and the beach area. She peered quickly into each one as she hunted for Fiona and Maria.

Isabelle was talking to the make-up girl, holding up flowers against Lara's hair. She was also watching Eddie. Chloe thought it was sweet she seemed to have a bit of a crush on him and luckily, Lara seemed completely used to it.

'Are we all finished with the run-through?' Chloe asked. 'Because if you don't need us anymore, I'd like to get off home.'

'Yes, all done.' Lara jumped down from the make-up chair

with her usual exuberance, dark hair still twisted into an intricate shape and dotted with hair jewels and flowers. 'We were just trying out a few styles for tonight. I love this one... Except, do you think I should have an extra rose?' She indicated the area just above her right ear.

'No,' Chloe said after examining the overall picture she presented. 'It would be too much.'

Isabelle agreed. 'If you have another flower when you get pictures from that angle it will hide some of your face.' She glanced over Lara's shoulder at the groom. 'What's the matter with Eddie?'

Eddie, who had been sitting on the wall next to the car park sipping a drink, was now walking up and down talking on his phone. He seemed angry, and pulled Lara to one side when he finished. They talked in low, urgent tones before Lara turned huge, distressed eyes on her team.

'Karim and Ali have missed the flight!'

There was a rumble of surprise and annoyance, before Kellie spoke. 'They really are a pair of idiots. I checked in with them this morning after what you said. All they needed to do was get on the bloody plane.'

Lara, tears in her eyes, was shouting at Eddie now. 'I told you not to ask them to be groomsmen! They are so fucking unreliable!'

Eddie looked furious too, his eyes cold and mouth set. He pulled his fiancée into a hug. 'I know, babe, and I'm sorry, but I wanted them to share the day with us. We've been friends for years though.' He turned to Kellie pleadingly, 'Can't you sort it?'

'I'm not a magician, Eddie,' she snapped, 'but I'll ring round and see if I can get them on another flight. Assuming I can, they'll just arrive later than everyone else and miss the party tonight. Unless you want to book a private jet for those two clowns, in which case they'll be here as soon as I can get one chartered.'

'Oh and they've got the suits!' Lara was crying. 'Did they check their luggage in? Why is everything going wrong?' Eddie released her and picked up his phone again.

Chloe squeezed her hand. 'It'll be okay.' She noticed the girl was wearing the little charm bracelet she had given her and felt touched by the gesture.

She sniffled, tears still falling, washing away her heavy make-up. 'I wish we'd just gone to Gretna Green instead of all this…' She tore herself away from Chloe and ran off down to the beach.

Eddie left a brief, curt message on someone's phone, sighed heavily and started after her.

Kellie was shouting for Maria and Ben, waving her phone around and scowling at everyone. The make-up artist was calmly washing her brushes, presumably used to celebrity dramas.

Chloe suddenly had an overwhelming need to be back at home, sitting in the garden with an iced drink, before going out to check on her animals before bed. Antoine was waving to her, impatient to get back for his party. She started back up to the car park, hoping to see Maria on the way. She noticed Eddie walk down to the beach, slip an arm round Lara while they bent their heads close together. When they eventually walked back towards the hotel, they were holding hands.

Gradually, the team, the camera crew and various hangers-on were beginning to pack up and head back to the hotel, leaving the cream-coloured gazebo milling with busy staff. A bar was being set up, and Maria, texting quickly, her face worried, looked up as Chloe said goodbye. 'Sorry, Maria, we really must head off. I just wanted to check it was okay to go?'

'Yes, of course, darling. Thank you so much for your input! I tell you what though, I could do with a bloody drink right now. Those complete idiots. All any of the guests had to do was get the correct flight, and now we're apparently missing the groom's suit,' she raged.

Lara and Eddie were now taking pictures, whispering to each other. Lara stole a quick kiss as they stood halfway up the beach, backs to the gently frothing waves, and Eddie responded, but his right hand held his phone. He appeared to be filming the whole thing.

'Think about that lovely Welsh farmhouse. Think hard about it, because by tomorrow night this will all be over, you will have done an awesome job and those two will be off on their honeymoon,' Chloe said to her friend. She frowned and pushed back a strand of hair. 'It's just weird not being able to appreciate being young and being in love though. I can't imagine constantly having to prove something to complete strangers on social media.'

'Don't be silly, darling, they might love each other but they also love all the fame and money that comes with it. You're just an old romantic. Which reminds me. I *still* haven't met your policeman friend, Finn... Oh, hang on...' Maria read a text and visibly relaxed. 'It's okay, the groomsmen got transferred onto another flight. It's not direct, which means they won't be here until tomorrow morning, but they will arrive in time. The suits will be arriving as part of someone else's luggage. Thankfully, it seems Eddie's uncle had the sense to take charge of them himself. I expect he knows what Eddie's best friends are like.'

'Well, there you go. I'll see you at the party tonight,' Chloe said.

'Are you bringing Finn?' Maria winked and Chloe flushed.

'No. He isn't invited.'

'Shame. I was so looking forward to meeting him,' Maria said. 'Perhaps we could all do lunch or something before I fly home on Sunday? Mandy will kill me if I don't even meet him. You've spoken so much about him I feel like there must be something going on...'

'We are just friends,' Chloe said firmly, but admitted, 'I do like him, and normally we see each other a couple of times a week, but it feels a bit odd at the moment when Mark keeps popping up. I mean, he must know I'm not going to spill any wedding gossip but everywhere I go he's lurking around. Then he writes those horrible articles. I wouldn't put it past him to be setting up all this stuff just to make stories out of it.'

Lara and Eddie had stopped to look at the party preparations, and then continued up the beach towards the hotel. His arm was around her shoulders, and she was leaning against him, as if for support.

Maria picked up a cardboard box filled with lace and flowers, her green eyes thoughtful. 'Word is Mark isn't doing well. Alexa told me *Wow* magazine chose someone else to cover the main feature and his freelance contacts must be getting bombarded with titbits. *The Daily News* has sent its own features editor over here, so they won't want anything extra.'

'Unless he can pull off another scoop,' Chloe suggested uneasily, thinking of the banner headline on Lara and Eddie's cursed wedding, about the strange happenings and about Danny's unsolved murder. It was exactly what Mark was known for, and the scoop never turned out to be something the subject wanted in the public domain.

'Chloe, come on!' Jordan had walked down from the car park, and was waving from the path that ran along the side of the hotel.

Chloe and Maria walked briskly across the sand and up the concrete path as music started to float from the beach. Chloe pushed her hair back. She was hot and sweaty, and couldn't wait to get back and jump in a cold shower and pour herself a Dark 'n' Stormy. The rum cocktail had always been Dre's drink of choice and Chloe felt it would be rude not to carry on the evening tradition.

Pleasantly distracted, hoping that at last maybe everything might be running smoothly, Chloe stopped short at the sound of a scream. High-pitched and terrified, it ripped the tranquil evening apart.

Chloe and Maria started running towards the terrace, following the path Eddie and Lara had taken minutes earlier. Chloe could see nothing amiss, and was bewildered by Lara's obvious hysterics, and Eddie's grim expression as he comforted his fiancée.

The thud of running feet from both directions indicated others were also hurtling to the rescue, and the narrow pathway was soon crowded, people spilling onto the immaculate flower beds, peering over shoulders, whispering. Chloe found she was clutching Maria's hand, as they both stared in horror.

The dolls were little wax replicas of Eddie and Lara, complete with Eddie's mop of blond hair and Lara's long, shiny dark locks. They were in full wedding dress, lying on the ornamental rocks with a circle of pebbles arranged around them.

In each doll a pin was stuck in their right eye, and the bride's dress was dabbed with what appeared to be bloodstains.

15

Lara was sobbing. 'It's disgusting. What's going on?'

'Just some idiot trying to scare us,' Eddie told her, but Chloe thought he looked just as shaken. 'Come on, Lara, it's not real, just a couple of dolls.'

'But... the spell... it's like witchcraft or something, like a curse,' she said, wiping her eyes with her fingers like a child. 'Who would hate us that much?'

'Babe, do you even need to ask? We knew it might be tough, but let's get through it and the most important thing is we love each other, okay?'

It seemed to be a sad statement to make when you just had to 'get through' your wedding day, Chloe thought, gently releasing Lara's hold on her arm. 'Eddie's right. It's not real. This is just someone with a sick mind trying to scare you. Don't let them win, Lara.'

'I know, and I know you're both right, but I can't get the curse out of my head now, and I broke my make-up mirror the other day so that's seven years bad luck and...' She smiled rather shamefacedly. 'I know, right? Sorry, I'm just freaking out, aren't I? I'll be fine later.'

'You'd better be, because you've two interviews before the party and you need to get your hair and make-up done for a bit of filming in your room before the two of you go and meet your guests at the airport,' Kellie, who had arrived back from the hotel, told her sharply.

Lara nodded without speaking, her eyes straying once more to the grotesque figures on the rocks, allowing Eddie to lead her away, his big arm cuddling her close to his side.

'Let's try and keep all this out of the papers,' Kellie said to Chloe.

'Well, I'd hardly be responsible for any leaks,' Chloe said defensively, glaring at her. 'Not only would it be immoral but also my business is tied up in the success of the wedding as much as anyone else's.'

Kellie pursed her lips, her chilly expression never altering. 'Okay then, at least we understand each other. You just remember those non-disclosure documents if you do happen to speak to anyone.'

Chloe watched the other woman walk away, fuming.

'She's a right bitch, isn't she?' Isabelle said, finally appearing with her box and a bulging bag. 'Oh! What's that?' She caught sight of the dolls and stepped backwards. 'I thought I heard a scream, but I was down in the party tent and the DJ is warming up, so I couldn't be sure.'

'It's nothing, just another one of the happy couple's stalkers wishing them well, I think,' Chloe told her.

'Horrible,' Isabelle agreed vaguely, her gaze lingering on the dolls. 'I wonder where the security guards are? You would think they'd be all over the place. When I came down with the flowers for the rehearsal this afternoon they wouldn't let me in the usual way. I even got my pass double-checked and got patted down.' She looked slightly offended.

Chloe, unsure how much she knew, muttered something

about harassment and glanced at Maria, who had by now recovered herself.

'You need to get the pass revalidated, Isabelle. I'm so sorry but there has been a bit of trouble, reporters breaking into the grounds and fans getting a bit too close.' She laughed, but it sounded forced and her expression was strained. 'You need to see James from the security team, or Maria. Sorry,' she added as Maria pulled a face.

'All right, I'll go and get sorted... James is such a Lara fan, he'll be mad someone is trying to upset her. He showed me all the pictures he has of her on his phone, and he got her to sign a few old magazines he had with her on the cover. He's kind of sweet about it.' She cast a final doubtful glance at the dolls. 'You don't think this whole wedding really is cursed, do you? I mean, I don't believe in black magic, and doing people harm. They do enough harm to themselves, don't they? It's just...'

'No,' Chloe said firmly, pushing away her own rising doubts about the wedding, and the fact the actual head of security was a Lara 'fan'. 'You must be shattered, Isabelle, I know I am. It's probably better if we forget about this. It's just some bully trying to get the better of everyone involved, thinking they're clever.'

'I hope you're right.' Isabelle trotted off, her long dress floating behind her, her brown plaits flopping neatly over her shoulders, bag spilling flower petals in a gentle rain onto the white concrete.

Chloe finally swung into the four-by-four beside Harry, almost shaking with exhaustion.

'What's going on?' Antoine and Jordan were riding in the back, impatient to get going. 'You've been ages and then suddenly a load of security guards ran down past.'

Chloe told them what had happened.

'Maybe some of the reporters are doing all this stuff. Not Danny obviously, but the other things, just to give them something to write about,' Jordan suggested suddenly. 'If it was your ex setting this up I bet he'll have a big story on it tomorrow,' he added, but then caught Chloe's eye in the mirror. 'Sorry, I didn't mean...'

'It's fine, don't worry. Kellie did just tell me not to spread any gossip,' Chloe said, winding down the window as Harry started to pull away. 'So I guess most people know about my connection to Mark.'

Maria rang as the weary Beachside Stables crew finally arrived home. 'I've just spoken to James, and we've reorganised the security for tonight. The dolls have been removed and we're all set for the party.' She paused. 'I'll see you later!'

Chloe tried to reassure her stressed-out friend. 'Come on, you're doing an amazing job and I was thinking, now that other wedding has been cancelled, afterwards why don't you stay on with me for a week and I can really show you Bermuda.'

'I'd love to, darling, as long as I don't have to muck out. I need to check with Mandy, though, because we were going up to see her aunt in Wales. But I must meet Finn...' Her voice lightened. 'I could be chief dog walker for your adorable little hound.'

The adorable little dog, sulking as Chloe was out late again, had torn up the end of the rug from the living room and taken it to her basket.

'There was no need to do that,' Chloe told her sternly, feeling guilty for leaving the animal. 'Ailsa must have walked you and given you your dinner so you aren't neglected.' Ailsa was always happy to do anything for Hilda, and the pair had come to an agreement over the chickens: Hilda would like to chase them, but confronted with Ailsa's steely gaze, pretended she didn't.

After a shower, Chloe sat on the sofa in her soft cotton pyjamas, enjoying her Dark 'n' Stormy in a tall glass jammed with ice. The dog crept over and climbed onto the sofa, too, head resting on her knee. She really, really didn't want to go to the party.

'You're a humbug,' Chloe told her, stroking Hilda's soft ears. She was just heaving herself reluctantly to her feet, and walking towards her bedroom, when her phone rang.

Kellie snapped, 'Those voodoo doll pictures are online. It's a news site and they won't tell us who sold them. The article is written by your ex-husband. I thought the name sounded familiar so I did a little research after the recent crap he's been throwing out.'

Chloe flicked on her laptop and tapped in the website. 'I'm so sorry, Kellie, but this has nothing to do with me.' She frowned at the screen. 'The very last thing I would do is give information to my ex.'

'He's been here ever since Maria arrived,' Kellie said, 'and Ben tells me he was at your house when we came over the first time.'

'He wasn't *at my house*, he was lurking in my driveway,' Chloe told her crossly. 'Look, I really don't care what you believe, but if you ask me I would have a chat with Ben again. *He's* the person who was talking to Mark that day, not me!'

Chloe's slightly dodgy internet connection finally allowed the news site to load and she peered at the spread. There were pictures, along with a very exaggerated article headed:

The Curse of Leddie...

Death threats and reported rifts amongst friends and family have led the happy couple to question whether they are really meant to be together. This latest incident comes after police admit they are no closer to finding Danny Bolan's killer...

Chloe felt she had read enough. 'Seriously, Kellie, my ex-husband and I are not on speaking terms. He's a sneaking, two-timing creep who loves himself more than anything or anyone else!'

Unexpectedly, the other woman laughed. 'Well, I wasn't expecting that! My ex is a bastard too. Anyway, it's all rubbish but all this negative press isn't helping the endorsements. Lara is going through the roof, but there isn't any more we can do. The security is so tight, I can hardly leave the room without an escort.' She sounded strained and exhausted now and Chloe felt a pang of sympathy, despite her earlier annoyance.

'I'm really sorry, Kellie, but I suppose the trouble is you have so many people around I guess it must be easy to find one dishonest person who doesn't know the couple very well, and is just out to make some money.'

'Or even a dishonest person who does know them well!' Kellie said mock cheerfully. She sounded as though she was regaining control. How odd to have appeased Kellie simply because they both had acrimonious break-ups. Some people were very odd, Chloe thought wryly.

'What about the bridesmaid who tried to sell the wedding dress story?' Chloe suggested, remembering Lara's late-night call.

'Maisie-Lynn? Little cow,' Kellie said venomously. 'Lara is too forgiving. I'm going to have my eyes on that girl from the minute she steps off the plane…'

Chloe let her rattle on, before saying firmly she would see her at the party. She took one more look at the sinister wedding dolls, shivering, before shutting her laptop with a decisive snap. But in her mind's eye she could still see the blood on the silk dress, mingling with the bride's hair.

Finn rang just as Chloe was slipping her keys and phone into her purse, ready to head out for the night.

'I just wanted to make sure you were okay? I was just

checking in with an incident report from Palm Bay Hotel after the wedding dress rehearsal. The dolls?'

'I'm fine thanks, Finn. Everyone was very shocked, but nothing actually happened. I'm just waiting for Peter's taxi now. It's the welcome party tonight. I wish you were coming.' Tired and overwrought, the words were out before she could stop them, and she felt her cheeks burn. She and Finn had always been casual about their developing relationship, keeping it firmly in the friends category. 'Sorry, I mean...'

He laughed, with no trace of anything but amusement and affection in his voice. 'I wish I was coming too!'

'Are you at work?' Chloe asked, still embarrassed at her blunder, and casting around frantically for something normal to say.

'I am. Another couple of hours and I think we'll have a breakthrough, so it will be worth pushing on.'

'On Danny's murder?'

'Possibly. Is your ex giving you any trouble?' Finn changed the subject.

So Spider had told him about the incident outside the Ocean Café, Chloe thought. 'No, he's busy writing vile things about Lara and Eddie.'

'Good, as long as he isn't bothering you,' Finn said. 'Well, I'll leave you to your party. Have a good night. And Chloe?'

'Yes?'

'Be careful.'

16

Chloe sighed as she put her phone into her purse and zipped it up tightly. Now she was expected to attend the party and be sociable, talk to strangers. She pulled a face in the mirror.

'The thing is, Hilda, I do love a small social gathering, but the bigger events at the gallery scare me, and this party is being filmed for TV, and photographed for magazines. It's a little terrifying,' she told the dog, who was lying nose on paws, also observing her reflection in the mirror.

She had chosen a pink silk sundress and sandals, and pinned her hair up with a flower-patterned clip she had bought at the community art and craft shop in Dockyard. Just for an hour, for the sake of her business, she could do some networking and congratulate the happy couple, Chloe told herself firmly.

Chloe was quite confident, as long as she managed to greet Lara and Eddie, she would then be able to vanish into the background and actually disappear out of a back door somewhere.

Peter was full of chat on the drive over to Palm Bay. 'You look very pretty, Chloe. Fancy going to a celebrity wedding party!'

'I think almost everyone who is working on the wedding has been invited, which is a lovely idea,' Chloe told him. 'Thank you for recommending Harry's transport business by the way. He's brilliant and so efficient.'

Peter nodded. 'He's a good boy.' He indicated left and drove carefully down the driveway.

Chloe could hear music, laughter and see thousands of twinkling lights arranged around the hotel and gardens. Now it was completely dark, it looked like the stars from above, reflected down on the Earth. The effect was magical and peaceful.

'Thanks, Peter. Please could you pick me up at midnight?' Chloe handed him his usual fare and a tip. That gave her an hour, she thought. She could do this, she really could.

'Like Cinderella?' he teased, face crinkling into laughter lines. 'No problem, I'll be here. You enjoy your party.'

Chloe walked slowly down the path from the car park, avoiding the main entrance, sneaking onto the terrace behind a loud group of glamorous girls.

The party seemed to be in full swing when she finally made her unobtrusive entrance into the main party tent. She caught Lara's eye immediately, almost as though the girl had been watching out for her.

'Chloe! I'm so glad you came. And we're both wearing the same colour!' Lara pushed through the crowds, flushed with excitement. She was looking stunning in a cropped-off pink top and wide trousers which appeared to be made entirely of silk ribbons. Her hair was in a long ponytail and draped over one shoulder. 'It was total chaos at the airport, with everyone arriving at once. Did Eddie tell you his uncle brought the suits? Eli and Karim will be here tomorrow morning.'

'Maria told me. Brilliant, I'm so glad,' said Chloe. 'You look stunning and I'm so happy for you both.'

Lara hugged her, showed her the charm bracelet hanging from one slender wrist. 'See? You were right, it's keeping me safe.'

A tall man grabbed her from behind and she squealed, then laughed as he whirled her away. She was soon chatting and air kissing, and Chloe breathed a sigh of relief as the cameras followed the girl. Eddie was laughing with a group of men who she assumed must be his groomsmen. He waved and grinned as she met his eyes across the chattering crowds.

Chloe felt as though she was in a rather extravagant fairyland dream. The hotel had certainly pulled off an epic party. The huge gazebo looked, in the semi-darkness, a bit like the sail of a boat. It was stretched across the main bar area, and a stage was set up in the middle with a champagne fountain.

It was a shame she couldn't have brought Finn, Chloe thought, as she accepted a glass of juice from one of the attentive waiting staff, and sipped it slowly. The familiar initial panic she found in any social situation was subsiding a little. There were so many laughing groups, it was easy blend in with the crowds. The gazebo sides were looped up with pink and white ribbons tied around little garlands of flowers, and fluttered like silk curtains in the evening breeze.

Finally, the night before the wedding, everything looked as it should, she thought. The white-painted hotel walls were lit with a soft glow, the terrace and beach alive with the sounds of laughter and the scents of the sea mingling deliciously with BBQ smoke. Lara and Eddie were standing, shoulders touching, talking to a group of older women. The bride-to-be might never have been the same tear-stained girl who earlier declared the wedding to be cancelled.

Occasionally the crowds would part and Chloe would catch

sight of her leaning up to her fiancé for a kiss, or his arm curling around her shoulders, drawing her close for a second before they moved on to chat to the next group.

Perfect. It would be perfect. She enjoyed the breeze lifting her hair, ruffling her dress. It was hot in the gazebo and already people were spilling out across the beach with their glasses and plates of food. Couples were wandering near the tideline, pointing in awe at the Longtails drifting lazily across the last touches of rosy sunset, or perched on the rocks, bare feet stretched out in the creamy pink sand.

The security team were evident on the paths to the hotel and she knew there would be some people stationed around the general area. The buzz of a drone made her glance up, but from the laughter from a large group of men, it seemed the drone belonged to one of the guests, not a journalist.

'Hallo, Chloe.' It was Isabelle, drifting along in her usual vague way. She wore a long dress of vivid crimson tonight, and it matched perfectly with the large red rose in her wavy hair, which fell in thick curls around her slim shoulders. 'Why are you hiding away in a corner?'

'You look lovely!' Chloe told her, ignoring the question. 'I haven't really spoken to anyone except Lara, although I have seen Maria and Fiona rushing around. The flowers look wonderful – you must be very pleased.'

'It does look wonderful,' Isabelle agreed, sipping her drink. 'Actually, Chloe, I wanted to talk to you about something personal, because you seem like a genuine person and close to Lara.'

Surprised, Chloe said, 'That's sweet of you but I hardly know Lara.'

'She seems to like you, though, and to want you around a lot, I've noticed. I feel connections between people,' Isabelle told her seriously. Her usual dreamy expression had been replaced by a ferocious intensity, her large hazel eyes full of fire. 'I'm very worried about her.'

Unsure just how much Lara had divulged to anyone else about her childhood and her mother, Chloe spoke cautiously. 'How so?'

Isabelle moistened her lips, and leant forward until her long hair brushed Chloe's hands. She smelt of the incense that had been burning in the florist's shop, slightly bitter and smoky. 'It's Eddie. I don't think he's right for her.'

Chloe blinked in surprise, glanced at the happy couple, who were now entwined on the dance floor, and back at Isabelle. 'Why not?'

'I hope you don't mind me telling you this but my own ex-husband was violent towards me.' Isabelle took a deep breath, but her heavily shadowed eyes were steady on Chloe's. 'Eventually, I managed to escape, but it took ten years of abuse before I found the opportunity and the courage to leave him.'

'I'm so sorry you had to go through that, Isabelle,' Chloe told her gently, still unable to see how this related to Lara.

'So am I. If I had only recognised the warning signs, I would never have married him, but I was young, silly and in love.' She glanced fleetingly at Eddie and Lara. 'Outwardly, my husband and I were a happy couple, but at home...' She shuddered.

'I'm sorry, Isabelle, are you saying you think Lara and Eddie...?' Chloe's tired brain finally clicked back into action.

'I know in the press it's always Lara causing the drama but I think he controls her.' Isabelle paused, before continuing dramatically, 'I feel the bad karma between them, the angry energy, and I know she can't marry him.'

'Isabelle, have you talked to anyone? Lara? Kellie?' Chloe wasn't sure what else to say. She had observed nothing but adoration between the couple. Although she suddenly recalled Antoine's comment the day she met the bridal pair. He had said he didn't like Eddie, had heard him on the phone, being angry. But that didn't mean he was violent towards his fiancée or anyone else.

'Chloe, I want you to warn Lara. She can still get away from him,' Isabelle said quietly. 'All the signs are there and all the warnings have shown her this is wrong.'

'The warnings?' Chloe found her heart thumping fast, her hand clenched on the glass. Isabelle seemed so sure, her talk of bad karma and mystic connections must be rubbish but it was giving her the shivers.

'Of course,' Isabelle's expression was grave, 'the death of her former lover, the signs from others who are clearly trying to express their own worries through other mediums.'

A shout of laughter drew Chloe's attention to the sea. Several guests were messing around in the water, dresses held high over bare legs, jumping the waves. Others were filming them on their phones, and the TV crew were unobtrusively lurking in the background.

Chloe tried to pull her thoughts together, and turning back to Isabelle, spoke quickly, 'God, I can't take her aside and tell her that her fiancé… is what? A potential risk? Honestly, Isabelle, I do appreciate what you're saying but I can't say anything when I haven't witnessed anything myself. Think about it. It'll just look like I'm trying to sabotage the wedding. Lara will be bound to tell Eddie.'

'What if she already knows? What if she's desperate for an escape, an ally to help her?' Isabelle moved closer and laid a hand over Chloe's. Her fingers were cool and bony, her hand very small and light.

Chloe, lost for words, totally thrown by the intensity of their conversation, looked away across the sand to the rolling waves. One woman had misjudged a jump and was staggering up the beach, soaked to the skin, shrieking with laughter. Back in control, Chloe turned back to Isabelle. 'I'm really sorry, Isabelle, but even if I did speak to her she'd just think I was mad. I... I am truly sorry you had to go through an abusive relationship and I'm glad you're safe now, but if you honestly feel there is something wrong with Lara and Eddie's relationship you need to talk to them yourself.'

Isabelle was silent, her gaze finally leaving Chloe's face, moving to the gathered 'wall' of the party tent. She reached out and gave one of the pink ribbons a sharp tug, loosed a cascade of lacy white material as the curtain fell. 'Fine,' she said quietly, ominously. 'I will. Because you know, this wedding can't go ahead. Everything is wrong.'

Isabelle turned without another word and threaded her way back through the mingling guests to the path that led to the garden and terraces. Perplexed, Chloe watched her go. What on earth was that all about? Clearly Isabelle had been deadly serious in her warnings, so would she really approach Lara herself? Her past experience had probably made her hypersensitive to emotions. Maybe the wedding had jolted her memories of her own wedding and the start of ten years of abuse, of living in fear. What was it called? Post-traumatic stress? But Isabelle was a florist and according to her résumé had worked on hundreds of weddings. Surely she couldn't be like this on each one.

Shrugging off her worries with an effort, Chloe decided she could probably get away with leaving now. It had been a long day, and tomorrow promised to be even longer. Peter would be back to collect her in twenty minutes.

She set down her half-drunk glass and turned towards the hotel. One last glance back made her smile and she felt her tense shoulders relax. Lara and Eddie were sitting together on the sand, her head on his shoulder, a group of friends and family spread around them, the sunlight catching his fair hair and her glossy dark locks.

The sandy beach, just turning a delicate rose in the sunset, formed a photogenic backdrop to the wedding party. Already thinking of falling into bed, she passed a cluster of guests when she heard the roar of a boat engine.

Turning back the way she had come, half expecting some romantic gesture, she could see a red-and-white jet-ski sitting, bobbing gently in the shallows. Both riders were dressed in black, their faces hidden by masks: a clown and ghost. Bewildered, and a little afraid, Chloe could see people pushing and shoving to get out of the way, a collective murmur of surprise and anticipation from the assembled party guests.

As the crowd parted, half intrigued, half fearful, she saw one of the figures had jumped off the jet-ski. He ran straight up the beach towards the gazebo. Chloe could see, half disbelieving, that he was carrying something in one hand. The sunset made the knife glitter as he continued swift and sure on his way, apparently heading straight for Lara.

17

Some people fell to the floor as he passed, scrambling to escape, but he paid no attention, continuing swiftly, straight for the group around Eddie and Lara. The security team was giving chase, but the man was quick and light on his feet, and the guards were hampered by a sea of screaming guests, dropped glasses and bodies lying inert on the sand. Chloe pulled out her phone, dialling 911, shaking with horror as she watched the drama unfold just below her.

The knifeman reached towards Lara, who shrank away, screaming. Chloe, speaking quickly into her phone, could see the head of security, James was shielding her. The attacker hesitated briefly, when the girl, in a blind panic, ducked under the side of the gazebo and started to run across the beach.

Her attacker was gaining on her until Eddie, who was also in pursuit, rugby-tackled him as he passed, hitting him hard. The two men struggled, but as other guests and security guards reached them, the assailant wriggled free from Eddie and made off towards the sea.

There was the roar of the jet-ski easily overheard above the screams of the guests, and the attacker was barely knee-deep when he jumped on the back, and, clinging to the waist of the driver, was borne away at high speed into the sunset.

Chloe quickly finished her report on the phone and ending the call, began to make her way back down to the beach, heart pounding. She noticed the photographers still taking pictures, the TV crew still filming, and dozens busy on their mobile phones, but the party had descended into chaos.

The crying, the blood on the sand reflecting the deep night tones of the sky horrified Chloe but she ran on shaking legs back into the tent to try and help. Some party guests were trying to help those who had fallen, but it was hard to see if the knife had caused any actual harm, or if those who were lying or sitting, had simply been hurt in the general panic. Others were standing in small groups huddled together, and the barman appeared to be handing out shots of rum and bottles of water, persuading people to sit down at the tables.

Chloe, looking frantically for Maria and Fiona, desperate to know if they were okay, reached the milling crowds. Unable to see her friends anywhere, but spotting Kellie near Lara and Eddie, she knelt down next to an elderly lady who was sitting on her own near the entrance to the tent, blood trickling from her arm.

'Sit down, help is on the way,' Chloe told her. 'How did you get hurt?'

'Oh, I fell and caught my arm on one of the tables. He never came near me... I don't understand,' the woman said, her faded grey eyes full of tears. 'Who would do that to a wedding party? Do you think he meant to kill Lara and Eddie?'

'He's gone now,' Chloe comforted her. 'Try to keep still.' She applied pressure to the wound on the woman's arm. It had almost stopped bleeding already, but she was very pale from the shock.

'Eddie's my grandson. Are you sure they're both okay?' the woman persisted.

Chloe looked round, and pointed. 'They're both fine. Look, I can see them over there talking to the security guards.' She could hear sirens, see the flashing blue lights up at the hotel, and felt a wave of relief.

'Thank goodness for that,' the woman said, and smiled at Chloe, her eyes losing focus as she fell into a dead faint.

Chloe sat with her, still holding her hand until medics took over. The police were quickly on scene and before she knew it Finn was striding down the beach, his team efficiently taking charge as he liaised with the uniform first responders.

Reaching the place where she sat, crumpled in the sand, he put out a hand and pulled her gently to her feet. 'Chloe! Are you okay?'

'Yes. I... It's just a bit of a shock. Is anyone really hurt? I didn't see if he actually attacked anyone or just went straight for Lara.'

The scene, which had been screaming chaos, was now well-ordered, secured and dotted with uniforms. The sea murmured peacefully, and the party area was now lit by several floodlights, which drowned the dancing fairy lights, turning the innocent romance into a stark crime scene.

Finn turned to give instructions to a group of uniformed officers before he turned back to Chloe. 'It's going to take a long time for us to gather statements from everyone, but can you tell me exactly what you remember. The more information we have, and the quicker we can get it, the more likely we are to catch the perpetrators.'

She took a long, shaky breath, and told him everything. From the moment the jet-ski had arrived on the beach, to the moment the attacker had been whisked away across the darkening waters.

'And your description of the attacker...' Finn was glancing

down at his iPad, which he was using to take rapid notes. 'You said average height, slim build and very athletic.'

'Yes. The mask hid his face the whole time, and he had his hood pulled up over his head too.'

'Not as tall as me?'

'No, more like my height, so probably small for a man,' Chloe said slowly. Finn was well over six feet five. 'And like I said, athletic and fast but not muscly like Eddie, more like a professional dancer or a gymnast might be.'

Finn regarded her thoughtfully. 'Was there any suggestion the attacker might have been female?'

She blinked, shocked. 'I suppose they could have been. I was thinking as well, while I was telling you... It was almost like an action scene from a movie.'

'How so?' Finn glanced quickly round as someone shouted his name, gave a quick thumbs up and turned back to Chloe.

'Well the last couple of days, I've been part of the whole thing, watching the TV crew and the photographer planning every move. I had no idea it was so... choreographed. Did you know they even have someone who works out all the camera angles in advance and sticks tape on the floor so Eddie and Lara know where to walk for each shot?'

'I suppose it makes sense,' Finn said thoughtfully. 'Go on.'

'Well, that's it really. I think everyone reacted so slowly because they thought it was part of Eddie and Lara's show to begin with. It was only when we all saw the knife everyone went crazy. I heard the TV crew talking with Lara and Eddie this afternoon about the party. The producer said they had to stay on the red X as much as possible.'

Finn looked down towards the tent, the orderly groups of guests waiting to have statements taken, the medics tending to the fallen. Clearly visible on a slightly raised podium to the left of the bar was a red-taped X. 'So how many people knew that's where Eddie and Lara were supposed to be?'

Chloe shrugged and shivered. 'Loads of people, I guess. People who should know, obviously, and people like me, who shouldn't know, but simply overheard the instructions.'

'How are you getting home?' Finn asked now, his hand on her arm, gentle and strong.

'Peter will be waiting up at the car park,' Chloe said. 'I must go if you don't need me for anything else.' She checked her phone and saw two missed calls from the probably worried taxi driver.

'No, I'd rather you got safely off home, and, of course, call me if you remember anything else,' Finn said gently. Another officer was calling him over towards the group standing near the tideline. 'Any worries, call me.'

Chloe was about to ring Peter and reassure him before continuing her hunt for Fiona and Maria, when she heard a shout.

'Chloe!' Maria hurled herself at her friend, hugging her tightly. 'Darling, are you all right?'

'I'm fine. Are you?' Chloe clung to her friend, feeling her tears. 'Look at us, both crying as usual at the slightest thing.'

'I'd say this was rather more dramatic than a sad movie, darling, but you're right, we are emotional old girls, aren't we?' Maria blinked hard while Chloe produced a packet of tissues from her purse and passed one over.

'Have you seen Fiona?' Chloe asked.

'Yes, she's fine but in a huddle with the police, the security team and the TV crew. They filmed it all, you see, so the chances are they'll have vital evidence and we can get this bastard. I bet it's the same person who killed Danny, don't you think?' Maria's voice was harsh.

When Chloe finally arrived home, having reassured Peter she would be absolutely fine on her own, and blessed her luck in having such good friends, she sank down on the rug and cuddled Hilda. The dog was delighted to see her and licked her face, until Chloe pushed her gently away.

The peace and quiet of her own home wrapped around her like a comforting woollen blanket. The white-painted walls, her framed photographs of island life, of Dre, the stamps of the nine parishes of Bermuda, her well-stocked bookshelves... It was a safe, happy place and she felt her tense shoulders relax. She pulled off the dress and pulled on striped cotton pyjamas.

'I should really go to bed now,' she told Hilda, who put her head on one side, wrinkling her nose, her beady eyes bright. 'But I don't think I can sleep yet.'

She made a mug of warm milk, and suddenly hungry, a plate of cheese on toast, which she shared with the dog. Flipping open her laptop, she held her breath as the pages slowly loaded.

With everything online, the news of the knifeman at the wedding party was everywhere. Unusually, Eddie and Lara seemed to be staying quiet on their social media feeds but speculation was rife. Most people seemed to think the same person must be responsible for everything from the funeral wreath, to Danny's murder, to the paint attack, the dolls, and now the party invasion. General consensus seemed to be also that he would now be caught.

Chloe, flicking through the photographs, reliving the terror, remembered Finn's comment about whether the attacker had been male or female. She also remembered, with a guilty jolt, her conversation with Isabelle earlier in the evening. Isabelle had said the wedding wouldn't, or couldn't go ahead... Chloe frowned, trying the recall the exact wording.

Could Isabelle be involved?

18

Chloe woke late the next morning to find there was huge publicity over the attack. It was, said the tabloids and social media, sheer luck nobody had died. One man was still in hospital, but he had suffered a minor heart attack when he ran away from the attacker, and was untouched by the knife. In fact, it seemed nobody had been actually directly hurt by the attacker at all. Even Eddie, who had fought him, sported no more than a black eye on his Instagram page.

She blinked at her phone and found a voicemail from Maria. 'Darling, I hope you're okay? Listen, I'm in a meeting now with Lara and Eddie but I just wanted to tell you I think the outcome will be we postpone the wedding until tomorrow. We need to give everyone time to recover from last night, and the police are still down on the beach this morning. Anyway, more later, love you!'

Chloe rubbed her tired eyes, and ran her hands through her hair, which was hanging over one shoulder in a long curtain. The logistics of postponing a wedding on the day it should be happening were beyond her, but she supposed Maria knew what she was doing.

Her phone buzzed again and she groaned, but it was just a text message from Finn:

Hope you're all right. All under control and let me know if you remember anything else.

Because she trusted Finn implicitly, she had rung him back before she went to sleep last night and told him about Isabelle's dire warnings. Chloe really didn't think Isabelle could have had enough time to leave the party, meet the jet-ski and run across the beach with a knife. She kept replaying the scene over and over. *Could* it have been a woman? Surely Isabelle wouldn't try to harm Lara – wouldn't she have gone straight for Eddie?

Although Danny's death would have made sense from Isabelle's point of view, Chloe thought suddenly, pausing, mug in hand as she went to open the back door. Danny had been hassling Lara…

Yawning and apologising, Chloe let a reproachful Hilda out into the garden, made her breakfast and stumbled out to the stables. Jordan and Antoine had already mucked out, and Antoine was getting ready to take the first ride out, three young men who wanted a nice fast beach ride.

'Are you okay?' Jordan asked. 'We saw your blinds were still down so we guessed you would be having a lie-in after last night. Were you still at the party when the attack happened?'

'Leave her alone,' Antoine told him. 'Go and tack up Mars, and make sure you pull his girths up tight this time.'

'It's okay,' Chloe said, sipping her coffee, inhaling the delicious smell of both her drink and the sun-filled yard. 'Thank you for not waking me and I'm sorry you had to do everything.'

'Why don't you sit down in the sun for a bit?' Antoine suggested solicitously. 'I'm taking this ride out anyway, so you don't have anything to do until midday. Jordan,' he shot a mischievous look at the younger boy, 'Jordan is going to pick up the droppings in the fields and tidy up the muck-heap.'

'What?' the teenager retaliated.

'You are,' Antoine told him. 'And you can take a few barrows round to your grandmother. She said yesterday that she wanted some for her flower beds.'

'Thank you both but I am honestly fine,' Chloe said firmly. 'I was there when it happened and it was awful. I was so late back because we had to give statements to the police, but luckily nobody died, and the people who went to hospital are hopefully making a good recovery.'

'Must have been scary. The news said the man had a ghost mask on, like one of those *Scream* ones?' Jordan popped his head over Mars' half door.

'Jordan!' Antoine said warningly.

'*All right!*'

Chloe was scrolling through the news on her phone, and she read a few bits out to the boys. The shock of what had happened had left her numb and exhausted and she was so grateful she had Jordan and the ever efficient Antoine to briefly take over. Lara and Eddie had both updated their social media, saying how shocked and distressed they were at the attack.

Chloe had half expected a phone call or text from Lara, but nothing had come in yet. 'I can't imagine how those two must feel, seeing their relatives and friends go through that.'

'Eddie tackled the man, didn't he? Nearly caught him, I read.' Jordan was back out in the yard wheeling the barrow up onto the muck-heap with vigour, avoiding the chickens. By the numbers, it seemed Chloe's birds had been joined by Ailsa's flock today. Jordan shooed them away.

'Yes. It seems ridiculous he wasn't caught, with Eddie, the security teams and a few of the guests all trying to stop him.' Chloe paused. 'He must have been watching us all afternoon,

Murder on the Beach

because when he ran through the gazebo he went straight across the shortest route. I mean, he didn't fall over the bar or the tables, or anything. He just went straight for Lara.' The more she thought about it, the more confused she felt. As she and Finn had discussed last night, the attack could almost have been staged. If the knifeman had been serious about hurting or killing anyone he could have done so quite easily.

She saw again in her mind's eye his run from the jet-ski through the crowd, straight towards Lara, and straight out of the side of the party tent after the girl. Of course, Eddie had tackled him and prevented him from reaching her. Perhaps, in panic he had seen how many people were after him and decided to abort his mission. But had his mission been to actually kill the bride, or to create a sensational story?

Even as the thought crossed her mind Chloe's phone buzzed with text messages. She glanced down:

Hi Chlo, want to talk about last night? Good fee for you. Mark x

She deleted her ex-husband's pathetic attempt at nailing a juicy eyewitness story without a second thought, and moved on to Lara's message:

Chloe I wanted to check u were ok after last night. Looking fwd to the wedding and we must stay in touch whatever happens xxx

Chloe stared at the words, frowning. Should she call her? The last sentence was worrying but perhaps Lara was just busy getting ready? Shoving the phone back into her pocket, Chloe started filling water buckets, giving her full attention to her business.

Jordan marched off with the first load of manure for Ailsa's garden, and Chloe watched him vaguely as he disappeared into her garden and turned to use the shortcut through the hedge to get into his grandmother's garden.

'Jordan!' she yelled suddenly, as the original hole in the hedge, generally used by Ailsa and her chickens when they visited, suddenly got a whole lot bigger. 'Not that way!'

Jordan, out of earshot, vanished into Ailsa's garden, and was soon hidden behind two vast spreading pine trees. Antoine rolled his eyes in the direction the teen had taken, and went to open the yard gate for the first clients of the day.

Chloe's phone rang almost without stopping for the whole morning, which wasn't a surprise, given what had happened. Distracted and stressed, in the end she left it on the diary in the tack room and went out to sweep the yard, relishing the hard physical activity which left her little time to think about the wedding.

Antoine's ride at eleven was cancelled, which was annoying, but at least, Chloe thought, it meant she had time to clean tack. She also managed to put in orders for feed and bedding and pay the farrier to change the horses' shoes. Thankfully the afternoon, cleared for the wedding, was free.

Picking up her phone, Chloe saw Isabelle had left a sharp voicemail. 'I told you there was bad energy around this wedding. I tried to speak to Lara this morning but, of course, she's very distracted by the attack last night. I'll try again later. You won't believe it but the police have actually questioned *me*.'

Mark had left a voicemail too. 'Chlo, I'm so shocked to hear about the attack last night. I do hope you are okay. Do pass on my best wishes to Lara and Eddie. I have a little wedding gift for them, perhaps I could give it to you to hand over tomorrow? I understand the wedding has been postponed? Would you believe it, the police turned up this morning to question me. Ridiculous!'

Unbelievable, Chloe thought. Clearly her ex-husband was

insane. She did wonder, quite seriously now, if Isabelle was slightly unbalanced. Surely she couldn't claim to have picked up some kind of vibes telling her the wedding was doomed. Or cursed? Could Isabelle be the source of the stories? Her mind was spinning and a crushing headache made her reach for her sunglasses and hat. One thing was for sure, Mark was not the attacker from last night. He was the opposite of tall, slim and athletic. But could he have set it up?

Chloe went back into the house, Hilda shadowing her as usual, and reached for the box of painkillers in her first-aid cupboard. Her heart was pounding and she could feel sweat on her face. She sat on a chair and slowly stroked Hilda's soft ears until she felt better.

'It doesn't matter who did any of these things, because tomorrow Lara and Eddie will be gone, far away from Bermuda, and things will go back to normal,' she told the dog firmly.

Hilda sighed and trotted off towards the sofa, returning with a piece of stinking, dried seaweed. It was clearly a gift and she dropped it at Chloe's feet, wagging her tail happily. Chloe tried to look stern, but laughed despite herself. 'I thought there was a bit of a strange smell over there...'

Her next caller was Maria. 'Darling, are you okay?'

'Well, sort of... I can't keep up with what's going on, and to be honest I'll be glad when tomorrow's over. How are you holding up?' Chloe asked, prodding the seaweed with her foot.

'Well, the good news is nobody in hospital is badly injured. A few stitches, and they kept Eddie's grandmother in overnight because she had chest pains, but she's fine now, and been given the all-clear. The bad news is the police haven't caught the attacker and his accomplice yet, although word is everyone from Isabelle to Mark is a suspect.'

'I'm glad everyone is okay.' Chloe could hear her own relief echoed on her friend's words. 'How are Eddie and Lara? I wanted to call Lara but, again, I felt she would be crazy busy and at least she has her friends to lean on.'

'Both of them are bearing up well. Eddie blames himself for not tackling the knifeman earlier, but on the whole, we're all good.'

'The wedding will still go ahead tomorrow then?' Chloe queried, thinking again of Isabelle and her dire warnings and gloomy predictions.

'Of course! I mean, it's been chaos rearranging yet again but most people have been offered double their usual fees. The only person who can't do tomorrow is the DJ. He's got to fly to Marbella, but Eddie's got a friend to step in. The thing is, darling...'

'Oh no... you want me to come over, don't you?' Chloe groaned, recognising the pleading note in Maria's voice.

'We'll send a hotel car. It will take one hour max, I promise. It's just to regroup and run through the revised schedule for tomorrow.'

Inevitably, Chloe, summoned by Maria, was chauffeured to Palm Bay Hotel for 2pm. The others were already seated in the conference room, half hidden behind a vase of fresh flowers, and a towering plate of scones, plus a jug of orange juice and one of coffee. Clearly Fiona was making every effort.

The hotel manager looked exhausted, worry wrinkling her pretty face, but she hugged Chloe and passed her a cup. 'Help yourself, and do grab some food, too, if you like.'

'Thank you for joining us, Chloe.' Kellie glared at Chloe and she met the gaze with a blank stare. She did have a business to run and could hardly drop everything at a moment's notice, as the other woman clearly expected. 'Right, everyone, Lara and Eddie are spending the day doing interviews in their suite and around the hotel. Your revised schedules for the wedding day are in front of you. Last night was... horrific, but I'm pleased to say nobody was seriously injured, so we are pushing ahead.'

Chloe, after exchanging glances with Maria, looked down at her sheet of paper. So this was it. After tomorrow Lara and Eddie would head off as a married couple. All deals would be done and the schedule completed. The thought made her feel a little sick. What else might be planned for them? Even with all the extra security an attacker had wrought havoc last night. She studied Ben's bent head. He was tapping away on his phone as usual and his icy body language with Kellie suggested they had just had an almighty row.

Could he be sabotaging Kellie's clients? Technically the couple were his clients too, but what if he had a secret agenda? As though feeling her gaze, he looked up, lips pursed. He didn't look dangerous, just exhausted and stressed, but who knew what went on in peoples' heads.

Isabelle was sitting quietly with the caterer, drawing doodles on her paper. She smiled fleetingly when Chloe caught her eye. Chloe wondered what had happened with the police. She clearly wouldn't be sitting here now if there had been the slightest evidence to tie her to the attack last night.

Kellie scowled at everyone, including James, the head of security who was working his way through a plate of pastries. Maria was sipping coffee, and Fiona was scribbling notes on a yellow pad. The happy couple were absent, Chloe noted in surprise.

Prompted by Kellie, James now spoke to the assembled team. 'We are working with the police to discover the identity of the perpetrator from last night.' He swallowed hard and cleared his throat. 'We all agree the threats leading up to the attack were possibly the work of one person, carefully arranged to take the media away from the couple's wedding plans and on to something rather more sinister. The attack at the party points towards the same idea. The jet-ski was rented from a centre in Hamilton for twenty-four hours. The owner found it drifting out to sea this morning.'

'Does he remember who rented it?' Fiona asked carefully.

James shook his head. 'No. Whoever did gave a false name. There is so much demand for water sports at this time of year, the place was jam-packed. The name was Mattie Scott, but as I say, it was false. There is no Mattie Scott on the island. The police are following other leads.'

'What if this person is the same one who invaded Lara's home in the UK?' Isabelle asked.

'You mean they followed Lara here?' Ben narrowed his eyes behind his large glasses.

'Unless it's someone who lives in Bermuda who decided to take advantage of the situation. A local would know who to hire to carry out these crimes,' Kellie said.

'I don't believe that for a moment,' Chloe disagreed hotly. 'All the trouble has been since Lara and Eddie arrived. It would have been easy for the stalker to catch a flight over here, and to work out how to hassle them once he got here. After all, Danny was on your flight and you never saw him.'

'Whatever.' Kellie waved her hand coldly in dismissal of Chloe's comment. 'We can't have anything spoiling the wedding. I will not have the police directly involved tomorrow or in camera shot. I want to keep a tight ship. Surely we can keep everything running smoothly for today and tomorrow?' It was a challenge and seemed to be directed at Fiona, who squared her shoulders.

'We are doing everything we can, and the security has been tightened again. It's best if Lara and Eddie stay in the hotel until tomorrow,' Fiona suggested.

James swallowed a mouthful of croissant and nodded firmly. 'No harm going to come to anyone on my watch.' Which Chloe thought sounded a little optimistic after last night. He and his team had let the jet-ski attacker run amok and then escape. Could James, the die-hard Lara fan, be responsible for anything? But Finn had said he knew and trusted him...

'I want the entire hotel on lockdown, Fiona,' Kellie added. Only those with passes will be allowed in or out and staff will have to be monitored. 'Lara is terribly upset,' she added.

Perhaps Kellie cared more than she had given her credit for, Chloe thought, or maybe she just wanted to soften her words.

'Lara and Eddie have over two million pounds tied up in endorsements for the event. Nothing can go wrong,' Ben told the room firmly, eyes cold and tone hard.

Hopefully nothing else would go wrong. Chloe sighed. 'I really need to get going...'

'Lara's a mess,' Ben stated, ignoring Chloe. 'Eddie is doing what he can but she needs to pull herself together...'

'Doesn't he get targeted as much by trolls?' Maria asked. She was taking quick notes, one eye on her phone screen, which kept flashing up messages.

'No, well, he still gets them but there seems to be something about Lara that stirs people up the wrong way,' Kellie said. 'But that's what got her so much airtime on *Tough Love* and one of the reasons she is famous now.'

Chloe considered this. She did feel terribly sorry for Lara, in fact, she found herself liking the couple far more than she had anticipated. They were so young to be running such a public empire and she had seen how stressed they were underneath all the glamour.

'A one-hour special of their reality show will follow the twenty-four hours leading up to the wedding, the wedding itself and the after party,' Kellie told them. 'We are hopefully going to be able show some edited footage from last night, depending on the police.'

Finally excusing herself, Chloe escaped from the room and went out to wait for the car which would whisk her back home.

'Chloe?' Isabelle and Maria had followed her out, and the latter called to her.

'Isabelle has been telling me she's worried about Lara,' Maria said in a low voice. 'She mentioned she'd already spoken to you.'

Chloe caught sight of the sleek black Palm Bay car coming round from the car park, and glanced at her watch. 'I don't know what to think at the moment.' She tried to focus. 'I can understand Isabelle's concerns but I still haven't seen a shred of evidence to support them. I mean, Eddie risked his life to save Lara last night! Sorry, Isabelle, I'm not saying you haven't picked up on something, just that I haven't seen it.'

Isabelle shrugged, and Maria just looked worried.

'Shall we just get the wedding over with?' Chloe suggested. 'Everyone is really stressed out, and I promise you if I see anything isn't right with Lara and Eddie I won't hesitate to act.'

'You're right,' Maria said, seizing on her friend's comments with relief. 'We are all jumping at ghosts and saying things we don't mean. Let's stick to the schedule and after tomorrow night, things will go back to normal.'

Isabelle said nothing, but fiddled with her purse, long hair falling forward to hide her face. Eventually, she looked up with a determined expression in her eyes. 'All I know is, the wedding won't go ahead tomorrow.'

19

By the afternoon, Chloe was beginning to feel normal again. The stresses of the wedding falling away as she went through her routine list of chores, laughed at the boys' continued banter, and took Hilda for a quick run down to the beach. As usual, the vast expanse of sea, spread gloriously under a baby-blue sky, the sand between her toes, the cry of the seabirds, soothed and restored her as nothing else could.

But by five she was restless. The horses were mucked out and led into the field for a bit of a break. Until evening stables there was nothing to do so she sent Antoine and Jordan home and wandered into her garden.

'What's wrong with you?' Ailsa was coming through the gap in the hedge with a basket.

'Just a bit worried about tomorrow, I guess. That and not enough sleep last night. This really is awful, Ailsa, and part of me almost blames myself for suggesting the Palm Bay Hotel to Maria. Fiona looks like she's about to have a nervous breakdown, and Maria the same.'

'Come to the Ocean Café with me for an hour. We can get

the bus in five minutes. I was going to ask if you needed any shopping but from the look of you, you just need to get out of here for a bit.'

Chloe was surprised how much the idea appealed. Wound up to breaking point by recent events, and trying to run her own business at the same time had given her no room for headspace. 'Won't it be closed?'

'On Thursday Spider stays open until eight.'

'Okay, give me ten minutes to lock up and put Hilda inside,' Chloe decided.

∾

'You could text Finn and see if he's around?' suggested Ailsa, quick, bright eyes mischievous. 'You haven't seen him much lately. Normally you'd be off on your days out, or admiring that boat of his.'

Chloe screwed up her nose as the bus rumbled west. 'He'll be busy after last night. It also seems odd with Mark on the island, and I know Finn feels the same. I wish everything would just go back to normal, and that Lara and Eddie were happily off on their honeymoon, Mark on a plane to London, and me and Finn back where we were.'

'Won't be long,' Ailsa comforted her, and picked up her huge shopping bags as they approached their stop.

∾

Finding solace and peace in the Ocean Café and the usual buzz of chatter, Chloe relaxed a little. She *had* sent Finn a quick text on the bus, just in case he was passing, but just now she sat in the sun with her coffee and a slice of rum cake, listening to Spider.

Spider was confident the perpetrator would be found. 'You said there have been a couple of other incidents leading up to this? Well, it's likely to be the same perpetrator, leading up to the main event, escalating the threat of violence until they actually do some physical harm.'

'But he hasn't caused any physical harm, apart from to Danny. If it was the same person. In which case the whole psychology is reversed because he started by killing someone,' Chloe pointed out as she sipped her coffee.

Ailsa tore a piece of croissant and dipped it into her cup. 'Maybe it's a gang. I thought all the other threats were these online trolls. Jordan showed me some of the comments. Vile, what makes people say things like that about strangers?' Ailsa commented between mouthfuls. 'And Finn said they don't often come out of hiding to carry out their threats, didn't he, Chloe?'

Chloe nodded thoughtfully. 'He also said that the profile would be different if they were looking for someone who actually wanted to physically harm Lara and Eddie. Those kind of people are actual stalkers who play in the real world, not behind a screen. Just as dangerous, but in a different way.'

'Right,' said Spider. 'The trolls play mind games and destroy mental health, and the others can use physical violence. It makes me sick to think what could have happened, but it sounds like he was almost doing it for effect, no?'

'He did lash out with the knife, but it seemed more like he was cutting his way through the crowd, almost making it more dramatic. There was a little girl in front of him at one point, before someone scooped her up, and he didn't even glance at her,' Chloe said, stirring her coffee. 'Lara was running away across the beach when Eddie tackled him from behind, but the more I think about it, the attacker didn't seem to put too much effort into chasing Lara. It's weird.'

'Could have been a publicity stunt gone wrong?' Ailsa suggested.

'I don't know. I feel like there's no way Lara and Eddie would have let that happen just to get some publicity. They don't need it anyway, everything they've done this week has been in the papers and magazines.'

'What about the camera crew? Did they get it on film?' Spider asked, making *just coming* gestures with his hands to a couple waiting to order.

'I imagine so. Finn said they were going to go through the footage,' Chloe told him. 'I still can't believe it happened.' She glanced down as her phone buzzed with a message. 'Finn's going to pop in for a quick coffee at quarter past.'

'Well, I'll go and get my shopping done then, and meet you back here for the usual bus, shall I?' Ailsa said, picking up her bags.

'Are you sure you don't need any help?' Chloe asked.

Ailsa waved away her offer with amusement. 'I'm not old yet. When I am you'll be the second person I call to carry my bags.'

'Who's the first person?' asked Spider, interested.

'Jordan, of course. That's what grandchildren are for, looking after the grandparents.' Ailsa was grinning, her eyes sparkling as she waved and walked across the sunny patio, down the steps to the busy road.

Finn arrived soon after, and waved at Chloe as he queued for takeaway coffee. Threading his way over to her corner table he smiled. 'Surprise?'

She smiled at him. 'You must be exhausted. I honestly didn't expect to see you here today.'

He sank down into the chair, and rolled his shoulders. His eyes were bloodshot with dark shadows underneath, but his smile was as solid and reassuring as ever. 'Well, I needed coffee, and I'm on my way to Palm Bay, so it was perfect timing.'

They sat without speaking for a while, enjoying the late-afternoon sun, watching Spider laughing with his customers.

Chloe sighed. 'How's the case going?'

Finn gulped some coffee. 'Good. Lots of progress today and I'm cautiously optimistic.'

'Oh good!' Chloe felt relief wash over her.

'I met your ex-husband this morning.'

'He did leave a message saying he had been interviewed by the police,' Chloe admitted. 'It sounds silly but while he's on the island I feel as though he's watching me all the time... He's not, of course,' she added hastily, seeing the concern on his face. 'He's only interested in digging up dirt on Lara and Eddie, but even seeing him at my house made me feel... odd. Mark's not dangerous, though, he's just an idiot.' She had kept her gaze down, stirring the dregs of her coffee, but now she risked looking at him, suddenly worried he might think she was having second thoughts.

To her relief he was smiling again. 'I can imagine it's not ideal to have him around, but don't worry, once the happy couple have left Bermuda after their wedding, I assume your ex will go too?'

She laughed, surprised at how worried she had been that their friendship might have faltered, how happy she was that it was doing nothing of the sort. 'He'd better. Would you like to do a day out next week, depending on work, of course, but I'd love to go and see Southlands Estate, and don't think I'm mad but I heard there is a haunted walking tour in St George's...'

'No way to a haunted tour! I'd be terrified.' He was laughing too, amusement lighting up his face, making his eyes sparkle behind his sunglasses. 'But Southlands would be perfect for you. Lots of old buildings to have a nosy around in. And we could have dinner in Hamilton afterwards if you like?'

'Perfect.' Chloe smiled at him. Her interest in old buildings was common knowledge amongst her friends and she took all the teasing good-naturedly. There was just something about derelict houses, crumbling forts, and magnificent ruins that caught her emotions. Was she nosy? She supposed she was.

'Have you heard from anyone at the hotel today?' He glanced at his watch, a serious expression replacing the fun of the past few moments.

'There was a meeting this morning,' she told him. 'Everyone is very stressed but I didn't see Eddie and Lara, and I think Kellie said the hotel was pretty much on lockdown.'

'Good,' Finn said grimly. 'With most of the wedding party leaving tomorrow night and Saturday morning, we need to get cracking.'

Chloe was silent for a moment, hardly liking to ask. 'Isabelle told me she talked to the police as well.'

'Yes. We've interviewed everyone who was at the party and more; family, staff, freelancers, film crew... They did manage to get some good footage, but unfortunately, the attacker and his accomplice's faces were very well hidden. I imagine they would have known the camera crew and photographers were going to be there. But there are some things you can't disguise.'

'Do you still think it might have been a woman?' Chloe asked.

He shrugged. 'We are keeping an open mind at the moment, but as I say we're nearly there. Meanwhile, I must head off, I'm afraid.'

Chloe also rose from her seat and went to pay the bill. Finn offered to settle it but she was adamant. He had paid for the Crystal Caves, so it was the least she could do to buy him coffee and cake.

Ailsa was walking up the hill, a bag in each hand, and Chloe called to her. She beamed at Finn and he and Chloe walked down the stone steps onto the pavement. 'Hallo, Finn. I was saying to Chloe I haven't seen you around much lately.'

Chloe felt her cheeks flame, for absolutely no reason, except that Ailsa spent a lot of her time matchmaking her friends, whether they wanted her help or not.

'Lots going on,' said Finn cheerfully. 'But we've got a date planned next week now, haven't we, Chloe?'

Ailsa nearly dropped her bags in delight at the phrasing and Chloe was sure her cheeks were even redder than they had been before. 'Um... We're going to have a look at the Southlands Estate... It sounds really interesting,' she finished lamely, acutely aware of Ailsa's intense interest and Finn's amusement.

The bus was late, but Chloe was happy to sit and chat with Ailsa, catching up on her family; Freddie, Jordan's twin, was doing well at cricket, and had been selected for some junior trials.

'That's great news. What does Jordan think? Is he still going to go for a sports scholarship too?'

Ailsa sighed. 'I'm not sure. His mum is just pleased he's holding down a job at the moment, and Antoine is very good for him. He spends so much time on his phone though! And just recently he's obsessed with this wedding. He idolises Eddie from what I can make out, and has even started to talk about getting money to qualify as a personal trainer, or even open his own gym. You know he's got an Instagram account?' She made it sound like Jordan was dealing drugs at the very least.

'I know about the account, but I didn't know about his ambitions,' Chloe told her as they boarded the bus and headed home. 'He works hard most of the time, and if he keeps up the riding lessons, as I said, he could maybe start taking rides out next year.' She smiled at her friend. 'I can see working in a riding stables might not be his life's ambition though.'

'As long as he develops some kind of ambition and it stays on the right side of the law, I'm happy.' Ailsa sighed.

Back home, refreshed after her outing, Chloe organised her animals for the night. She gave the horses some carrots and wondered if she might grab a quick swim in the balmy evening. Fiona rang as she was walking down to the beach.

'I'm just going crazy at the moment. Please tell me you are all on schedule for the horse bit tomorrow?' Fiona sounded very unlike her usual bubbly self.

'Yes, of course,' Chloe told her soothingly.

'I just want this all to be over. Everything has been so stressful from the moment they arrived. I mean… the bookings are going through the roof so I'm massively grateful to you and Maria for recommending the hotel, but I feel like every time I get one thing organised, one piece in place, another pops up.'

'I'm so sorry, but just think, the wedding is tomorrow so in twenty-four hours they'll be gone and you can go back to normal, with loads of extra bookings,' Chloe comforted her.

'You're right and I shouldn't whinge. A lot of hotels would give anything to be in our position, but this threat of violence was just the final straw. All the guests are terrified and the security bill alone is going to be enormous.'

Chloe rang off, feeling uncomfortable. Hilda was nosing around the rocks, and Chloe threw down her towel and phone before wading out into the waves. The silky water closed over her, but she didn't swim far. Exhausted by recent events, she lay back and floated, letting the tide carry her body, staring up at the softening sky.

Later, in the velvety darkness of the night, Chloe went out into the garden, listening as always for the swell of the waves, the call of various night birds and the scents of the coast and her garden. It calmed her, as it always did, and she went back inside to sleep.

But her thoughts still niggled. Who would have thought the happy couple would be pursued by stalkers, trolls, double-crossing bridesmaids and a knife-wielding maniac... And if Finn still hadn't made an arrest, what could the perpetrators possibly have planned for the wedding day?

20

Chloe woke with a jolt to early sunlight glittering through the shutters, and blinked at her watch. It was 5am. The day of Lara and Eddie's wedding. The uneasy feelings returned and she flung herself out of bed, bare feet hitting the cool tiles with a slap. Hilda was delighted to have her get up so early and tucked into her breakfast with gusto, before running out into the garden.

She went down to the stables early, and had tacked up three horses – Candy, Star and Mars – for the first ride of the day. Two women had booked in for an 8am trail ride before they had to catch their flight home. It would be business as usual until the Beachside Stables team were required to report for duty at the hotel.

'If I was them I would've just eloped and got married in secret,' Antoine said as he brushed Candy's long black tail, which was covered in straw.

'Can't though, can they?' Jordan said, yawning. 'They're making millions out of this.'

'Sad,' commented Antoine.

'You're just jealous nobody wants to sponsor the underpants you're wearing at your wedding,' Jordan retorted.

'Really? Tell me they didn't…' Chloe was giggling as the boy put his pitchfork down, fished out his phone from a voluminous tracksuit pocket and scrolled down Eddie's Instagram feed.

'Look! He's wearing these new underpants from ESS MEN,' Jordan said, pulling a face. 'And he says he'll be wearing them today to get married in.'

'Too much information,' Antoine said, but he was laughing.

'I hope nobody is going to gatecrash the wedding ceremony,' Chloe said. 'That would be horrendous.'

'Of course they won't. I think practically every security firm on the island is currently at the hotel and stretched along the beach. My mate says they've hired boats and a helicopter for the big day,' Antoine told her reassuringly.

Chloe was distracted on her ride, and her clients were happy to enjoy the trails in silence. They were friends on a cruise, and were enchanted with the Bermudian flora and fauna, and the stunning coastal views.

Had Isabelle mentioned her worries to Lara by now? Surely she would see they were only projections of her own unhappiness. It must be odd, being so involved in the wedding business, when your own marriage had been so unhappy. But she really couldn't see Eddie was in any way abusive or controlling towards his fiancée. If anything, he was extremely tolerant of her mood swings and sudden impulses.

A beautiful day, with a light wind and just a few clouds scudding across the early morning sky. Chloe sipped her coffee and checked her messages. Just the one from Maria reminding her to bring the saddle just in case Lara lost her nerve. She had, she said, cordoned off a secluded area where they could hang up the haynet, so the mare was relaxed before her big moment.

Chloe smiled, and hoped Goldie would appreciate her film star moment.

Antoine had taken the next clients out and Chloe thought there was just time for her to take a quick mind-clearing ride for herself.

'You go for it,' Jordan said, yawning. 'I might catch up on some sleep,' he added cheekily. 'Why did those women want to ride so early? Weird.'

'Eight a.m. is not early. But if you want to chill out in the garden be my guest,' Chloe told him.

She tacked up Candy, calling to Hilda, who trotted obediently behind. Candy was a big grey mare, placid and strong, and she ambled along the trails, but this morning Chloe wanted to go faster so they flew along the beach, splashing waves with galloping hooves. The tide was out so she found herself taking the circular route, skirting the Palm Bay Hotel beach, trotting briskly along the trail which led to the rocky cove beyond.

Her mind cleared and content now, Chloe halted the horse, dismounted next to the sea, slipping off her shoes to paddle with Candy in the lazy ripples. The sun was just starting to heat the sand and the cool deliciousness of the water was welcome to both horse and rider. Candy stretched her nose down and snorted at the waves, clearly knowing from past experience it wasn't nice to drink!

Hilda was busy with some seaweed on the tideline, and Chloe called to her dog as she checked her watch and remounted. They rounded the corner into the next bay, where tall rocks hid secret coves, only accessible at low tide. Hilda shot off into one of these, presumably to explore another pile of weed brought in by the tide. Chloe narrowed her eyes against the sun's brilliance, frowning in the direction of Hilda's barks.

The pile looked like it could be salvage off a ship. She

nudged Candy into an easy canter to catch up with the dog. The horse's hooves squelched on the wet sand, hard shoulder muscles digging in, before slowing as they reached the cove. Chloe tugged her to a halt.

The body was lying half in the water, and as the tide moved, gave an illusion of breathing, of life. Had she fallen from the towering stack of rocks? Chloe gasped, shouted at Hilda to leave it alone and jumped down into the wet sand. Her legs almost gave way, and she had to lean against the horse for a moment before she could loop the reins over her arm and bend down to the body.

She looked so peaceful, lying on her back, hands on her breast, with not a mark on her body as far as Chloe could see. In her hands was her wedding bouquet. She looked like an ancient sacrificial bride. No signs of violence apart from bruises on her left forearm.

Shaking, Chloe forced herself to check for a pulse, fumbling a little as Candy pulled back against the length of her reins. A moment of panic at her instinctive actions made Chloe falter. Should she leave the body where she was and call for help? It looked like the girl was dead, and her flesh was icy cold… Just as Danny's had been.

There was nobody else on the beach, and she definitely showed no signs of breathing. Chloe was shivering and gasping a like a fish out of water, emotion catching at her throat as she yanked her phone out of her pocket, dialling 911.

She found herself watching the still face as she spoke to the emergency call handler, hoping that against all odds the girl might suddenly give a cough and wake up.

By the time the medics and police arrived to take over, Chloe was still standing, staring at the body, unable to process the situation. Candy had wandered a little way along the beach, reins hanging loosely, but Chloe was focused on the dead girl, willing her to wake up, willing it to be a nightmare.

It was only now she noticed the significance of the clothing. It wasn't just a summer dress – it was the wedding dress. The one Lara had been going to wear for the ceremony to ride triumphantly down the beach like a fairy princess.

The beautiful silk and lace was now limp and soaked in seawater. Her long dark hair flowed out across the sand, dotted with the diamante clips she had chosen for her wedding day. And the flowers. Those stunning roses Lara had selected for the bouquet were also knotted into the bedraggled strands. On one slender wrist was the charm bracelet Chloe had given her.

One of the police first responders came back from a preliminary search along the beach shaking his head. 'Nobody else around and nothing to see. There are tracks leading from the tideline back up into the woods, probably a quad bike or something, but nothing there now. And it isn't necessarily connected to this girl.'

Chloe was trying to give her statement but still shaking from shock. 'At first I thought she'd had an accident, maybe taking selfies from high up on the rocks like she was earlier in the week, then I realised she was arranged in that position, you know, with her hands across her breast and her wedding bouquet laid over them.'

The police officer nodded. 'Did you see anyone else on your ride today?'

'No, well maybe a couple of runners on the top trail, but I wasn't paying much attention. Certainly nobody on the beach near here.' Chloe's voice gave a little catch as she recalled the pretty elfin face, the spark of excitement in her eyes when she rode Goldie, her overenthusiastic approach to everything. 'Whoever killed Danny must have killed Lara, mustn't they?' she added dully.

The officer said nothing, merely taking a couple more notes, so she could sign off her witness statement. 'We may need you to come down to the station at some point, just to clarify a few points as the investigation progresses.'

'Yes, of course,' Chloe said, rubbing her eyes. 'I know you already know this, but I just want to make sure...' She told him what Isabelle had said about the wedding, reiterating the connection between the events leading up to the wedding, and Isabelle's dire warnings.

Statement complete, Chloe sat watching Candy wandering further up the beach, feeling utterly exhausted and unable to move even if her life depended on it. Could Isabelle have killed Lara? And Danny? Surely if she was going to kill anyone it would have been Eddie, the object of her strange obsession.

Finn arrived at the crime scene as Chloe finally climbed back into the saddle. Hilda was sitting in the shade of a rocky outcrop, panting, her quick bright eyes missing nothing, but always returning to her mistress. There was now a white tent over Lara's body, and police tape cordoning off the beach. A few people had gathered on the other side of the tape, snapping photos. Two police officers headed over to move them on, and Chloe watched them arguing.

'Chloe!' Finn waved, strode across the beach, spoke briefly with the uniformed officers and moved towards her, where she now sat motionless. 'You found the body?'

Her eyes filled with tears again and she brushed them away. 'Poor Lara. Who would murder a bride on her wedding day? I mean all the stuff that's been going on is horrible, but this is it, she's actually dead.'

He passed her a packet of tissues, dark eyes concerned. 'I checked in with Brian, the officer who took your statement... You said she and her fiancé were fooling around on the rocks earlier in the week taking pictures?'

'Yes, they were... I thought she must have gone to take some pictures and fallen. She's in her wedding dress,' Chloe told him, sniffing. 'I thought it was an accident, but afterwards I saw she was arranged. I know there was a photo shoot planned for the magazine, but she would be ready far too early for that.'

'No sign of anyone else? Eddie?' Finn asked gently.

Chloe looked away from the activity and shook her head. 'No! If Eddie was with her he would have called for help... Oh, you mean he might be involved?' Her heart slammed painfully against her ribs, as she considered Isabelle's words. 'I thought Isabelle...'

The sun was beating down now, as the full force of the golden day brought swimmers and tourists down to the beach. Further up, nearer the woods, a small group of runners pounded out of the shade and onto the white sand. They halted by the cordon, pointing and exclaiming at the blocked path.

Finn's team had set up two tents now, and more officers had arrived, several zipping up white suits and pulling on elasticised booties.

Finn put a gentle hand on her arm. 'Isabelle has disappeared. She didn't turn up for work this morning and her staff reported her missing. It was a big day for them and she should have been at her shop ready to take delivery of the last flowers at 4.30am, and spend the morning with her team setting up at the hotel.'

'So she *is* the murderer?' Chloe licked her dry lips. 'Oh G od, unless she isn't, and someone else...'

'...someone else has taken her,' Finn said grimly.

21

'We have to keep an open mind,' Finn said. 'Are you sure you're all right?' He was watching her face with concern.

'I'm fine. You get back to work, and I'll see you later on,' she told him firmly, trying to stop her hands from trembling on the reins. Her legs felt like jelly, but luckily Candy was bored with all the waiting around and strode willingly away across the sand. Chloe rode up the beach, calling to Hilda, and was let out of the police cordon.

∼

Antoine was already tacking up for the next clients, and he called to her as she rode slowly into the yard. 'Are you okay, Mrs C? I tried your mobile but you didn't answer.'

Chloe slid off the horse and closed her eyes briefly, before she told him what had happened. 'She was lying right under that stack of rocks, you know with the arch in the middle and the rock pools, so, of course, all I could think of at first was that she had fallen. But then her hands and the flowers...' She shook her head to try and clear the chilling murder scene from her mind.

'Oh my God, poor Lara!' He came out of Star's stable and took Candy's reins. 'You sit down, I'll do her. That's terrible. I can't believe it! Where's Eddie? Was he with her? Is he okay?' He rattled out the questions, shock evident on his face.

Chloe hadn't thought of Eddie's safety, and instantly felt guilty. She sank onto the little wrought-iron chair under the hibiscus and stared out at the brilliant blue sea, inhaling the salty air. Slowly the shaking stopped, and Hilda sank down at her feet, panting. She bent down and stroked the dog's ears. 'The police don't know anything yet. I've just come straight from the beach and it only happened about an hour ago. Finn told me they are keeping an open mind. I didn't see anyone else on the beach.'

Antoine leant against the fence, eyes narrowed in the sun. 'An open mind how?'

Chloe told him about Isabelle.

'So she could have been abducted?' He narrowed his eyes against the sun, dangling Candy's bridle in one hand. 'Or she could have been the killer?'

'Who knows? I can't think straight at the moment, because, as you mentioned, we don't know if Eddie is safe, and if it wasn't Isabelle who killed Danny and Lara she might be in terrible danger,' Chloe said. She tried to pull herself together, walking over to the tap and filling a fresh bowl of water for Hilda.

The action calmed her, and she turned back to Antoine. 'I'm going in to have a quick shower, and a cup of tea. Can you take the ride out and then I'll do the eleven thirty group? Not that there's any hurry now the wedding... now the wedding is off.' Again, in her mind's eye she could see Isabelle's earnest face, her mind focused on one thing, *The wedding must never happen. Lara can't marry Eddie...*'

Murder on the Beach

'No problem. I can do both rides if you like?' Antoine offered quickly.

'I'll be fine, but thank you.' She glanced around. 'Just a minute, where's Jordan gone? Is he up in the fields?'

Antoine rolled his eyes. 'I don't know. He wasn't here when I got back from the ride.'

'Okay, he's probably nipped over to Ailsa's house for a nap, and lost track of time. He was complaining about the early start when I left,' Chloe said, getting up and walking wearily towards the garden gate, Hilda trotting behind her.

She felt slightly better after a hot shower, and combed the salt out of her hair. The mirror showed her summer tan had deepened, despite regular applications of sunscreen. There were deep wrinkles across her forehead and a fan of lines around her eyes, which just now reflected her grief at the recent discovery.

A bride had been murdered. The glow faded as her thoughts turned back to Lara. Eddie would be devastated, poor boy. Was he okay? She needed to make calls, she needed to speak to Maria, to Fiona, probably to the police again, but all she wanted to do was sit in her calm and peaceful house and grieve for a girl she had barely known.

Surely Eddie wouldn't have killed her. They had seemed so in love, so happy.

Her mobile was ringing as she dressed and made her way quickly back to the kitchen. Seeing Mark's number she ignored it. Bastard. Word spread quickly and she had no doubt every celebrity journalist on the island to cover the wedding would now be searching for an exclusive on Lara's tragic death. It made her feel sick.

Both Maria and Fiona's phones were busy so she left a brief message on each, ashamed at how thankful she felt not to have to talk about Lara's death at the moment, aware many hours would soon be spent going over and over what had happened.

By the time she went back out to the yard, Antoine had taken his ride out, and the next clients, Milo and Angelica were just arriving. He was elegant and grey-haired and she was green-eyed and immaculate.

'Good morning, Chloe. Sorry, we're a bit early,' Milo said in his usual courteous manner.

She smiled. 'No problem, I'll just get the horses ready, if you'd like to sit down...' She indicated the table and chairs. 'How are you both?'

Angelica launched into a list of places they had been in the last week, and Chloe noted a few of the most exclusive restaurants in Bermuda. It seemed they had also attended parties and entertained constantly at their rented house, which sat on its own private island.

Neither of them mentioned Lara so Chloe decided thankfully the girl's death had not yet reached their social set. The last thing she wanted to do today was speculate on Lara's death when she kept seeing the sweet, heart-shaped face and closed eyes, all that life and vivaciousness drained away, leaving a pretty shell, but nothing more.

'Are you all right, Chloe?' Angelica asked, peering at her.

'I'm fine, thank you. You're riding Candy and Milo will be taking Angel.' She smiled at them.

Chloe set off with her two clients, forcing herself to participate in the small talk, pushing her suddenly aching muscles to ride. Why did everything hurt? *Come on, Chloe, sort yourself out*, she thought. Business first, there would be time enough later to think about Lara, to talk to everyone connected with her and the wedding. Everyone except Mark, she thought dryly. Any trouble from him and she would certainly be calling on her friends again. Ailsa would relish the chance of another argument, and she was pretty sure Antoine was more than a match for her ex-husband. This was her turf, her home and her friends and the sooner Mark left the island, the better.

She led Milo and Angelica along the Railway Trail. It was pleasantly shady for much of the way and the horses plodded happily along the pine-scented track while the couple chit-chatted, exclaiming over the views to the coastal side, telling Chloe how they were considering buying a home on the island.

'Although we were horrified by the attack on that wedding party at Palm Beach Hotel,' Angelica said eventually. 'The poor family. We have shares in the water-sports business which hired the man the jet-ski so we feel very bad.'

It seemed like years ago. The party, the speculation, Isabelle's warnings, Chloe thought.

'But the manager on duty couldn't possibly have known what the jet-ski would be used for,' Milo said quickly. 'It is unfortunate the security cameras face towards the storage area, not down on the beach, but I'm sure the police will catch these criminals.'

'Yes,' said Chloe, thinking she couldn't possibly tell them another crime had been committed. She wanted to stay numb, working on autopilot, without stopping to allow her grief to flood out.

When they had gone Chloe made sandwiches and took them and a jug of iced orange juice out to the yard as Antoine clattered back with his group.

'Have you found Jordan?' Antoine asked when they were finally alone again and he was tucking into lunch.

'No, I tried his mobile, then his mum and Ailsa but they all went to voicemail,' Chloe said. 'I thought his days of skipping off work were over, but it doesn't matter. Not after what's happened, I mean. I'm dreading looking at my phone now. I switched it off when I took the ride out.'

'Check it now,' Antoine said gently. 'Don't wait until you're on your own. I had a look online and there is the usual crazy stuff. Eddie is fine, and nobody else is missing apart from Isabelle.'

Chloe smiled gratefully at him. 'You know with all this going on I've hardly asked you about your own wedding.'

He shrugged and finished off the sandwiches. 'Louisa's got a dress, we're having a party on the beach, my mate's doing the music and my mum's doing the BBQ and drinks. Oh, and we've got the licence to get the legal bit done first in Hamilton. No hassle, just a party with our friends.'

She nodded, thinking of the contrast between the massive celebrity wedding and the sweet simplicity of Antoine and Louisa's union. 'I'm looking forward to it.'

'Now get on with checking your emails and phone,' he told her.

Chloe braced herself, checking the missed calls, messages left in shocked, hushed voices from various members of the team. Even Kellie sounded as though she was almost in tears, although whether from the lost revenue or from her client's death, it was hard to tell. She instantly felt bad for having such a horrid thought. Maria wanted to come over, but there was nothing from Fiona. Chloe could only imagine the chaos of the rearranged, now cancelled wedding, and hoped her friend was okay.

Lara's friends were on the island and Eddie's family. How terrible to wake up on the wedding day to such news. She couldn't bear to even think what they would be going through. It was such a cruel thing to do. Obviously no sane person would murder anyone anyway, but to kill the bride on her wedding day brought a whole new level of sickness to the crime.

Lara's cold skin and expressionless face haunted her thoughts. She kept remembering the way her hair had swayed in the water, like a gentle mermaid had arisen from the sea to rest on the sand in the sunshine.

She wondered whether the online trolls were happy to see the object of their hatred finally dead, or whether they would feel remorse at hunting her down, making her last days a misery. She hoped they would be haunted by what they had done for the rest of their lives.

'No messages from Jordan,' Chloe announced, having checked the final email in her inbox. 'You may as well have the afternoon off. We cleared everything for the wedding, so we can turn the horses out into the top field, and I'll get them in for evening stables. Go and make sure you're ready for your own wedding.'

'If you're sure, you are going to be okay?' he said doubtfully.

'I'll be fine. I think I just need an hour on my own, and Maria is going to come over. Oh, and I can see Ailsa's back so I'll grill her and find out what's happened to Jordan,' Chloe said firmly.

Ailsa was already coming through the hole in the hedge. 'Chloe! What a terrible thing to happen. That poor, poor girl... Jordan was just showing me the articles online...'

'Is Jordan with you?' Chloe asked.

'Yes. I came home and found him asleep on the sofa. He told me you said it was all right to have a nap?'

'I did say that, but I didn't mean take the whole day off,' Chloe said. 'Oh, it doesn't matter anyway, not with everything that's happened today.' Tears were threatening again and she closed her eyes briefly, squeezing her eyelids shut tight.

Ailsa took her hand. 'Do you want to talk about it?'

Chloe opened her eyes again and blinked the tears away. 'I honestly don't think I can at the moment. I suppose after we find out what really happened it might get easier...'

'The police found Isabelle's van,' Ailsa told her.

'They did? Where?' Chloe's heart did a double thump, and she found her hands were clenched.

'It was hidden in one of the trails off South Shore Road, about a hundred yards from the entrance to Elbow Beach, but on the other side. Peter told me he drove past in his taxi and there were police all over the place setting up cordons.'

Jordan emerged sheepishly from Ailsa's house as the two women were speaking, and his grandmother yelled at him, 'Come over here!'

But Chloe wasn't interested in his excuses about falling asleep and forgetting the time. She waved a hand. 'It doesn't matter, okay?'

～

It was getting late by the time Maria arrived, her face tear-streaked, eyes shadowed. She got out of the taxi and went straight into Chloe's arms. Without speaking, they linked hands and walked out into the yard.

'I can't stop thinking about her,' Maria said eventually. 'And the poor families and wedding guests are all trying to dodge the press, or book interviews with them, depending on whether they are cashing in or grieving.'

'How's Eddie?'

'In bits. The police still haven't found Isabelle. Do you really think she did it?'

'Who knows. Maria, I was looking at Lara's last posts on social media...'

'The video from this morning?'

'Yes. It must have been posted just before she died.' Chloe couldn't help herself, scrolling through the posts covered in Lara's professional, glossy smile:

'Hi Lovers! It's my wedding day. I can't show the dress yet, but I

wanted to show off my amazing nail polish. I always use Perfect Tips, which are available in a range of colours...'

Chloe stared at the video. It was very short, showing just a tiny teaser of the dress, half of Lara's face, and, of course, her nails. She twisted her hands this way and that, showing off the nail polish.

'Looks like she was standing up on the rocks by then. So whatever happened to her happened right after she shot this ad,' Maria surmised. 'The police were all over it when they asked me questions. Kellie told me later it was all planned, getting ready early and going out to do the Instagram things, before they had a photo shoot.'

'Where was Eddie?'

'In bed,' said Maria. 'Go back to the previous post...'

Chloe did, and sure enough there was Eddie fast asleep. Lara had captioned the post:

My gorgeous husband-to-be getting his beauty sleep while I get some work done.

'I keep looking at it, wondering what she was thinking, and how sad it was that her last post should have been an advertisement,' Chloe said heavily.

The sky was softening and the beautiful pastel hues merged with the heat of the day, as though an artist had smudged a gentle finger across the scene. Eddie and Lara should have been saying their vows, watched by a hundred guests, and a film crew, pledging their love in front of the ocean as they had planned.

Chloe's phone buzzed with a text and she sighed, extracting it from her pocket:

Hi Chloe. Please can I see you? It's urgent. Come to the hotel. My room is 6005. I'll send a car. Eddie x

22

'What could he possibly want to see you about?' Maria was perplexed.

'I don't know, but it says it's urgent,' Chloe answered, frowning. 'Shall I call him?'

Maria shrugged. 'I guess so. I mean, Lara did like you a lot. Maybe he feels like he needs to talk?'

It was the last thing Chloe felt like doing, but she rang the number anyway.

'Hi, Chloe.' Eddie's voice was flat and exhausted, far from his usual exuberance. 'Sorry to ask you to come over but I wanted to talk... About Lara, you know, and what she said about you being the double of her mum.'

'Eddie, I...' Chloe started, her heart sinking. She caught herself. The poor boy had just lost his fiancée, and if he wanted to talk about her, she should let him. He should have been toasting his marriage with champagne.

Instead, Lara had been murdered, and God knows what was going through this boy's mind, Chloe thought. The cruelty caught at her heart every time she flicked past a news item on the couple, or heard a fragment of gossip.

'Please, Chloe. I won't keep you long and I can send the car right away.'

Maria made a face at Chloe, who shrugged her shoulders.

'You're going over to Palm Bay?' Maria queried, as Chloe rang off.

'I can't not,' Chloe replied.

'All right, darling, I understand. You're a good person. Shall I have a rummage in your kitchen and make us some dinner?'

'I thought your handbag had suddenly got bigger,' Chloe told her. 'Are you staying the night?'

'As long as you don't snore,' Maria said, smiling through her exhaustion. 'I can't cope with another night at the hotel. I just need to escape for a bit before I can cope with the rest of the fallout tomorrow.'

Letting herself and Maria back into the kitchen, Chloe poured a glass of iced water for each of them and sat down at the table. She kicked off her shoes and wriggled hot toes against the cool floor tiles, before hunting for her flip-flops. Hilda joined in the search, tail wagging in delight.

'What's she got now?' Maria was smiling indulgently as the dog brought out, not a flip-flop but what looked like a piece of old leather.

'No idea. She's always picking things up off the beach,' Chloe said. She chucked the object at the bin, distracted as someone knocked on her door.

'Hallo!' The voice was accompanied by clucking and Chloe smiled. 'Come in, Ailsa, it's open!'

Her neighbour appeared, and two chickens slipped in, almost tripping her up. 'Chloe, I've brought you some of my fishcakes for dinner... Oh sorry, I didn't realise you had company...'

Ailsa was a gossip, but her heart was pure gold, and Chloe considered herself very lucky to have her as a friend. She introduced Maria, and added, 'You're so kind. Do you want a drink?'

'It's been all over the news tonight, the murder,' Ailsa said, setting the dish down on the table. Her hair was scraped back into a messy bun, and her dark eyes were sharp and bright, almost hidden amongst the wrinkled tan of her skin. She was wearing a bright-green dress and, as usual, her arms jangled with bracelets. 'It's tragic, and the poor fiancé must be devastated.' Her mouth hardened into a thin line. 'Two murders in a month. It never happens in Bermuda. It's just shocking!'

Unnoticed by Ailsa, another chicken pattered through the door, little claws click-clacking as it hurried to join its sisters under the table. Chloe frowned at it, but decided to ignore the intrusion this time. 'Ailsa, I need to go out. Can I leave you and Maria to it? I shouldn't be long if you want to stay. Help yourself to drinks and there's ice in the box. I shouldn't be more than an hour.'

~

Chloe arrived at the Palm Bay Hotel feeling rather nervous, and emotional. Everywhere reminded her that Lara and Eddie should be enjoying their party down on the beach by now, and she was dreading facing the groom.

The driver said he would wait, and settled back with a newspaper. Banner headlines screamed about Lara's murder but she hurried away. Reception was quiet, but she had to sign in with security before the receptionist phoned up to Eddie's room, asking if he was expecting her.

Finally, heart pounding, she was knocking on Eddie's door. He must have been waiting, because he opened immediately.

'Chloe, thank you for coming.' Eddie's face was pale, his eyes red, and his hair standing up in greasy tufts. 'I'm sorry to get you out so late.'

'Oh, Eddie, I'm so sorry about Lara,' she told him, laying a gentle hand on his arm, covering his collection of plaited leather bracelets. In his misery he looked younger than Jordan, she thought, blue eyes forlorn and mouth down-turned as though he was trying not to cry.

'I can't understand who would kill her. I can't see why...' Eddie caught himself. 'You must be wondering why I needed to see you.'

'Sort of. I know Lara thought I looked like her mum, and she was right but...'

'It wasn't that...' He smiled ruefully. 'I... I wasn't sure if you'd come if I told you the real reason I needed to see you.'

Bewildered, Chloe smiled back. 'Go on.'

'I need to know what happened. You found her, Chloe,' he grabbed her hand and held it between his, 'you found her and I need to know exactly what happened. I know it sounds crazy but the police won't tell me anything but you were there...'

'But I don't understand. I found her body, Eddie, and that was it. It's not something you want to hear, honestly, and it's not something I want to go over again,' Chloe told him. His hands were cold and dry.

'Please, Chloe,' he said, blue eyes tearful, 'I just want to know.'

∼

Maria stared at her. 'Really? He wanted you to tell him how you found Lara's body?' The ice in her glass clinked as she took another drink.

Chloe, discovering she was starving, tucked into Ailsa's home-made fishcakes, and helped herself to salad. 'Yes. I don't know, but it seemed to help him. He seemed relieved after I'd gone through it, and he said he was struggling with not knowing what had happened to her. He said he blamed himself because he was asleep when she left, and he should have been looking out for her.'

'Well, I told the police the security team should have gone with her,' Maria said firmly. 'But Ben told me she snuck out an hour earlier than she should have done.'

Chloe paused with a mouthful, and looked hard at her friend. 'You said Kellie told you it was all planned.'

'Well, she did, but Ben said later Lara was just out a bit early and gave everyone the slip. Why are you looking at me like that?'

'It's nothing. Let's sleep on it, and if you're sharing my bed no snoring.' She grinned at Maria.

∽

Waking early, despite her exhaustion and the sudden stab of pain as she remembered the happenings of the day before, Chloe left Maria asleep. She crept into the kitchen, closing the bedroom door quietly behind her.

Hilda was waiting for her breakfast, sitting right next to the bowl staring at it, just in case Chloe should forget where to put the food. Yawning, Chloe made coffee and started to tidy up the plates and glasses from last night. She washed up and then swept the kitchen tiles, pulling open the back door to allow the fresh morning sunlight to flood inside.

Hilda was now busy at the bottom of the garden and Chloe was regretting not bringing her clothes out of the bedroom with her. She could hardly go out to the yard and start work in blue striped pyjamas.

She opened her laptop and started to flick through her emails, but soon found herself looking at Lara and Eddie's social media accounts. Lara's last tragic post still tugged at her heartstrings.

The mail arrived and she wandered out to pick up her post, idly sorting bills. A plain white envelope with an untidy handwritten address made her pause. Dumping the bills on her desk, she slit open the envelope. A note and a memory stick. She sat down to read it, her hands shaking.

Maria wandered out of the bedroom, dressed in red silk pyjamas. 'You should have woken me, darling. Have you been up for ages?' Her expression sharpened as she caught sight of Chloe's face. 'What's wrong?'

Chloe stood up slowly, trying to collect her thoughts. 'I've just had a letter from Lara.'

23

'Should we see what's on the memory stick or give it to the police?' Maria asked, sinking down onto the sofa.

Chloe sat down next to her. 'I suppose if she posted it just before she died...' She was rereading the letter:

Chloe,

I'm sending this to you because I know you'll give it to the police. I didn't want to live a lie and I want to set everyone straight about what really happened. I can't trust anyone else but you're a good person.

Love,

Lara x

Maria stared at her. 'I need at least a gallon of coffee before I can even think about this. Is it a suicide note?'

'Suicide? God, I don't know.' Chloe brushed away her tears. 'I also need to get changed and run down to the yard. Look, I'll get hold of Finn and see if he can come over. Lara says to give it to the police,' Chloe said, already dismissing her idea of popping it in her laptop there and then. 'And that's what we will do.'

The boys had already started mucking out when Chloe appeared and she apologised, explaining Maria had arrived late last night and stayed over.

As she had expected, Antoine was very sharp with Jordan, but both assured her they could cope fine when she said she had some business to attend to.

Finn arrived twenty minutes later, and Chloe left him chatting with Maria, while she ran in and picked up the letter and memory stick.

'Finn, I know you can't say much, but do you have any idea who killed Lara?' Chloe asked, when she returned.

He read the letter, placed it carefully in a plastic bag with the memory stick and looked back at her. 'Honestly, at the moment we are still following up leads. But this is very helpful and I'm glad you called me.'

'I saw in the news this morning that you issued a statement saying the autopsy showed she drowned,' Maria said.

He said nothing, but nodded slowly. 'Yes, she had water in her lungs.'

Chloe said hastily, 'Sorry, I shouldn't have asked. Just... Isabelle's all over the papers today, portrayed as some kind of satanic killer, who has now run away, whereas she might be in danger.'

Finn nodded. 'You know what the press are like, and, unfortunately, we have no control over what they publish. I can tell you we've arrested the knifeman and his accomplice from the pre-wedding party. We did manage to get some decent footage from one of the magazine photographers in the end. He saw the jet-ski coming in, and assuming it was maybe a party piece, he started taking shots with a zoom lens. Luckily, he got them just before they stopped next to that rocky outcrop to pull on their masks.'

'And you knew who they were?' Maria wrapped her hands around her mug of coffee, green eyes intense.

'We were able to find out, and then to circulate images to everyone who had been either at the party, or out on the water in the area between the hotel and the water-sports centre at that time.' Finn paused. His face was grim, but he was clearly pleased at this progress. 'Both men have been positively identified by a couple who have shares in the water-sports business. They realised they were out on the water that evening and saw the pair ditch the jet-ski. They didn't realise it was their jet-ski until later, because it was a second-hand one bought in as a job lot and it hasn't been painted up in the business colours yet.'

'That wouldn't be Milo and Angelica, would it?' Chloe asked curiously.

He flashed her a glance. 'It might be. Do you know them?'

'Yes! I met them at one of Jonas' and Melissa's parties at the art gallery. They book a ride about once a month when they are in Bermuda,' Chloe told him. 'Who are the men anyway?'

'Basically a couple of criminals for hire. They live on a boat and spend time sailing around Cuba mostly, as far as I can gather. But they also have links to organised crime in the UK.'

Chloe let out a breath. 'Did they say why they did it?'

'No. They aren't talking at the moment but I think someone hired them to put on a show. So far they have no connection to Lara and Eddie that we can trace, but we do have a DNA match from Danny's body, which, along with other evidence we have gathered proves that certainly one, probably both, were involved in his death,' Finn said.

'Mark left a message on my phone saying you had interviewed him and he might have done something stupid, but he didn't kill Lara,' Chloe said suddenly. 'I completely forgot but I saved the message in case you needed to hear it.'

'We did interview him,' Finn said. 'But I think I can say at the moment I don't think Mark killed her.'

Something about the tone of his voice made Chloe turn to look at him. '*Did* you really think Mark could have killed her?' Maria asked with interest.

'He admits he did see her that morning. He swears he found her up on the rocks and just wanted to talk to her.'

'She would have been terrified,' Chloe stated. 'He said such vicious things about her childhood, her life and she had read them all...'

'Yes.' Finn sighed. 'It's possible that she turned to run away, or even just fell because he startled her, but that is only a theory at the moment. The head injury could have been acquired after she fell into the water.'

'You said she had water in her lungs? He left her to drown?' Chloe pointed out.

'Possibly, but she did also have that little-known heart condition called Long QT. It's the kind of thing that sometimes gets people when it's never been identified and they just suddenly suffer a cardiac arrest,' Finn said. 'Is there any more coffee in the pot?'

'Of course, I'll just bring it out,' Chloe said.

She returned with the coffee and a bag of pastries from yesterday, to hear Maria saying earnestly, 'I really hope it wasn't Eddie who killed Lara. They seemed like such a sweet couple all along. I don't get why Lara was on the rocks without security though... Chloe and I were discussing it earlier.'

'Did you reach any conclusion?' Finn asked with interest. 'I know what Chloe's like when she's on the case.' He caught Chloe's eye and she grinned back at his teasing. For the first time since she had found Lara's body she found herself smiling naturally, without the shadow of grief.

Maria was tapping her fingers on the table, frowning. 'Lara

did send Eddie a text at six fifteen, saying she would be back soon, but he didn't wake up until ten, and by that time you'd found her...' Maria continued, 'Her wedding dress was hanging in the suite of extra rooms the hotel provided for the wedding. I remember her saying how generous Fiona was being, and how she had five outfit changes planned for the big day.' Maria shook her head. 'I really can't see either her or Eddie being involved in organised crime. For a start the press would have nosed it out already. Sorry, Finn, but it's true.'

'I found her at half eightish... If Mark scared her and she panicked, and fell, I'm not sure I can see Mark walking away. I mean, he's a complete idiot, but he would have seen a heroic rescue as a great story,' Chloe mused, and Maria nodded in agreement.

'As you say, but he's adamant they had a chat, he got a selfie and he walked away leaving her alive and well and busy taking pictures on the rocks.'

'She was under a lot of pressure,' Chloe said. 'What if she went out with the intention of harming herself?' She met his glance and sighed. 'Sorry, I'm getting carried away with my amateur detective bit, aren't I? I just feel so involved. I mean, nothing compared to her poor friends and family.'

He sighed too. 'Witnesses claim to have heard the couple arguing late last night, but it's hard to tell if that's a genuine statement or people who want to be part of the whole circus. Honestly, this is going to be a nightmare to investigate with all the media interest. Sad enough that a young girl is dead in tragic circumstances, but horrific that everyone wants a piece of it.' He glanced sideways at Chloe. 'Do you think we scared Mark off?'

'I hope so.' Maria looked down at her phone, which had just started buzzing. 'Sorry, it's one of the wedding suppliers, I need to take this.' She smiled apologies at Finn and walked out of earshot, red silk pyjamas fluttering in the ocean breeze.

Chloe gave a wry smile. 'I think Mark's got the message. It's good to know you don't think he killed Lara though. I know it's his job, but I hear him talk and wonder how on earth I ever fell for him in the first place. He's so... shallow!'

Finn said seriously, 'People make mistakes, and I'm just glad you came to Bermuda, however it happened.'

She peered at him over the rim of her coffee mug. 'Dre must have had it all planned out because she made her will two years before she died, leaving me the house and stables. I often feel like she's hanging around, keeping an eye on things, like a guardian angel or something.'

'If anyone would be a guardian angel it would be Dre. She was a wonderful woman,' Finn said. His phone rang and he hastily pulled it out of his pocket, answering the call, and making a 'sorry' gesture to Chloe.

She nodded, understanding, and sipped the last of her coffee, considering. There were so many loose threads still to be tied up, but the main one surely had to be where the hell was Isabelle?

Finn returned first. 'Sorry, got to head off but I'll keep you updated. Thanks for breakfast and please apologise to Maria for me.'

'Of course, and no worries. Let me know if you still want to come for dinner tomorrow.' Chloe said hastily, 'Once I've got Jordan trained up, we might even be able to manage lunch too!'

'You could even have a weekend away,' Finn suggested as he collected his coat from the kitchen.

'I've always fancied New York for a weekend.' Chloe looked at him, unable to decide if he was teasing her or serious, bearing in mind their previous conversations. She could feel herself flushing red, and pretended to be looking down at the empty mugs.

'I'll bear that in mind.' Finn was laughing now. 'About eight thirty tomorrow night?'

She waved as he made a thumbs-up gesture before walking briskly round the corner of her house. Chloe finished clearing the mugs and plates as she waited for Maria to come back. When her friend returned her expression was grave.

She was brandishing her mobile phone. Scrolling through her photos with an elegant pink fingernail, she finally proffered the screen to Chloe. 'Eddie found this outside his room when he got back from the gym this evening.'

Intrigued and slightly alarmed, Chloe leant in and studied the photograph. It was on the floor outside Eddie's hotel room. A pretty but sinister little arrangement – a heart made out of flowers and twigs, and inside the heart a note on pink paper. The writing was simple and clear:

Eddie,
Stay here with me,
Lara x

24

'It must be a hoax or something. Someone's idea of a joke...' Chloe's voice faltered as she saw Maria didn't believe that either.

'Kellie thinks Isabelle must have been in the hotel and somehow left this,' Maria said firmly. 'Shit, has Finn gone?'

'Just left. He got an urgent call, but get the hotel to deal with it. They can report it, you don't have to do it all for them.' Chloe touched her friend's hand. 'Maria, Isabelle is still missing. There is no chance with all the security she could have got into the hotel. She can't possibly have left this.'

'No... I don't know, Kellie sounded so certain. And it does seem odd. You get a letter from Lara today and now Eddie does too. Maybe yours was a hoax too?'

Chloe considered this. 'I don't know. Look, all this is horrible, but Finn has it under control. The police here will solve the case. We just need to keep them updated on anything that happens. And it doesn't matter what Kellie thinks, because you don't work for her anymore!'

Maria nodded, and picked up her phone again, turning it

over in her hands. 'You're right, there isn't anything I can do. Eddie had his passport with him, the idiot, and he says that's missing now. Instead of leaving it in the safe he took it down to the gym in his pocket. He put his stuff down while he worked out. Says it was fairly quiet and he wasn't paying attention to anything, just trying to work through his grief.'

'Why don't you stay here today? Just hide out in my house while I take the rides out. You can use my laptop if you need to,' Chloe suggested.

Maria sat down at the table, and put her head in her hands. 'I'm completely exhausted. I'm a wedding planner not a counsellor slash detective.'

'You're right, so leave them to it,' Chloe said firmly. 'I need to be back down the yard now, but make yourself at home. Seriously, you're amazing but don't try and take on any more at the moment.'

∼

Chloe left Maria alone, and let herself into the yard, speaking to each horse in turn and dodging Star's teeth. Hilda was busy digging in the muck-heap and Chloe called her away. The stable cat was lying on the roof of the feed room, half hidden by the flowers, long ginger tail hanging down.

Jordan was up in the top field with a shovel and wheelbarrow, picking up droppings, and Antoine had popped down to the local saddlers as soon as it opened to pick up Candy's bridle, which had been restitched.

Two rides later and it was time for evening stables. The boys were subdued by recent events, although Chloe talked brightly about Antoine's approaching wedding, and deliberately avoided any mention of Lara and Eddie. She sent them home at five, thinking they probably needed to be with their families more than anything.

It was so hard to continue as though nothing had happened. Chloe had caught the boys peeking at their phones throughout the day, and when she popped back to the house for a snack, Maria showed her the mound of flowers and candles on the beach where Lara's body had been found. She had captured hearts. The public outpouring of grief had been extraordinary on social media, but the vile comments and speculation continued as well. It was such a waste, Chloe thought, with a stab of grief.

Maria was an easy house guest, spending most of her time working. Chloe felt she had almost wound the clock back to when they used to share a flat together at university. Although, as she told Maria with a smile, they were both far more domesticated now.

In the last few months Chloe had started cooking again and to take her mind off recent events she decided to make a nice dinner for herself and Maria. Mark had always preferred either to eat out, or cook for them both. He had fancied himself as a bit of a chef, and made it clear her cooking was considered below par.

Chloe had found Dre's collection of recipe books, tucked away in a corner of the bookshelf, and had begun to recreate the delicious meals of her childhood. It was a pleasure cooking for herself if she fancied.

Tonight was Bermuda cassava pie, which was traditionally served at Christmas, plus a Bermuda fish chowder. The chowder was dark and flavoursome, although Chloe eased up on the dark rum. The garlic and allspice soon made the kitchen smell delicious. She left it to simmer and poured a glass of wine. A perfect comfort dinner and a welcome distraction from her thoughts. What exactly was on the memory stick Lara had sent her?

Maria was having a shower when there was a knock on the front door. Definitely a stranger. Everyone else used the back door.

Mark appeared at the door just as she had finished, and she frowned. She had half expected one last visit before he left the island but she hadn't been looking forward to it.

'Can I talk to you for a minute, please, Chloe? Not for long because I've got a flight to catch. Look, the taxi's waiting.' He looked shattered, sunglasses pushed up on the top of his head and face lined with exhaustion in the sunlight.

Chloe peered round and saw Peter sitting at the end of the driveway, engine off, newspaper spread out across the steering wheel. 'Fine. Come in.'

He walked carefully through the house to the kitchen, where he stood, hands braced on a chair, facing her. 'I wanted to talk about Lara's death. I want you to know I had nothing to do with it.'

'I believe you, and so do the police,' Chloe told him. 'Surely as long as the police aren't going to arrest you, you can just go home and forget about it.'

'I can't... Look, I saw her go out that morning, early. I was waiting to see if I could get any snaps of the build-up for the actual wedding, or any guests who would be up and about for quick quotes.'

Chloe raised her eyebrows and opened her mouth to speak, but he continued.

'Don't look so judgemental, it's my *job*, and people have been very happy to give me the odd titbit.'

'So you followed her to the rocks?' Chloe asked, interested despite herself. 'Was she wearing her wedding dress?'

'Yes... I took pictures, and when I saw her standing on top of the rock, I took a few more and she turned and saw me... She was... shocked. I tried to talk to her, explain who I was...'

'That must have gone down well,' Chloe commented.

'Yes,' he agreed. 'She asked me why I hated her so much.'

Silence for a moment as Chloe experienced another flash of grief, and Mark was clearly feeling sorry for himself. Maybe, hopefully, even a bit for Lara too.

'I told her it was nothing personal, it was my job. She went off on one saying I should tone it down and stop persecuting people.'

'I see. But you parted friends?' Chloe said sarcastically.

'No, after a bit she just told me to get lost because she needed a bit of headspace, and then ignored me. I took a couple more pictures and walked away. When I left her it was about six forty-five.'

'Mark, did she have her flowers with her?' Chloe said suddenly.

'The police asked me that and no she didn't.' His eyes were sharp. 'But when you found her she had the bridal bouquet, didn't she?'

'It wasn't the full one, but yes, flowers from her bouquet,' Chloe said, frowning. 'Did she say why she was in her wedding dress?'

'No. She seemed... a bit upset. Not just because I was there... I've never seen her without make-up and her hair was down, blowing in the breeze. She looked like a kid in her mum's clothes playing dress-up,' he added uncomfortably.

Chloe squeezed her eyes shut briefly and then opened them to see him watching her, ill at ease, guilt in his face. 'You'd better get going or you'll miss your flight.'

He moved away, shoulders drooping. 'I'm glad you've got a

good thing going here, Chloe. I am honestly glad you're happy and things have worked out for you.'

She met his eyes, and felt nothing but relief. It was closure of a sort. 'Goodbye, Mark.'

Chloe stood at the door until the taxi moved away and turned back inside as Maria stepped out of the bedroom.

'I was just coming to kill him, but I could hear you had it all under control.' She hugged Chloe. 'I'm so proud of you.'

Chloe hugged her back. 'I'm proud of me too, and I'm glad he said what he did. He's not evil, just an idiot. I was thinking of taking Hilda for a quick walk. Do you fancy half an hour on the beach?'

Hilda was already bouncing joyfully at hearing the familiar word, and Maria laughed at her antics. 'Love to come for a wander, but what about your delicious dinner?'

'It's ready and it'll keep warm in there until we fancy eating. I just need a quick shower and change out of these horsey clothes.'

She turned the oven down low, and had a shower, before combing her wet hair out and pulling on a pistachio-green sundress. It was long and covered the bruises on her legs. She paused and inspected them, not even remembering how she had got them. Working with the animals, lugging bales of feed and bedding, not to mention mucking out and grooming, had given her more muscles than she had ever had.

Not to mention a gold tan, which made her blue eyes flash almost turquoise. The wrinkles on her skin were a badge of honour, and old age was far less terrifying than it had been just a year ago. In fact, she was grateful for every bag and wrinkle because it meant she was alive. Alive and happy.

She went back into the kitchen to find Ailsa's hens had pushed open the back door again, and seemed to be happily roosting on the rug next to the sofa. 'Out!' She shooed them away into the garden and they went protesting and squawking in annoyance.

They could sit outside for dinner, she thought. Dre's recipe book was still open on the worktop and the smell of cooking made her memory dance. Dre's picture on the wall could have winked, or it could have been an evening illusion. Chloe liked to think Dre was her guardian angel, but it wasn't something she ever discussed with anyone but Finn, not even Ailsa or Maria.

Sometimes she would be certain she could smell her grandmother's perfume in the bedroom, or would find an old novel, bookmarked carefully with a personal item; a hair band, a swatch of fabric, or a handkerchief. Dre would approve of her dinner with Finn, as Chloe hoped she would be proud of the continued expansion of the riding stables business.

Maria was giving the horses carrots in the yard when Chloe caught up with her. 'You know, I'm going to miss all the animals when I'm back home,' she said. 'And the view. And the sunshine.'

'Are you going to be all right after this? I mean financially?' Carefully, Chloe turned the opposite way to her normal evening rambles, well away from any tourist spots.

'The insurance will cover it, so yes, thank God. I feel so sorry for all the suppliers and everyone who helped pull this together at the last minute, but I've made sure they all get paid,' Maria said.

They wandered down along the deserted coves and scrambled across the rocks that divided the pristine hidden beaches. The gentle tumble of the waves, the smell of salt and clean summer air, working its usual magic on her senses, Chloe glanced at her friend. 'How are you feeling now?'

Maria stopped to examine a blue blob of jellyfish, prodding it with her shoes. 'Better, I think. I can see why you love this place so much. And I like Finn,' she added, winking at Chloe. 'Oh, what's Hilda carrying?'

Chloe called the dog, who looked rather sheepish. Chloe gently eased her prize from the animal's jaws. 'Yuck! It's that bit of leather she had yesterday. She must have pulled it out of the bin.'

'Nice.' Maria was laughing. 'I really must get a photo of this sunset. It's incredible.'

Chloe shoved the leather band in her pocket and walked slowly down the sand. A lone runner was making his way across the trail higher up, and a few boats were out in the distance, near Elbow Beach.

Chloe slipped off her shoes and climbed across the rocks towards the next beach. She checked Maria was following, but she was still taking photos on her phone, standing high on a rocky outcrop, dark hair flying out in the Atlantic breeze. Just as Lara must have done before she fell to her death, Chloe thought sadly. She jumped down and walked more slowly now, wet footprints marking the sand, only to be smoothed away by the next frothy wave.

Hilda barked, and Chloe looked up, startled. But it was just another runner, loping along the sand. The woman lifted a hand in greeting and continued on her way.

They wandered back to Chloe's house in companionable silence, enjoying the ocean breeze, laughing occasionally at Hilda's antics as she tried to chase the seabirds soaring high above.

Ailsa was in the garden as Chloe opened the little wrought-iron gate from the yard, and Chloe's heart gave a little jump at her expression. 'Ailsa, what's wrong?'

'It's Betsy! She's been missing all day, and a friend just called to say she thinks she might have just seen her on the road heading towards Elbow Beach.' Ailsa gave a reluctant grin. 'I know, don't start with the chicken jokes, it sounds crazy, but I'm so worried.'

'Why didn't your friend pick her up?' Maria asked sensibly. 'Can't they go back and bring her home?'

'He doesn't like chickens,' said Ailsa dolefully. 'I'm going to have to walk up there...'

'No you won't,' Chloe said firmly. 'Did Jordan leave his scooter tonight? I think he said a mate was picking him up for a football game?'

'Yes, he did,' Ailsa said, brightening.

'Okay, so Maria can go in and sort out dinner and drinks, and I'll take the scooter and the cat basket and if it is Betsy I'll catch her and bring her home. She always comes for bread, doesn't she?'

'She does. Are you sure, Chloe?' Ailsa asked.

'Positive.'

Her friend smiled at her neighbour. 'Why don't you come to dinner too? Chloe's done enough for about six people.'

'Well, if you're sure, I'd love to,' Ailsa agreed. 'Chloe, the keys are on the red peg next to my front door. Have you got a basket?'

Chloe rushed off, confident the problem was sorted, only to rush back ten minutes later. 'Sorry, Ailsa, the scooter's out of fuel.'

'Oh that boy!' Ailsa sighed. She was lifting bowls down from a cupboard while Maria poured drinks. 'Thank you anyway, Chloe...'

'No, I can still go. I'll just run down the trail with Hilda. It takes me right to Elbow Beach,' Chloe offered, unwilling to be beaten, despite the luscious cooking smells drifting around her kitchen.

'But it's nearly dark!' Maria said, pausing with a handful of spoons and a bottle of wine.

'I can take the shortcut. Honestly, it's fifteen minutes tops and no hills.' Chloe smiled at Ailsa, knowing how much she loved her chickens.

∼

Ten minutes later, Chloe and Hilda were running along the top trail, which led under pine trees and ran in an almost straight line to the next headland point. Hilda was alert and excited at this unexpected additional walk, and kept close to her owner, ears flapping as she loped along.

Reaching the road, Chloe spoke to Hilda, who was well-trained with traffic, and the dog walked to heel. No sign of Betsy, but Chloe could see she wasn't on the long straight stretch to the right. There was only a black four-by-four sitting well into the side of the road with the lights off, so she turned left. To her delight, she caught sight of the plump brown chicken immediately, and reached in her pocket for the breadcrumbs.

A car drove slowly past, but Betsy was sensibly walking along the very edge of the road, and Chloe let out a breath of relief. The next car was the blacked-out four-by-four, which went past, braked at the bend and then stopped, and reversed into a lay-by.

Chloe and Hilda were gaining on the errant chicken now, and she hardly paid any attention as the driver got out of the vehicle ahead.

'Chloe?'

She looked past the chicken. 'Eddie? Oh, damn!' Betsy had also reached the car, and, clearly unnerved, had plunged into the undergrowth, squawking.

'Was that a chicken?' Eddie asked, bemusement in his expression.

'Yes, it belongs to my neighbour. If I can catch her I don't suppose you could give me a lift home, please?'

'Of course. I was just heading back to the hotel. I've just been visiting the caterers to thank them for... well, you know,' he said, his voice trailing off.

With Eddie helping they managed to entice Betsy towards the basket, but unfortunately, Hilda, who had been well behaved with the chickens for ages now, couldn't cope with Betsy being offered a treat and bounced at her. The chicken flapped its wings and squawked, running back down the bank at the side of the road. Eddie made an unsuccessful grab at her, and was left with a sharp scratch on his hand.

'Bad dog, Hilda!' Chloe scolded. 'Oh, Eddie, I'm so sorry. Here, have a tissue...' She fumbled in her pockets, and a packet fell out, followed by a load of rubbish, including the leather band she had confiscated from Hilda earlier.

She passed Eddie a wad of tissues, and looked up from gathering the contents of her pockets to see why he didn't take it. 'Eddie?'

He was staring at the leather band. 'Where did you get this?'

She turned it over in her hand. 'Hilda found it on the beach the morning...' She stopped as she met his gaze, and then glanced down at his wrist. There was silence for a moment, and then she said slowly, 'She found it on the beach when I found Lara. It's one of your bracelets, isn't it? You always wear four, but last night when I visited you, there were only three on your wrist...'

He was still smiling, rather uncertainly now. 'I did lose one, so thank you for finding it. It's a bit chewed so I might give it back to Hilda.'

Chloe was thinking fast, still staring at him in the deepening twilight. The picture Lara had posted of Eddie in bed had showed his left forearm carelessly flung across the covers. He had been wearing all four bracelets when Lara left the room. He had asked her to describe the scene, to tell him everything she had seen on the beach...

'You lost your bracelet the day Lara died. You lost it on the beach where she drowned. That's why you wanted to talk to me. You wanted to know if I'd found your bracelet,' she told him, breathing fast, heart thumping so hard it made her chest hurt.

'Yes.' He smiled again, but his eyes were blank, assessing. 'But what a shame you had to remember.'

25

She moved before he did, running across the road in a blind panic, the opposite direction she had come. He was after her in a second, his long athletic stride easily catching her, grabbing her arm.

Chloe screamed and struggled, but he held on. Even as she panicked she heard growling and Hilda threw herself at Eddie, snapping and snarling. He kicked out, swearing at her, but she dodged and finally bit him hard enough on the leg to allow Chloe to wrench herself free.

She heard a squeal from Hilda as Eddie must have kicked her again and she felt a flash of fury, but carried on running. The anger gave her the strength to propel herself down the bank and into the trees. The jungle closed in around her, with only narrow animal paths to follow. She ran blindly, as fast as she could, and gradually, as the first impetus gave out, she slowed, aware she could no longer hear her pursuer.

Had she lost him? Eddie was much faster than her, but she knew the territory, was used to the trails and the jungle, even if she had gone totally off course and just now had no idea where she was. Where was Hilda? She thought she had heard a bark, and hoped the dog would run home.

Ailsa and Maria would raise the alarm when she didn't come back. Eddie would surely cut his losses and drive away. He had been going in the direction of the hotel, she remembered, slowing to a walk, but his car had been stopped on the edge of the road further along.

Eventually, her breath coming in gasps, legs aching, and sweat pouring off her face and body, Chloe stopped to get her bearings. She found her phone still wedged in the inner pocket of her trousers, and pulled it out, almost sobbing with relief. No signal. Not even one bar.

In disgust, she shoved it back in her pocket, and took a long calming breath. *Come on, Chloe, you can do this.* Everything looked different in the darkness, but she forced herself to be still. It was a clear, hot night and the moon and stars shone brightly to guide her. There was no sound of her pursuer or of valiant little Hilda. Hopefully, she had gone home, Chloe thought again, pushing through her panic that her dog was badly hurt. Hilda was smart enough to avoid Eddie, she was sure of it.

Had he killed Lara? He had certainly been involved in some way. The guilt and horror in his face when she picked up his bracelet had given him away totally. Had he somehow suspected she knew something and been following her?

Dismissing this as fantasy, and properly lost now, Chloe edged down the bank amongst the undergrowth. She hoped it wasn't poison ivy that brushed her hands and bare legs. Remembering she had a torch in her pocket, she fumbled for it. All the rest of her tissues, odd pens and pencils, wrappers and notes seemed to have fallen out on her hasty flight from Eddie, but the little rectangular hand-torch was still there.

She lost her footing near the bottom and slid the rest of the way, landing with a clatter amongst some loose rocks. Cursing her clumsiness, she leapt up and was about to continue when she heard a voice.

'Help! Is someone there?'

'*Isabelle?*' Chloe whispered to herself, recognising the florist's voice but unable to see her. She cautiously switched on her torch, swinging the beam low across the ground. It was a mossy green area, between two high banks. The sound of water trickling made her thirsty. But Isabelle wasn't anywhere to be seen.

She walked further, noting a beaten path, very overgrown, to her left. To her right it seemed to lead into a rocky bank. She shone the torch again, wondering if she had imagined the call. Almost instantly she could see the answer. It wasn't a rocky bank at all. When she swung the creepers and vines away, it was the entrance to a cave.

After another swift glance around, Chloe stepped into the darkness, risking another call. 'Isabelle, are you down here?'

'Chloe? Yes. Help!'

Chloe tripped halfway down the steps, which were shallow but slippery, and dropped her torch with a sharp crack. The light went out and she cursed her haste. Carefully now, she climbed to her feet and picked up the torch. Relief made her almost giddy as she flicked the switch and a welcome beam of light shone down into the cave.

She reached the bottom of the short flight of steps, ducked her head and picked her way carefully across the rocks, stopping short at the sight of Isabelle.

She was half sitting, half lying on the remains of a rotting wooden platform, which jutted out across a dark, oily-looking pool of water. There seemed to have been a similar set-up to the Crystal Caves, but for some reason this cave had been abandoned.

The walkway strung out across the water, half broken, and sticking up from the darkness to meet the pale stalactites from above. She knelt beside Isabelle, slipping her hands behind her back, finding them bound with plastic cable ties. 'Isabelle, it's okay, I'm here!' Her first thought was to get them both out of the cave and ask questions later.

'Oh, Chloe, it's so dark, so very dark...' She was crying. Her face was streaked with dirt, a bruise spread across one cheek.

'Isabelle! How did you get down here? Who tied you up?' Chloe spoke clearly, ignoring much of the woman's rambling, and put a gentle hand on either side of Isabelle's face. Perhaps she was delirious. Beneath her feet the platform creaked. 'Are you hurt?'

'He said I would never be happy, you know. He said he would hunt me down and kill me if I ran away. I left home early one morning and got the bus with just one suitcase in my hand. I had saved money for a flight and when I got home to Bermuda, when I walked into my cousin's home, I knew I would be all right. But now he's found me again...'

'Your ex-husband?' Chloe was bewildered and then comprehension dawned. 'You mean your ex-husband, don't you? Is he here in Bermuda?'

'No, I don't think so... Sorry, what were you saying?' Isabelle's expression cleared suddenly. 'Chloe, he killed Lara and...'

'Isabelle! We need to get out. Can you stand?'

But Isabelle jerked away from her, her hair tangled, falling over one shoulder. 'I was driving down to the hotel early, Chloe, and I saw Lara standing on the rocks. She was just standing there in her dress, staring out to sea. Her hair was blowing out in the wind. I was worried, so I pulled over by the toilet block, but when I got out she had stepped down and I heard voices.'

'Whose voices did you hear?' Chloe, desperate to get out of

the cave, could see Isabelle was equally desperate to tell her what had happened.

'I heard Eddie. Lara sounded hysterical and he was trying to calm her down. You know how I feel about him so I stayed, just listening.'

Chloe held her breath.

'There was a shout and a scuffle. I couldn't see what was happening, and I was scared. I waited until there was no noise. By the time I got down to the rock they had gone. I was relieved, thinking perhaps I had been mistaken and they had simply gone back to the hotel, argument or whatever resolved.' Her voice changed. 'But then I saw her, lying half in the water... I could tell she was dead.'

'Why didn't you call the police? An ambulance?'

'I fetched some flowers from the van and made her a bouquet, sent her soul away to a better place but then Eddie was back,' Isabelle gasped in fear, 'he was right behind me, and his face was so... so evil. He asked me what I was doing, if I had picked anything up. At least Lara is safe now, away from him.'

'Isabelle, she's dead!' Chloe exclaimed.

'I know, but Eddie has the proof I killed her!' Isabelle shot back. 'I could see what was going on. I told you what I had observed, but when I tried to ask Lara if she was really okay, she brushed it off. So all I could do was try to watch over her, make sure she was at least okay while she was in Bermuda.' Isabelle fixed her gaze on Chloe's, eyes suddenly clear and filled with painful memories. 'Eddie is very clever, but then so was my husband.'

'What do you mean?' Chloe stared at her, mind whirling with confusion. It felt like some crazy dream, 'And you just said Eddie killed Lara, so what proof are you talking about?'

26

'Eddie killed Lara, that's what I'm trying to tell you,' Isabelle said angrily. 'Why don't you listen?'

'Did Eddie bring you down here?' Chloe asked, watching as the torchlight bounced eerie shadows off the rocky walls, the stalactites glimmering above the dark water. She kept peeking over her shoulder, thinking she heard someone coming down the shallow flight of steps behind them.

'He tried to blackmail me into keeping quiet.' She paused and shifted her weight a little, giving a squeak of pain. 'I told him I'd seen what happened and I was going to the police.'

'So you *do* know what really happened to Lara?' Chloe asked quickly. 'What did you mean when you said Eddie had proof you did it?'

'He killed her. I didn't see all of it, but what else could have happened? She was alive, and then he was there and she was dead. When I wouldn't give in to his stupid blackmail, he took me away in my own van, brought me here, and left me for hours. I tried to run away from him, on the beach, but I slipped and hurt my ankle,' Isabelle told her.

'But Eddie always seemed to be...' Chloe felt she had

stumbled into a nightmare. Was her torch battery failing? She thought the light seemed a little paler, a little weaker.

Isabelle said shrilly, 'Stop defending him! That's why I knew if I said anything nobody would believe me. My ex-husband was the same. I could be bruised and bleeding but they would all believe him, always. He set that up himself. He could have set all of it up this time too,' Isabelle muttered.

Chloe thought she seemed confused, previous trauma merging with present-day trauma. But then she had been in a cave for two days. 'Isabelle, have you had food and water?' She swung her torch and was relieved to see a couple of plastic water bottles with the caps off and some sandwich wrappings.

'He left me some but it's been hard to eat and drink with my hands behind my back, I can't feel my arms at all now,' Isabelle's words were rushing out again. 'After he pushed Lara off the rocks and drowned her, he left her lying in the sand. She looked so sad, so ungainly, so I arranged her body and left her flowers.'

'I know, you already told me what happened.' Chloe was beginning to feel slightly desperate and Isabelle wasn't giving all the answers, despite rambling on about Lara's death.

'My ankle hurts,' Isabelle moaned, as she tried to move again.

Can you put any weight on it?' Chloe urged. Would Eddie come back down here to check on Isabelle or would he assume she had run home and raised the alarm? It seemed sensible to assume the latter. He had the car, and once he had stopped searching he would surely be heading for the airport.

'I stopped in the lee of the rocks and listened, peeped round to see where they were. I was... afraid. His voice was so filled with anger, but she was... she wasn't giving in. I suppose she thought he'd never hurt her,' Isabelle said sadly. 'I could see her face from where I was, but not his, and he suddenly pushed her forward, jumping with her into the sea. The tide was out so the water was only maybe knee-deep. I heard her scream and I heard sounds of a struggle. I wanted to help her but I was so scared and I...' Isabelle trailed off.

'Did you see anyone else on the beach that morning?' Chloe asked.

'No, just Eddie and Lara. He had seen me go down to the body with the flowers, you know, when he came back. I suppose he might have considered killing me, too, but instead, he took the video and used it to blackmail me to keep quiet,' Isabelle said, repeating herself again and again in that quiet, defeated monotone, until Chloe, nerves stretched and taut with fear now, wanted to scream.

'Look, Isabelle, I need to go and get help. Are you sure you can't get up? If you lean on me? There's no phone signal down here at all.'

'No, I think I busted my ankle trying to run away from Eddie. It was agony and I heard something snap.' Isabelle seemed to be testing her weight in the darkness again, and she gave a sharp gasp of pain. 'No, I've been trying since I've been down here, but I can't put any weight on it. I can't even crawl. He had to carry me down here. I told you this already!'

Chloe thought quickly. 'I'll go and get help. I'll run really fast and call the police as soon as I get a signal on my phone.'

Isabelle made a sound that was halfway between a whimper of pain and an acknowledgement of the plan. Chloe found her face in the torch beam, but she looked resolute enough.

'Go now and hurry,' was all she said.

'I'll leave you the torch,' Chloe told her. 'It's a clear night and I can easily see outside.' She wedged the torch into the platform so it shone across the water, giving the captive some welcome light in her dark prison.

Isabelle nodded gratefully, then mouthed one word: 'Hurry!'

Chloe ran carefully back across the rocky floor, and up the

steps. Out of the torchlight it was pitch black and the going was treacherously rough. One wrong move and their chance of escape would be finished.

She reached the top of the steps, gasping from her efforts, blinking in the moonlight. Her first thought was a flash of fear that Eddie would be waiting for her, but the empty path into the jungle reassured her. After a moment to get her bearings, she plunged into the undergrowth.

Rounding the first corner she was brought to an abrupt halt by Eddie. She screamed and lashed out, but he held on grimly.

'Let me go!' Chloe yelled. As his other hand wrapped around her mouth, effectively silencing her, she heard another voice, felt another figure slide out from the trees.

'For God's sake shut her up, Eddie, and let's get a move on.'

'Kellie?' Chloe twisted her head away from Eddie's hand and turned to stare at the other woman. 'What the hell is going on?'

'Shut up,' Kellie snapped. As usual, she looked immaculate, and was dressed in a black suit, with a small rucksack on her shoulders. 'Eddie, bring her down into the cave.'

'Eddie?' Chloe tried again. She stopped dead and swung round towards Kellie. 'This is crazy! I have no idea what's going on. You can't do this. Maria is waiting for me at my house. I said I'd be around in an hour max. She'll call the police.'

Eddie looked uncomfortable, shooting little glances at Kellie for instructions, but still hanging on grimly to Chloe's arms.

'Down into the caves,' Kellie repeated, shoving Chloe so hard she nearly toppled over. 'We don't have much time.'

'Why are you doing this?' Chloe pushed back against Eddie's strength. She was fairly sure he wouldn't hurt her, but had he killed Lara? And where did Kellie come in?

Together, captors and captive started to climb down the steps into the cave where Chloe had found Isabelle. The darkness was broken by the beam of Kellie's torch. She continued in silence, and Chloe felt her fear start to rise again. She pulled back a little against Eddie's hands, wanting to see if he would stop her. He did. The fingers tightened and he gave her a little shove so she stumbled again.

Finally, they reached the bottom and turned towards the rotting remains of the walkway and platform. Isabelle was still huddled in the corner, her face sharp and pale in the torchlight, and Chloe tried to smile reassuringly at her, but Isabelle's bleak expression said she had given up.

Kellie turned briskly to her accomplice. 'Eddie, tie Chloe up.' Finally, she turned to Chloe again. 'We aren't going to hurt you – we just need you out of the way so we can get off the island.'

'Why are you helping Eddie?' Isabelle had found her voice again, but it came out squeaky and breathless with fear. 'He killed Lara!'

'It was an accident!' Eddie snapped back at her, as he wrestled with cable ties from Kellie's bag.

'Don't talk to them,' Kellie told him. 'Now tie her up and put her next to Isabelle.'

'The police will be here soon!' Chloe said in desperation, moving away from Eddie again.

Kellie grabbed her arm, her face a mask of smug satisfaction. She was in control, Chloe thought, and she wanted them all to know it. 'No they won't. How could they possibly find you down here?'

Eddie did as he was told, despite Chloe struggling and wriggling her hands away several times. She still felt his heart wasn't quite in this. But it was no good, her wrists were firmly fastened, and she was pushed onto the platform next to Isabelle. Chloe felt the whole thing shake as she lost her balance and almost fell on the rotten, slimy wood. Below, the blackness of the water could have been hundreds of feet deep, and she bit her lip in terror.

Murder on the Beach

Kellie surveyed them with satisfaction, hands on hips, a grim smile on her face. Eddie had confiscated their phones, and she took them from his hands and dropped them into the water.

Eddie made as if to move away but Kellie grabbed his wrist, and tapped her watch. They stepped to the side of the cave and talked in low voices, Eddie protesting about something, but Kellie overpowering him with sharp words. Eventually, she left, sports shoes making a quick light tap on the rock and she jogged out of sight.

Chloe stared at Eddie, who looked away awkwardly, staring at his hands. After a while he pulled his phone out of his pocket and started scrolling through, just as though it was perfectly normal to be sat opposite two bound women in a dark cave.

'Eddie?' Chloe was fairly positive Kellie had gone now. 'Eddie, what's going on?'

He shrugged, so Chloe left it a while and then asked again, 'Where's Kellie gone? You might as well tell me. Isabelle and I can't escape. Why are you still here?'

Eddie looked up, put his phone back in his pocket and sighed. 'I'm not going to hurt you. Kellie's just gone to sort things out and we need you to stay down here until we get off the island.'

'But the flight must have gone by now!' Chloe said.

'She's getting hold of a private jet,' Eddie said reluctantly.

At least he was talking now, Chloe thought. 'Did you kill Lara?'

He put both hands up and raked handfuls of hair back, shaking his head. 'No! At least I didn't mean to. It was Kellie… she set everything up…'

He stopped again and looked towards the entrance to the cave, but there was only the steady drip of water and the immersive darkness beyond the beam of torchlight. 'Everything Lara and I did together was an act, to get as much money and exposure as possible and she was about to screw it all up,' Eddie continued.

'What do you mean? You weren't in love at all?'

'We weren't supposed to be. Kellie was our manager right from the start, when we both went on *Tough Love*, and she told us how to play everything.'

Chloe could almost see this. Two pretty dolls with their strings pulled by a master puppeteer.

'But it was going wrong. Lara began to tell me she had fallen in love properly, and if I felt the same way we should give it all up and just be normal, buy a place abroad somewhere and live off the money we'd already earned for a bit.'

'Did you feel the same?'

'Yes, I mean no, I mean, she was cute and I really liked her but I…' he glanced away again, 'I've been with Kellie since she signed me.'

'You mean you've been sleeping with Kellie?' Isabelle was incredulous.

'It was an act with Lara and it was going so well. I was sure she knew what she was getting into, but last month she started saying if I didn't love her for real, she'd had enough, she couldn't keep the pretence going any longer. I'd had a couple of slip-ups with other girls, including Kellie… Lara didn't know but she suspected.'

'So you proposed?' Chloe said sarcastically. The ties were really biting into her wrists and she couldn't shift her weight any further without toppling into the water. Every time she moved an inch the rotting, slimy wood seemed to crumble a little more, tilting her towards the icy water below.

'I told Kellie we were in trouble and she planned the whole thing. I didn't know quite what she was going to do but she said she would get us as much money as she could before we had to cut Lara loose.'

Murder on the Beach

'You *knew* Kellie was going to *kill* her?' Chloe heard her voice rise in shock.

'No! Oh no, and Kellie was planning it all. She did all the stuff in the run-up to the wedding. Everything. She went a bit far with the knife attack but seriously, do you know how much the pay is for a decent story and pictures? We were raking it in, and we weren't even married yet.'

Eddie's eyes glittered as he talked about money, Chloe noticed. His whole expression became fanatical, grasping and greedy. There was no trace of the Eddie his fans thought they knew and loved. He had lied to them all, betrayed everyone.

'Did Lara have any idea what was going on? Your family and friends?'

'Nobody knew. Lara did suspect a while back when she saw a sneaky press photo of me and Kellie leaving a party, and looking a bit too close. But I told her it was a one-off, a mistake, and Kellie actually cried, and told her she would never do anything to hurt her, she'd been drunk, etc.' Eddie paused to take a breath. 'But the night before the wedding, she caught me with Kellie. It wasn't planned, it was just, you know, spontaneous... Bad timing, yeah?'

Chloe stared at him, speechless, breathing in the darkness, the dankness of their prison.

'I laid it on the line, told her Kellie's plan. All she had to do was go along with it until after the honeymoon, and then we could do a break-up story, you know, pressures of fame, all that, and she would be free. We would have banked as much as we could and Kellie said then I wouldn't lose public sympathy, because I would still be carrying on. She's already put me forward for some more reality TV stuff and now I've got a platform I can...'

'Wow. You told her you didn't love her the night before your wedding? Do you have any idea what kind of bastard that makes you?' Chloe said furiously. 'Lara was vulnerable and you used her in the worst possible way.'

'Hey, she had no complaints before she started with the falling-in-love thing. I never signed up for that.'

'You really are a complete bastard. What really happened on the morning she died?' Isabelle asked.

She seemed to be gaining strength and courage now she had an ally. Albeit, Chloe thought dryly, an ally who was also tied up.

Eddie shrugged. 'She slept on the couch on the other side of the suite, but I heard her get up early. I didn't take too much notice, but I was keeping an eye out, you know, in case she thought of doing a runner. I saw her put on her dress, so I asked her what she was doing. She told me she had thought it through and decided I was right, we should just play along with everything until we broke up. She told me she had the nail polish endorsement to do, and the jewellery photos, and she'd see me later.'

'And you believed her?'

'Kind of. Not enough to be sure, which is why I still rang Kellie and told her what happened. She said we needed to make sure she wasn't going to blow us out, or run, so we followed her to the rocks. Lara stood right on the edge, and I knew right away she was going to jump, and that wasn't going to play along with the plan...'

Chloe found she had tears streaming down her cheeks. 'She was taking the only way out she could see.'

'I shouted at her, and she screamed back, saying... saying a lot of stuff.' He looked away. 'Kellie was trying to reason with her as well. I'm not proud of it, but I told her if she really felt that way she could kill herself after the wedding.'

There was a shocked pause and the words seem to echo around the darkness, repeating again and again inside Chloe's head. 'Oh my God, and to think I felt sorry for you,' she finally said in disgust.

'She jumped, and I jumped after her. We struggled, me trying to pull her out, and Kellie was down on the beach by now. Suddenly, she just went limp in my arms, and I dropped her under the water, couldn't seem to grab her. She... she just died and it wasn't my fault. I know now from the autopsy it was her heart, but at the time I had no idea.'

'So you left her?'

'Kellie said to leave her on the beach, said she must have drowned and I held her down too long or something. We checked and she wasn't breathing. Kellie said we would have to go with it. She was furious, but she made sure we hadn't left anything on the rocks, got me to sweep away our footprints in the sand. I must have dropped my bracelet when we were struggling. I didn't notice until we were walking back.'

'So you came back to get it, but by that time Isabelle, who had been there all the time, had found the courage to go to Lara,' Chloe supplied.

'Yeah, I saw her bending over the body, and that was when I thought of filming her. When she turned and saw me, I asked her what the hell she thought she was doing.'

'I told him I had seen him kill Lara and I was going to tell the police,' Isabelle said. 'But he told me if I did, he would go back to the hotel straight away and tell them he had seen me with Lara, and show them the footage.'

Chloe sat in silence for a moment, thinking about the tragic loss of life, how at any time the chain of events could have been stopped. But Kellie and Eddie, in their greed had pushed the girl to her limit. 'And now you think Kellie is just going to come back for you?'

'Of course she is, we've been together ages, I'm part of the plan,' he said confidently.

'Eddie, what did Kellie tell you to do to us?' Chloe asked, amazed he hadn't thought it out for himself.

He shrugged. 'Nothing, just to watch you until she comes back for me. She'll be back any minute.'

'But we know what happened!' Isabelle burst out. 'And even if we didn't, you and Kellie attacked us both and kept me prisoner in this cave for days. You can't get away with doing exactly what you like, Eddie, no matter how rich and famous you are.'

He sat, didn't even look at her. He was scowling at his phone in the darkness, walking away, apparently trying to get a signal.

Chloe hissed at Isabelle, 'Did you have to say that? Now he's twigged he needs to kill us!'

'I bet Kellie told him to do that anyway.'

'I bet Kellie isn't coming back for him,' Chloe shot back.

Eddie walked back, still looking at his phone, one hand nervously pushing his hair from his forehead. Then he looked at the two women, huddled on the rotten platform, hands bound, flinching away from him.

Chloe was never sure what he intended, but his expression suggested some sort of violence. But as he stepped onto the walkway, there was an ominous creaking, a crash, and the platform fell into the pool below. She fell with it, hurled backwards, feeling the wood disintegrate, a broken plank hit her arm, and the icy water closed in, filling her nose, her mouth...

'Isabelle, are you okay?' Chloe yelled, as soon as she had surfaced, kicking hard to stay afloat in her panic, spitting water and coughing to clear her throat. She thanked her lucky stars she was a good swimmer again now, but she had never tried to stay afloat with her hands tied behind her back.

'I'm here!' Isabelle was spluttering, her voice edged with terror. She was bobbing close to Chloe, her body jack-knifing in an apparent effort to keep her head above water.

'Eddie, you need to help us or we'll drown with our hands tied like this!' Chloe tried again, spitting another mouthful of vile water. She could see Eddie crouched on the edge, peering in. He had obviously leapt back just in time to save himself. He turned back to his phone.

'Eddie!' Isabelle screamed.

27

He looked up from the screen in frustration. 'Shut up! I need to get out of here, and I need to think, okay?'

Isabelle made a choking noise, and disappeared briefly under water before resurfacing again. He shot an anxious glance at her, before chucking his phone across the floor and swearing. 'This is all your fault, Isabelle! If you hadn't interfered with Lara's body, Kellie would have been able to push the suicide option, and we would have got away with it.' His voice was heavy.

'But now you won't get away with it, Eddie, because the police are already on their way,' Chloe said firmly, trying to stop her voice shaking. 'Maria is staying with me, and I told her I'd be back in an hour. For God's sake!' She wasn't sure how long Isabelle could keep afloat, and it was impossible to help her with her hands tied.

'She'll never find you.' He was looking at his watch again, picked up his phone, and this time vanished into the shadows. They could hear his heavy tread as he, too, climbed the steps.

Ten minutes later he was back, wild-eyed and panicked.

'Has she gone without you?' Chloe guessed. 'Eddie, we can

help you. You're right, you didn't kill Lara, and Kellie made you do everything else. We'll tell the police...'

'No! Nobody else knows, and I need time to get out of here.' He looked at them bobbing in the icy water, in a clear moment of indecision. 'Sorry, I'm really sorry but I need to get out of here!'

He ran swiftly back towards the main steps as Chloe and Isabelle thrashed about trying to stay afloat.

Isabelle was gasping, and Chloe shouted at her to try and keep on her back. The rocky ledges were steep in this area but hopefully lowered further on and Chloe thought it might be possible to boost themselves up onto the dry land. She was trying to remember the layout of the cave, but had only glimpsed it in torchlight when she first descended the steps. 'Kick your legs!'

'I can't, Chloe, I'm drowning!' Isabelle's voice rose in panic and then finished in a splutter as she accidentally took in a mouthful of water.

Chloe managed to kick her way towards the ledge, but struggled to get up to dry land. Each time she fell back into the water, and each time she took in a great gulp as she sank under before she could force her way back to the surface. Her feet grazed the rock where the sides of the pool fell in a rough step formation. She yelled this information to Isabelle, who managed to get close enough to half stand on the bottom, shoulders resting against the side.

'How are we going to get out?' Isabelle gasped. Her long hair had come loose from its plaits and was streaming around her shoulders, floating in the water.

'We might have to wait for the police. Maria would have called Finn by now,' Chloe said, trying to sound confident. There wasn't enough room on the ledge for both women, so she kept balancing with a toe, then floating for a bit. She had never been so thankful for her regular ocean swims as now. 'Maria and Ailsa knew where I was going... And Hilda... I think Hilda went home after Eddie lashed out at her. She'll find us.'

She was just trying again when they both froze in the semi-darkness. Running footsteps echoed around the caves, and Eddie appeared on the walkway, panting and peering into the darkness.

'Chloe? Where are you?' There was something that could have been desperation in his voice. 'Isabelle?'

28

Isabelle put her mouth close to Chloe's ear. 'Why is he back?'

Even as Chloe shook her head, Eddie called to them, 'I've come back to help you! Where are you?'

They could hear him fumbling for the torch, clicking it on and starting to scan the water.

Chloe thought quickly. Had Kellie deserted him as they had suspected? If so, had he come back to try and redeem himself by rescuing them? Or had he come back for revenge?

The two women kept quiet, huddled together in the deepest recesses of the rock. The darkness seemed friendly now, keeping them safe as the torch beam swung this way and that.

Of course, it wasn't long before the light picked them out, and Eddie yelled in relief, 'Are you okay? Why don't you say something?'

Chloe found her voice. 'Eddie, you shoved us in the water when we were bound hand and foot, what do you expect? A medal?'

He was coming swiftly around the side of the cave, slowing as the path gave out and he had to climb, torch between his teeth. Reaching the women, he put the torch down and bent over, extending his hand to haul them out.

Both women shrank back. Chloe tried to keep her voice as calm as she could through chattering teeth, 'Eddie if you really want to help you need to take my arm and pull me up.'

She almost held her breath as he reached down again, hand closing over her upper arm, grunting as he hauled her up across the rock to safety. He repeated the action and soon Isabelle was huddled next to Chloe, staring wide-eyed and fearful.

When they were all on dry land he spoke again. 'I couldn't leave you to maybe die. It was all Kellie, you know. Lara's death was an accident, but it was all her. She was blackmailing me because we were sleeping together. She kept saying she would tell Lara... I mean Kellie had me beaten up!' His face was earnest, blue eyes full of charm and honesty, but his smile was more of a baring of teeth, a gesture of desperation.

He had clearly been rehearsing his speech on the way back down to the caves. It was just as clear his accomplice, and the true orchestrator of Lara's downfall, had deserted him. As further proof of his good intentions he took out his penknife and cut the remaining bonds from their hands.

Chloe rubbed her wrists thoughtfully. If they could keep him happy, make him think they would go along with his version of events until the police arrived... it seemed like hours since she had left Maria in the house, but it could only really be one.

But volatile Isabelle, crouched like a drowned rat, water streaming off her long hair and clothes, had other ideas. 'You only came back because Kellie's taken off without you! You killed Lara and tried to kill us and you think we'll stick up for you to the police. No chance. You're a slimy, lying bastard who deserves all he gets!'

With that, Isabelle took them both by surprise and gave Eddie an almighty shove into the water. Unfortunately, there was very little room for movement, and Isabelle's violence also dislodged both herself and Chloe.

Eddie was thrashing around, swearing, the torch having been jettisoned somewhere on the rocks. 'You bitch! I was going to save you...'

His voice suggested he no longer had any desire to save either of them and Chloe mentally yelled *'Nice one, Isabelle'* as she swam out of the danger zone. But Isabelle, as already proven that evening, was not a good swimmer, and splashed helplessly out into the middle.

She could hear Eddie yelling and splashing somewhere to her left, further out. She reached the rocks with a powerful front crawl, swimming into the shallows, her knees brushing seaweed, and her elbow catching on a sharp rock. She gasped in pain and then began to take long, slow breaths, keeping her eyes above water, hidden amongst the rocky outcrop like a sea creature spying a predator.

But Eddie was grabbing at Isabelle now, and she couldn't just leave her. Chloe slid from her hiding place and moved forward in a powerful underwater dive that took her straight towards the struggle.

She surfaced and shook water from her eyes as the police ran into the cave. Powerful torchlight illuminated the struggle, but Eddie wasn't finished. Isabelle, taking advantage of the confusion, began kicking towards the edge of the water, but Chloe found her neck enclosed in Eddie's arm.

'Don't come any closer!' he yelled, voice echoing around the rocky walls, bouncing off the ceiling.

To her horror, Chloe felt, through her icy skin, the point of a knife in her neck. Eddie must have held on to his knife but lost the torch when he was pushed into the pool.

'Eddie? Bermuda Police. I'm Inspector Derrick Carmichael.

We aren't coming any closer. We want to help you and not get anyone hurt.'

Chloe vaguely thought she recognised the voice. Someone she had met at the Ocean Café perhaps? She saw Isabelle being helped ashore and dragged to safety, but with the knife at her throat she didn't dare speak.

Eddie tightened his grip as best he could, wrapping a strong hand over her mouth. 'Be quiet or I'll kill you,' he hissed.

She and Eddie were both treading water, which made her position even more precarious as both their bodies were moving and sometimes the point jabbed harder, sometimes tracing a line up towards her ear. Either way would be deadly if he did stab her.

Feeling his massive strength around her neck, Chloe hardly dared breathe, but couldn't help gasping with the effort of staying afloat. Fear made her heart pound painfully against her ribs, but Chloe didn't dare fight him. She tried to let herself hang like a dead weight.

The police officer was talking again, and she could see medics in the shadows, Finn, and Josanne. She remembered Derrick now. He had been waiting in the coffee queue at the Ocean Café a few weeks ago, before she had ever heard of Lara and Eddie. Finn introduced him as a new recruit, with a background in hostage negotiation.

He was talking calmly and confidently. 'Tell me what you want, Eddie, and we can arrange it.'

'I want a car to the airport and a private plane to take me to... to Spain,' Eddie said suddenly. 'And I'm keeping Chloe right up until I get on that plane. You can see the knife, and how close it is to her neck. Even if you try and shoot me, I'll still manage to kill her. And that will be your fault.'

With that Eddie began to swim slowly backwards, dragging Chloe with him. The lights followed them, but he was able to manoeuvre them both into a crevice. Again, the rock shelved beneath their feet and they stood, both panting, his arms around her, the knife point just below her jaw.

Terrified Eddie was going to cut his losses, she began to struggle, but he held her arms firmly, panic in his voice. He said softly, 'Don't worry, I won't really hurt you, I just need you as a hostage in case anything goes wrong.'

'Eddie, why don't you just tell them what happened. Lara's death was an accident and you haven't hurt anyone. Kellie is the one who set everything up,' Chloe said persuasively, watching the knife. Would he actually use it?

The inspector was talking again. 'Can you come over to the edge? We can get both of you on dry land while we organise a plane.'

'No chance!' Eddie shouted back. 'You get everything done and then Chloe and I will come out. You stay back!'

Chloe couldn't stop shaking, her hair streaming down her back like a mermaid, legs and arms battered from the rocks. She sat, hunched, arms around knees, watching him. Surely he must know there was zero chance the police would meet his demands.

'Eddie, come on. It's Kellie who deserves to be arrested, not you. Once the police find out it was all her...'

'What if it wasn't all Kellie?' Eddie hissed. 'Maybe I enjoyed killing Lara, and maybe I'll enjoy killing you.'

'What do you mean?' Chloe didn't like the way this was going.

'I'm not stupid.'

That was questionable, thought Chloe.

'Kellie underestimated me. I know loads of stuff on her, and I know where she's gone. I'm going after her. The bitch made her money but when it got tough, she bailed on me. I'm not coming over like some idiot. I'd get a lot for interviews on my own and maybe a book deal.'

Chloe decided he had finally lost the plot. 'Eddie, you'll make a lot more by being the good guy who got tangled up with Kellie's blackmailing. Believe me, one of my friends is a journalist, and she always says...' Chloe paused, what the hell did this fictional friend say? '... She says the public always want someone to love and someone to hate in every story.'

'Really?'

Was he actually falling for this? 'Yes, and Eddie, I can back you up.'

'Isabelle won't.'

'Isabelle is... she's been under a lot of strain,' Chloe told him urgently. 'Come on, Eddie.

'She's crazy.' But the knife was wavering, and his grip was weaker. 'It might work. You could say Kellie pushed you both in and I came back to save you.'

'Yes, just like you planned originally,' Chloe said soothingly. The whole thing was farcical. Here she was, Chloe Canton, having a conversation in a cave with a murderer, albeit by his own admission, an accidental one.

The police inspector was talking again. 'We've got your transport organised. You can come out now. We'll stay right back.'

Chloe was quiet, but scanning the cave she had seen two things. Firstly, a large rock positioned right next to her, and secondly, the ground shelved steeply to the left of the cave entrance. If she could wait until Eddie was distracted, she could bash him over the head with the rock and dive straight out into the pool.

If she headed fast and straight to the police on the other side, with the element of surprise, she thought she could make it. There was plenty of light now from the first responders. It was her only chance, because she was no longer sure Eddie wouldn't hurt her. He was desperate, his eyes gleaming, darting in the torchlight, twisting his big hands and shifting his weight from side to side.

At any time he might decide to cut his losses and just kill her. She couldn't risk it.

She waited until the inspector repeated his sentence, pretended to be tucking her head down on her knees, cowed and obedient. Eddie wasn't stupid, he had eyes on her the whole time, but the knife was further away.

'Eddie?'

'I want...'

Eddie was distracted for that split second, so she exploded upwards, throwing the rock at his head, shoving it as hard as she could into his skull, and in the same movement launching herself in a straight dive into the dark waters, powering off in a front crawl towards the walkway.

He was yelling, but she carried on until she reached the crumbling wooden structure at the far end, hauling herself up, stopping dead as a shadowed figure blocked her way.

A torch showed her the distinctive uniform and she gasped in relief, stumbling onwards, grabbing the police officer's outstretched hand and allowing the woman to help her up the bank.

As she reached the top, she twisted round to see Eddie was overpowered by officers who had clearly crept around the ledge behind the cave while the negotiation had been going on.

Chloe was disorientated, freezing cold and very grateful for the blanket someone draped across her shoulders. She could see her fingers clawing at the wool, white and wrinkled, nail beds tinged with blue, but she couldn't feel them at all.

Finn was beside her now, pulling the blanket around her. 'Are you all right, Chloe?'

She nodded. 'I'm fine, honestly.'

He looked at her hard but was soon called away as another

officer shouted urgently from the walkway. 'Can you make sure she gets checked over by the medics?' he said to the woman officer. 'Chloe, once this is wrapped up I'll come back, okay? Go to hospital and I'll pick you up when you're done.'

She nodded again, extreme weariness sweeping over her body, muscles aching. Her right shoulder was agony when she moved it but she hoped it was just a strain.

Medics, the BFR and police officers were swarming through the caves, and she could hear the extraction of a raging Eddie from the water.

'Is Isabelle okay?' she managed to ask the police officer who had helped her out of the water.

'She'll be fine. She's been taken to hospital just to get checked over,' the woman said kindly.

'What about Kellie? Did she get away?'

'I'm not sure. Let's get you checked out and then we'll take your statement,' the police officer said.

∼

Chloe was pronounced fine by the medics. Her cuts and bruises were all superficial, her shoulder wrenched but not broken, and she would be able to go home and recover. She blinked sleepily at the large digital clock on the wall. It was half past four in the morning. For some reason she found it surprising. It seemed like at least a whole day had passed since she first saw Eddie on South Shore Road. Was it really only seven hours?

'At least we now know who was behind all of this. Isabelle, even though the evidence pointed towards her, was like a wrong puzzle piece being shoved into the picture,' Finn said thoughtfully. He took her arm as they walked back to the car. 'I was so worried when Maria called me and said you'd gone tearing off to find a chicken and never come home.'

'There wasn't time to think after I met Eddie on the road, and later I had no phone signal. The only thing I could think of was Maria and Ailsa knew where I was going, and Hilda might be able to find me,' Chloe said simply.

'If Hilda hadn't come home and found Maria, we might not have found anything until it was too late,' Finn said soberly. Then he smiled. 'You seemed to have dropped half the contents of your pockets between the road and the cave, so it wasn't a hard trail to follow. Don't panic, I've got a bag full of tissues, a lipstick and other bits...'

Chloe half-laughed, hysteria was nudging at her emotions, and she felt slightly tearful again. 'Hilda deserves a medal, but I expect she'd prefer a dog chew.' She stopped and yawned widely, before turning back to Finn. 'Isabelle was truly terrified of Eddie or I think she would have come forward much earlier and explained what really happened the morning Lara died. I think she might have been suffering from some kind of PTSD after what happened with her ex-husband. She seemed to think he had manifested into Eddie.'

Finn held the car door open for her. 'She will be offered the help she needs now. And Eddie will face numerous charges, and spend a long time in prison.'

'What about Kellie?'

He grinned. 'She did catch a flight, but she will be met by police when she steps off the plane.'

'Where was she going? Back to London?'

'No. She caught the last flight out of here, to New York, but we suspect she was intending to do a quick change and fly to Spain. She has a holiday home out there.'

They drove slowly along the road, and Chloe finally began to feel warmer, pushing her blanket away. 'It was the money for Eddie. The fame for Lara. But I think out of the two of them Lara was easier to understand. She was desperate to be liked and she looked for her own validation from her social media fans. I suppose once you get caught up in that kind of life... But she also realised what was happening to her, the strain it was putting on her mental health, and that was why she wanted to get out.'

'You said Eddie told you he never really loved her?' Finn's tone expressed his distaste.

'He was focused purely on the money.' Chloe sighed. 'I'm just so sad she never got to live out her fairy tale.'

'Well, Eddie will be brought to justice, which I know is a poor second, and all those trolls on social media have taken a hammering of their own in regards to the vile comments regarding Lara's death,' Finn said, pulling up on the driveway and parking in front of Chloe's house.

She smiled at him. 'Dinner didn't quite go how I planned last time, so how about lunch on Wednesday?'

'Perfect.'

As he drove away she walked wearily into her home and sank down, filthy and exhausted, still half wrapped in her blanket. From the magazine on the coffee table, Lara's pretty, vivacious face laughed up at her. But now she knew what to look for, she could see the sadness underneath. She hoped Lara would be pleased Isabelle was getting the help she needed, and that Eddie and Kellie had been caught.

29

Ailsa appeared at the door and Chloe's eyelids flickered open again, taking in the kitchen clock. It was now past ten. She had overslept!

'Are you all right, Chloe?' the older woman started towards her, concerned. 'I went down to the yard. Antoine said you had left a message. Maria was here and she told me you were sleeping. She's just popped down to the police station to give a statement and help with their enquiries so I said I'd come over and see if you needed anything when you woke up.'

Chloe blinked at her, sleepy and weak. 'Did you find Betsy?'

'What? Not yet, I think a cat or something must have got her, but it doesn't matter, after what happened. *Chloe!* Are you awake?'

'Yes. No, sorry.' Chloe hauled herself together. 'I must have a shower, and then I'll be coherent. Feel free to grab a cup of tea if you've got time.'

Chloe's phone rang as she walked slowly to the bathroom. It was Maria, her voice quick and excited. 'Hi, darling, are you okay?'

'I'm fine. When are you coming back?'

'In about an hour. They've got Kellie in New York, arrested her as soon as she stepped off the plane, and she's admitted everything but tried to put the blame on Eddie! She's saying it was all his idea. Honestly, the police here are so brilliant. They've managed to find out Kellie was raking huge amounts of cash from Lara and Eddie's earnings, and all her other clients. She made plans to disappear to Spain just after Lara and Eddie got back from their honeymoon. That poor girl, Chloe. I can't get over how evil those two were, just using her. It makes me feel sick.'

'Me too,' said Chloe, feeling the familiar catch of sadness in her throat as Lara's name was mentioned. They could all be triumphant Eddie and Kellie were caught, but it wouldn't bring the girl back. 'Look, I'm just going to have a shower. Tell me all about it when you get back?'

'Of course, darling. You looked like death when you got home last night. That's why I asked Ailsa to come and sit with you, I was so worried...'

∽

When Chloe emerged from the bathroom twenty minutes later, wet hair tied up in a ponytail, wearing a striped dress, Ailsa, as she had known she would be, was sitting at the kitchen table, two mugs of tea already made.

She had also made a large plate of sandwiches and was flicking through the magazine. She tapped the feature on Lara and Eddie's wedding with a battered fingernail. 'Sad to see something like that go so wrong.'

Chloe thanked her for the sandwiches and told her in more detail what had happened down in the cave last night. Ailsa fed a few crumbs to the chickens, who had wandered in at the door and settled under the table.

'He seemed so charming and normal,' Chloe said slowly. 'I think the worst thing is how much he deceived Lara. She honestly thought he loved her.'

'But he had his eye on the cash, you say?' Ailsa was nodding. 'And if he was with that Kellie woman as well...'

'Yes. He admitted it to me,' Chloe told her. 'Kellie was behind everything that happened in the lead up to the wedding, and all the things that were leaked to the press. Everything was planned.'

'Even the knife attack at the pre-wedding party?' Ailsa was shocked.

'He says he told the man to wield the knife but not hurt anyone. Finn told me they arrested the knifeman this morning after a tip-off. He was stupid enough to come back to Bermuda in the hopes of blackmailing Eddie.'

'Bet that was a nasty shock for the groom-to-be,' Ailsa observed.

'Yes! It came back to bite him. I suppose it would have been easy for him and Kellie to get in touch with Lara's trolls under another name, feeding them information. The other thing that wasn't down to him was the stalker, and Isabelle.'

'Poor woman,' Ailsa commented. 'I hear she's doing well in hospital though.'

'Yes, she's finally going to get the help she needs.' Chloe sighed. 'She was the only one who saw through Eddie, and she tried so hard to warn Lara. But I can imagine Lara just laughing it off. I mean, who would think your enemies were so close to home?'

'I suppose for him it was the final strike when Lara said she wanted to give it all up.'

'He said that was when he knew the wedding had to go with a bang, and they needed to make as much money as possible. Kellie managed to convince him to cover up Lara's death. In his mind, he was now ensured continued income as the devastated fiancé who never managed to walk his tragic bride down the aisle. But Kellie never intended to keep helping him, or for them to end up together. He was a dupe as much as Lara was, really.'

'It's shocking, it really is. People forget what they need to live, I think. Good health and good friends are all you want really. Lots of other bits and pieces but those are the main ones,' Ailsa said firmly.

∼

A week later Chloe had recovered enough to help set up for Antoine and Louisa's wedding reception on the beach, and join in the general excitement at their upcoming nuptials.

Right on time, at ten minutes past twelve the happy couple arrived at Beachside Stables in Peter's taxi, after signing on the line at the registry office in Hamilton, and Chloe joined the receiving line, throwing flower petals as bride and groom ran down the trail to the beach, laughing.

Ailsa stood behind a table of food, and Harry was mixing drinks, and handing out ice-cold bottles of beer from a massive bucket. With just twenty close friends and family attending, Chloe found she knew everyone, and enjoyed herself immensely.

'This is how a wedding should be done,' Antoine told her, as she went over and hugged the bride and groom, offering her congratulations.

'It's just perfect for you two,' Chloe said, smiling at them. They were so in love, and it would be nice to think they might actually live out their fairy tale. 'Everyone wants something different for their big day, don't they?'

Louisa leant in and kissed Chloe's cheek. 'We wouldn't have been able to afford to get married and find a place of our own at all if you hadn't come to Bermuda. It wasn't that long ago Antoine was freaking out about not having a job. Oh, and thank you for the lovely wedding gifts.'

Chloe had finally settled on one of Melissa Aliente's paintings from the Stone Gallery. It was done in her trademark delicate watercolour, and depicted a couple walking along a vast empty beach. Their hands were linked, and overhead the blue skies seemed full of promise. Chloe had also added a small crate of her home-made candles tied with a blue ribbon.

'It's a team effort at Beachside Stables. I certainly couldn't do without Antoine,' Chloe told her, noticing Jordan wander past with a very pretty girl laughing next to him.

As the couple moved on, Louisa's long white lace dress trailing in the sand, Finn came up and passed Chloe another glass. 'I don't normally enjoy weddings, but this is more like a beach party.'

She clinked glasses in a toast, and nodded towards Louisa and Antoine. They were now laughing and hugging friends and relatives. 'It's perfect.'

The smell of a barbeque began to drift along the beach, luscious scents mingling with the music and the laughter.

Later, joining the other guests, Finn and Chloe danced on the beach, barefoot, sand beneath their toes. Her hands in Finn's, her friends all dancing and laughing around her, she decided she would have been perfectly happy if it wasn't for her sadness at Lara's death. Would Lara have approved of this wedding? Chloe had a sneaky feeling she would have done.

EPILOGUE

The day after, Finn finally made it to lunch, and Chloe settled them outside in the sunshine, shaded by the fig tree. She had made her version of her grandmother's fish chowder, and had enjoyed a pleasant moment of nostalgia as she stirred the fish, bacon fat and vegetables. Adding black rum and sherry peppers had made it smell heavenly.

Finn grinned appreciatively. 'I remember Dre making this. She would occasionally invite a whole load of people over, and lay on the rum and the fish chowder.'

'Did she?' Chloe smiled, intrigued at this new slant on her grandmother. 'I don't ever remember her being very sociable when I was young. It was always just me and her doing things...'

'Oh she was very selective about who she liked and who she didn't. Invitation to her garden parties was strictly for those in favour.' He laughed. 'Anyway, it must be my turn to cook for you next. Even my sisters admit I'm a decent chef when I have to be. And I want to show you the boat before her official launch.'

Chloe laughed. 'I'll hold you to that. Should I bring a bottle to crack on her bows before we set sail?'

'Of course!' He set his glass down and leant back in his chair. 'Actually, there is something I need to tell you, Chloe...'

She studied his face, noting the sudden serious expression. 'Is anything wrong? What's happened?'

'It's okay, nothing bad. I just wanted to wait until we had eaten to give you this.' He passed her a brown envelope.

'What is it?' Intrigued, Chloe opened it, and a sparkle of metal fell out onto her palm. She held it up to the light, balanced on her palm. 'But I gave this to Lara!'

'I know, but we have been able to release her belongings now. She had made a will, you know,' he added thoughtfully. 'Before she became famous actually, which is surprising.'

'Wow, I don't think I made a will until I was about forty-five!' Chloe said. 'But she was a savvy girl in every way, except when it came to falling in love. Don't tell me she put the bracelet in her will before she died?'

'No. Sorry, just the way my thoughts were going. The will might take months to get sorted out and then it will have to go through probate.' He leant back in his chair, eyes serious, holding hers, watching her face. 'She left a note.'

'So she did mean to kill herself that morning?' Chloe asked sadly. She pulled her hair back from her face and tied it up in a ponytail. The heat from the midday sun was intense and she could feel sweat trickling down her back. 'Let's move the umbrella round so we get some more shade, I'm boiling.'

Finn obligingly unfolded the white umbrella and angled it across the table and chairs, where it cast a welcome shadow of coolness. Chloe stretched her legs out, wriggling her bare feet on the grass, as her mind showed her a picture reel of Lara, from the girl's first day on the island, to the very last time she had seen her.

'It seems she probably did have that in mind. Her final video, the one she never posted, and the one I can't show you yet, because the process is still ongoing, pretty much confirms everything Eddie said.'

'She found out about the affair but felt she had to carry on?' Chloe suggested.

'Yes, but Eddie didn't tell you that at first. He assured Lara it was a one-off, a mistake, but later changed his story and told her the truth, that the whole relationship was faked and set up by Kellie.'

'Presumably that was why they pushed the wedding forward, because Lara was becoming more unstable?'

'Yes, Kellie admits Lara was threatening to pull out and tell the truth, which would have lost them millions, not to mention hers and Eddie's careers would have been over.' Finn paused. 'Danny discovered the truth about Eddie and Kellie, and he came to Bermuda to tell Lara face to face.'

'So they had him killed?' Chloe said incredulously.

'Yes, Kellie's brother has criminal leanings. He's been a big-time drug dealer for years and it seems she asked him for help. He knew the right people and it was done. Then they ramped it up with the funeral wreath, the dolls, the painted pagan symbols, which didn't actually mean anything but were enough to scare everyone. Everything was arranged by Kellie and her brother.'

'But Lara wasn't meant to die?' Chloe asked.

'No. It seems her death really was an accident, but Isabelle ruined it by interfering with the body, with the best of intentions, and she turned it into a murder enquiry. Eddie and Kellie were terrified of being implicated, so they blackmailed Isabelle.'

'And Hilda found Eddie's bracelet,' Chloe said slowly. 'It was when I pulled a tissue out of my pocket, and it fell out too. Eddie's face was just horrified and so guilty, even if he hadn't said a word I would have known. But I don't think Eddie would have killed us, not until the end when he felt cornered.' She shivered at the memory. 'Kellie's different. She might easily have left us there to drown.'

'I'm just glad you're safe,' Finn told her. 'We have been able to release Lara's belongings now. Her best friend has taken charge of everything and is packing up her stuff from the hotel.'

'Maisie-Lynn?' Chloe was surprised.

'Yes. It seems they had a falling out but were reconciled before the wedding.'

'She sold a story to the press,' Chloe told him.

'Yes, she told me,' Finn said soberly. 'She regrets it very much, and she's talking about the charities Lara wanted to support and how she wants to carry on with what her friend started.'

'But Lara's bracelet?' Chloe queried, turning it over in her hand so the charms caught the sunlight.

'Lara stated in the note she had few friends she felt she could really trust, but when you met someone you just knew. That was how she felt about you, according to Maisie-Lynn.'

'She said I reminded her of her mum.' Chloe felt her lashes wet and a small tear escape. She turned away, embarrassed. 'Sorry, I just think it was so sad, and now she's dead.'

'She wanted you to have the bracelet back, to keep you safe,' Finn stated.

Chloe blew her nose and carefully fastened the bracelet around her wrist. 'She was a lovely girl and I feel like I knew her for ages, instead of just a few days.'

'She was. That is one of the hardest parts of police work,' Finn said. 'We can see justice done, but we can't bring back the dead.'

Chloe pulled herself together, and picked up her glass. 'A toast to Lara.'

He tapped his glass on hers, and they sat in the warm garden for a moment in silence, before he changed the subject. 'Have you heard anything from Mark?'

'No, not a single phone call or email. I actually think it was good for both of us to meet up again, to get some kind of closure. Now we both know exactly where we stand.' She shaded her eyes against the sun, smiling up at him, grateful for the change in conversational direction. 'I think I can safely say he won't ever be coming to Bermuda again.'

'And that makes you happy?'

She didn't even have to think. 'Yes it does. He will always be part of my history, but I've changed so much since we split up, and there isn't the slightest chance he will ever be a part of my future.' It was a strong statement but she meant it with every word she spoke.

'I don't think Bermuda liked him either,' Finn suggested with a cheeky grin.

They finished the lemonade and smiled at one another in perfect understanding. Finn seemed about to say something when Ailsa burst through the hedge.

Chloe stood up, instantly concerned. 'What's wrong?'

Ailsa beamed at them both and pointed to her flock of chickens, who had, as usual, followed her straight into Chloe's garden.

'Oh, Betsy's back, I'm so glad!' Chloe smiled, and then glanced back down to where the chicken was marching towards the table. 'Oh, *Ailsa!*'

Finn was laughing as she bent down and gently held out her hand. Betsy was now sitting happily under the table with five tiny chicks, who were cheeping and fluttering their little wings.

'I reckon they must be around two or three weeks old, because they've got their wing feathers,' Ailsa said proudly as she reached them.

Finn poured three glasses of lemonade and held up his own. 'Another toast must be in order, I think!'

Chloe could hardly drink for laughing. She tried hard to catch this one glittering, happy, sun-drenched moment and store it in her memory. Her friends, her home, and her health. Ailsa was right, who needed anything else?

Finn caught her eye and winked, and she grinned back. Okay, well maybe a little something else was needed.

Below them the waves rolled lazily onto the beach, while the Longtails swooped and danced on the hot breeze.

THE END

AFTERWORD
CHLOE'S BERMUDA

Bermuda is definitely an island to fall in love with, and if you are planning a visit, you can follow in Chloe's footsteps and enjoy some of her favourite places:

The Crystal Caves

The limestone caves in St George's parish are a major tourist attraction and Chloe first visits with Finn in this book. The Crystal Caves, which include both the Crystal Caves and the Fantasy Cave, are the largest on Bermuda and you can book ahead or just pitch up and take a tour. Numbers are limited so try to avoid peak times. The steep steps down into the caves aren't suitable for those with reduced mobility, and it's certainly a long climb back up again! But well worth it. The caverns and stalactites are awe-inspiring and quite beautiful. There is a small café, and lush gardens which are easy to access.

The caves are open 0900 until 1700, but do check the website before you head out there. The bus stops right outside at the bottom of the driveway.

Alexandra Mosher Jewellery Store and Studio

Located at 5 Front Street in Hamilton (close to the Hamilton Ferry Terminal). Perfect for wedding gifts, or just to treat yourself, the designs are hand-crafted and really beautiful. The store also smells gorgeous so you feel pampered from the moment you step inside!

The Bermuda Railway Trail

Chloe spends time walking and riding along this beautiful trail path as the series continues.

Two famous American visitors, Mark Twain and Woodrow Wilson started a petition in 1908 to ban the motor car. It worked and by 1931 the twenty-two mile railway track was finished. The Bermuda Railway Company operated until 1948, until the lifting of the motor car ban in 1946 made the enterprise unviable.

Now **The Bermuda Railway Trail** is a hiking and cycling path and is a great way to explore Bermuda. If you get tired, the trail is never far from a main road, so you can pick up a bus or taxi.

Horseshoe Bay

This is a magnificent sweep of sand, and one of the most popular beaches in Bermuda. There are a couple of concessions – a café, toilets, showers, shop and the parking is plentiful. If you walk along the bay, away from the main beach, you can explore the picturesque coves beyond, like **Chaplin Bay**.

Southlands Estate

Chloe and Finn make plans to visit this historic estate for an afternoon. The limestone quarry, which forms a fascinating part of the extensive gardens, has its own history. In the 1800s limestone blocks from Southlands quarries were used to construct many buildings in Hamilton City. The estate has its own beach, **Marley Beach**. Just above the beach are several rental studios, which would be perfect for those looking for a romantic getaway.

Horse riding

Beachside Stables, the equestrian personalities and establishments are entirely fictional, but if you fancy some riding on the island, try **Watson Performance and Trail Horses** in **Warwick Parish**. Mike Watson is a professional horseman and offers lessons and trail rides on beautiful quarter horses.

St Catherine's Fort

In *Murder on the Island*, Chloe and Finn spent the day in and around *St George's* and *St Catherine's Fort* and beach and they are around a 5km hike from the town. If you can drag yourself away from the beauty and history of the town, including **The Unfinished Church** on Government Hill Road, the fort and beach are well worth a visit. Break your hike at **Tobacco Bay Beach** for a drink in the café, before continuing uphill. This beach is also one of the best for snorkelling, with its beautiful, clear shallow waters. Snorkel gear can be rented from the kiosks on the beach so you don't need to lug everything around if you are hiking further up the hill. The towering limestone rock formations are a haven for marine life, and like Chloe, you might spot blue parrotfish, angelfish and grouper.

There is also an excellent bus service for those less mobile.

The Royal Naval Dockyard

Dockyard is easily worth a day of exploration. Although the community shop run by Emma (in *Murder on the Island*) is fictitious, there is a local produce store, and other shops nestled amongst the former military buildings where you can pick up rum cakes, souvenirs and essentials.

The imposing grey stone buildings are fascinating and a trip

Afterword

up to the **Commissioner's House** and the **Museum** is highly recommended.

The Clocktower Mall

Although the **Stone Gallery** is an author creation, **Clocktower Mall** does indeed contain some wonderful galleries, clothing stores, jewellery makers and crafters. After chatting to the busy creatives you will definitely want to stop off at the **Haagen Dazs Bar** and sample some luscious ice cream.

Snorkel Beach

Snorkel Beach is located within the walls of Dockyard. The small beach has a safe, shallow area for children in the daytime and a lively music and bar scene in the balmy evenings.

The Swizzle Inn

Bermuda has two national drinks; firstly, the 'Dark 'n' Stormy', which is made with Gosling's Black Seal rum, ginger beer, and a twist of lime. Its origins trace back to WW1 when sailors discovered adding a splash of local Gosling's rum to ginger beer made a tasty drink. Secondly, the 'Rum Swizzle', a punch, was invented at **The Swizzle Inn** in 1932. Patrons are said to, 'swagger in and stagger out', so you have been warned!

The original **Swizzle Inn** is Bermuda's oldest pub. Situated in Hamilton Parish on Bailey's Bay and great for families.

Sister pub ***The Swizzle (South Shore)*** is in Warwick Parish on South Shore Road. There is a bus stop opposite the pub. Chloe drops in for a bite to eat (in *Murder on the Island*) after her hike around **Tom Moore's Jungle**.

Both pubs have an excellent, varied food menu too.

Fishcakes

When Chloe first arrives on Bermuda (in *Murder on the*

Afterword

Island), her neighbour, Ailsa, gives her some home-made fishcakes. There are a great many different recipes for codfish cakes, and these are traditionally served as a Sunday breakfast dish. These became a popular dish when traders in the 18th century used to trade salt (made by evaporating seawater) for codfish from the incoming fishermen. For a luscious, indulgent breakfast try codfish cakes, and Portuguese donuts.

Tom Moore's Jungle/The Blue Hole

Chloe sneaks off for the day in *Murder on the Island*, challenging herself to an adventure and ends up here. The jungle is in Hamilton Parish and the bus stops right across the road from where the trail starts. The going can be a little rough, but the jungle isn't huge (approx twelve acres) and you reach **The Blue Hole** after about fifteen minutes hiking. The signage isn't great but the paths are all well trodden.

The views from the coastal path are stunning, and you can dip into the sea for a swim if you don't mind the sharp rocks. There are a lot of caves in the jungle and they are fascinating. Signage asks that you don't swim in these beautiful natural rock formations, but you can go right underground to take pictures. Just watch your head as the roofs are often low!

The Blue Hole is nothing short of amazing, which is why I wanted Chloe to experience it at a time when she was rediscovering herself. The water is ice cold and vivid turquoise. On the other side of the jungle is **Tom Moore's Tavern**, perfect for a drink and snack, or if you return the other way, **The Swizzle Inn** is just half a mile up the road, and is where Chloe stopped to refuel.

Getting around Bermuda

Chloe uses the bus for most of her trips and the public transport system is economic and efficient. Taxis are expensive

Afterword

but safe, and if you are staying in a hotel, most will have some kind of complimentary transport.

Scooters are available for hire at various outlets but do take care if you do this as the roads in Bermuda can be very steep and twisty with plenty of blind corners.

For more information, including wedding and honeymoon ideas, visit: **www.gotobermuda.com**

A NOTE FROM THE PUBLISHER

Thank you for reading this book. If you enjoyed it please do consider leaving a review on Amazon to help others find it too.

We hate typos. All of our books have been rigorously edited and proofread, but sometimes mistakes do slip through. If you have spotted a typo, please do let us know and we can get it amended within hours.

info@bloodhoundbooks.com

Printed in Great Britain
by Amazon